THE RUTLAND IDENTITY

THE RUTLAND IDENTITY

Michael Dane

The Book Guild Ltd

First published in Great Britain in 2024 by
The Book Guild Ltd
Unit E2 Airfield Business Park,
Harrison Road, Market Harborough,
Leicestershire. LE16 7UL
Tel: 0116 2792299
www.bookguild.co.uk
Email: info@bookguild.co.uk
Twitter: @bookguild

Typeset in 11pt Adobe Garamond Pro

Printed and bound in Great Britain by 4edge Limited

ISBN 978 1916668 614

British Library Cataloguing in Publication Data.
A catalogue record for this book is available from the British Library.

For my children

PROLOGUE

Berlin, 1991

Bernard was retiring. He had retired before, of course – more than once actually. He had even been dead once for about six weeks, until the KGB learned that he wasn't. But this time, he really was retiring – *retiring* retiring.

The first time he retired, he had been a mere sixty and even Brigadiers were not allowed to work past sixty. But Bernard had been in Berlin since 1945. There was too much in his head to allow him to simply salute one last time and disappear. There was nobody, literally nobody, who could match Bernard's knowledge of that extraordinary, divided city.

And so, he had gone home on a Friday evening as the retired head of Military Intelligence in West Berlin and returned on Monday morning as some sort of civilian contractor. Bernard never bothered to find out his exact title, grade or status. He simply returned to his desk and immersed himself in the world of lies, subterfuge, deceit, betrayal and all the other little games, puzzles and stories that had been his life for thirty-five years.

The last time he had retired was simpler.

But this time, it was different. This time, he was genuinely retiring and he was going home. Home to the village where he had been born. Home to England. He was seventy. The wall had come down the previous year. Suddenly, his intimate and detailed knowledge of every liar, traitor, dissident, coward, hero, con artist, chancer, high-flyer, lowlife, spiv, pimp, patriot, zealot and cynic in the city, East and West, was no longer valued. And neither was he.

In a few minutes, there would be a brief – what might you call it? Ceremony? That was surely too grand a description of what was certain to be a rather sad little affair. Some embarrassed civil servant who barely knew him and who knew nothing about what he did, what he had done, would make a short speech. Somebody would give him a hastily purchased knick-knack[1] and he would be gone.

He had one last thing to do first, though. It was probably pointless. It was almost certainly pointless, but Bernard had made a promise to himself many, many years ago and it had to be done.

Gisela had been his agent for thirty years. She would not have been Ian Fleming's idea of a secret agent, which was part of the reason that she was so good. She was a mousy-haired, plain, dowdy woman, somewhere in her mid-fifties. Gisela was a spinster. Bernard was of the generation that still used such words.

She travelled each day from the little apartment she shared with Brunhilde, a small brown-and-white dog of uncertain pedigree and malevolent disposition, to the same office she had occupied since the wall went up. She was, in Bernard's opinion, the single most important human intelligence source in East Berlin.

The German Democratic Republic, East Germany to its enemies, was a massive bureaucracy. And the Stasi, the Ministry of State Security, was even worse. And sitting at the apex of the pyramid of bureaucracy was the accounts department, where Jakob Schneider had made pedantry, petty-mindedness and intractability his life's work, and Gisela's life – who was his secretary – a misery.

Jakob took his role as a custodian of the public purse very

---

1   In fact, it wasn't a hastily purchased knick-knack. They made him a knight. He would have preferred a Berlin snow globe – at least he could have used that as a paperweight.

seriously. No payment would ever be authorised without the correct paperwork, and he frequently took it upon himself to go beyond the official requirements to satisfy himself that the money of the peoples' government was being wisely used for the advancement of peace and socialism.

Most organisations have somebody like Jakob. It is a bit of a mystery as to why more of them don't end up, as Jakob had, floating in the River Spree. At least, it was assumed it was Jakob. Headless corpses are hard to identify.

Jakob had been particularly parsimonious with respect to making payments to East Germany's agents in West Berlin. Every Pfennig had to be accounted for. Every expense had to be detailed and justified. And all of it had to be typed… by Gisela. And so, each month, by various means – sometimes exotic, sometimes mundane – a list of every Stasi agent in West Berlin, their activities and their sources would find its way to Bernard's desk. All thanks to Gisela.

But Gisela had disappeared shortly after the wall had fallen. To have been a Stasi employee, even a secretary in the accounts department, was deeply unfashionable in the Berlin of 1990. Gisela would not receive a retirement present, a few kind – or, more likely, indifferent – words from a middle-ranking bureaucrat nor a state pension. She would be, had been, cast adrift in an uncertain world.

That was why, as the clock ticked towards five, Bernard was writing a report detailing the assistance that Gisela had provided over the decades and imploring the authorities to find, rescue and reward his top agent – codename Gustav.

*

Nottingham, 1997

Frank was also retiring. And he had been dreading this day. Not retirement itself. He had managed to persuade himself that he had had enough, done his bit, run his race. He was ready for his pipe and slippers. Of course, he had had the pipe for years. No, Frank had been dreading this day specifically – this day, this occasion.

Today was Frank's last day as an officer of Her Majesty's Customs and Excise, Friday 26th September 1997. It was also his sixtieth birthday, but that was not as significant – at least not to Frank. He had been a customs officer for thirty-nine years, 279 days. It said so on his pension statement. And today was his last, so there was going to be a 'do'. Everyone got a 'do' when they retired. Kind words were said, an inappropriate gift was purchased with the proceeds of a whip-round, and everyone knocked off early and went to the pub. If it was no more than that, Frank would consider that he had got off lightly. But he was Frank McBride. It probably wasn't going to be like that.

Frank lingered in the pub with Joe Lake – his... what was he? Underling? Protégé? Successor? – for as long as he decently could before trudging back up the hill to the office. Lake had said nothing. Was this because the 'do' would be embarrassingly poorly attended? Was it because it would be embarrassingly well attended? For once, Frank couldn't read the runes. And that was rare. Frank prided himself on his ability to sniff the air, feel the vibe, sense the mood. Perhaps he was getting too old. Perhaps it was the right time to retire. Or perhaps he had just trained Lake too well.

As the pair rounded the corner into Clarendon Street, McBride had his answer. There were cars parked everywhere – not just cars, Customs cars. Unmarked, but if you knew, you knew. They were on both sides of the street for a hundred yards. The car park would be overflowing, too. McBride's first thought was that the room wouldn't be big enough. That was good. If people were uncomfortable, perhaps the excruciating ceremony might be briefer.

There were two deputy chief investigation officers, half a dozen assistant chiefs, people Frank had known for years – in some cases, decades. Some of these people were almost as famous as Frank McBride. None were as notorious.

Frank stood to one side. His pipe, unlit, clenched in the corner of his mouth. Lake wondered if he had a spare or two because he was likely to bite right through the stem if things became too mawkish, sentimental, effusive – you know, excruciating. And in the circumstances, this was pretty likely. The room was far too warm. It was September, every window was open. McBride could hear a dog barking outside. But it was still too warm.

Alan Hawkins, who technically was McBride's boss, in the same way that the coach at Santos was technically Pele's boss, appeared to have appointed himself master of ceremonies. He began, predictably, with the tale of how he and Frank had first met. There was a certain amount of teasing, some oblique references to some of the lowlights of Frank's career. That little incident in Bangkok and the subsequent demotion. The occasions when Frank had taken the invitation to speak his mind a little too literally.

And then there were the successes, the triumphs, the achievements, culminating with Frank's most recent case – his final one – Operation Bagration. Frank bit down hard on the stem of his pipe and tried to imagine that he was somewhere else. Anywhere else. Only then did he notice that Michelle was in the room.

Michelle was Frank's daughter and the reason why, to the astonishment of everyone, he had chosen to spend the last few months of his career in Nottingham – the smallest and most obscure office in Customs' National Investigation Service. She was also about to become his landlady. Michelle and Simon had bought an old farmhouse out in Rutland and Frank was going to live in its converted barn next door. Michelle looked a little anxious, preoccupied. If it hadn't been Michelle, he would have said that she looked shifty. But Michelle was never shifty.

McBride pushed the thought to the back of his mind as he subconsciously realised that Hawkins was reaching the final straight. He should probably pay attention to this bit, maybe give some thought to the few words that he would be expected to say in response. Michelle was edging towards the door. It was probably too warm for her. She couldn't be, could she? She couldn't be pregnant?

"And so, Frank, we thank you. We thank you for everything that you have done for everyone here. And although I don't suppose you'll miss us, we are worried that you might miss having a loyal and faithful colleague to order about. And so, we got you one."

Frank was puzzled. What on earth was he talking about? Was this going to be a blow-up doll in a Customs uniform? It had better not be. Hawkins knew him better than that, surely. He scanned the room looking for knowing grins. But he saw none. No. He saw one, Lake's. But it wasn't the sort of grin that people wore when they were in on a joke. It was something else. The crowd of people nearest the door were trying to shuffle away to make room. There was a sort of hum that Frank couldn't quite identify.

"Michelle! We're ready!"

The door opened. Michelle entered. Frank could just see her head through the throng of bodies. Those closest to her were smiling, but smiling in surprise. McBride couldn't see the reason.

"We hope you'll be very happy together."

The crowd parted and Frank could see.

"Happy birthday, Dad! We got you another retired has-been. Thought it might keep you out of mischief! He's called Rocky."

The springer spaniel leapt into Frank's arms. Everybody cheered. Later, maybe for years, people would tell the story. But nobody believed them. It didn't matter how many witnesses, it was simply incredible. Literally incapable of being believed. But the people who were there knew what they saw.

Francis Daniel McBride OBE – The Tartan Terror, Big Bad Frank – was in tears and Rocky was gently licking them away.

ONE

Rutland, 1998

It was Thursday, and Thursday was pub quiz day at The Old Volunteer. The brewery lorry had been late and so George Bowman hadn't yet had time to compile the questions. Some publicans delegated such tasks to a customer-quizmaster, but George would have considered that a dereliction of his duty as a landlord.

George took his duties seriously. Well, not his duty to the brewery, obviously. Or the VAT man or the National Insurance people. Actually, if he were totally honest with himself – and George was the type of man to be mostly honest most of the time – he didn't really feel he owed a duty to his customers. His duty was to the trade and his own, slightly skewed, sense of the code of the publican. The code of the publican was written in brown ale on a piece of papyrus handed down from the pharaohs and it resided in Burton in a golden tabernacle, shaped like a beer barrel. No, it didn't. Of course it didn't. It existed only in George's head or perhaps his heart.

Other publicans may also have had their personal codes, but George believed that his was the one true faith. It was what people these days call an organic document, which is a fancy way of saying that George could change bits of it if he wanted or if circumstances required. He had been forced, for example, to modify his views on the subject of lager over the years. And he was now willing to accept that the world of wine actually extended further than 'dry' and 'medium dry'.

George owed everything to beer. It was in his blood. Not in the sense that it would be detected by an in-line intoximeter or a breathalyser, except on Sunday nights and the early part of Monday morning – then it would. No, beer was part of his DNA. George's paternal grandfather had been a cooper. He had spent almost fifty years making eighteen-gallon barrels at the Everards Brewery in Leicester. His other grandfather had been a drayman.

His father had spent forty years at the brewery, rising to be the manager of the bottling plant. George himself had started collecting glasses at The Wagon and Horses when he was thirteen. For George, the brewing, distribution, care and sale of beer was not a career, it was a vocation. A sacred trust passed down the generations. And inheritors of a scared trust did not let other people write their quiz questions. No, they bloody did not!

There were people he knew who simply took their questions from one of the many books published specifically for this purpose. George used these, too, but they were just a primary resource, along with the slightly tatty exercise books containing scribbled questions and answers from old episodes of *Mastermind* and *University Challenge*. His quizzes were bespoke, designed specifically for the clientele of The Old Volunteer. His customers were a little better heeled than most, a little better educated and a lot older.

*

The Old Volunteer was not like George's previous pub, The Iron Duke. As well as representing different ends of the military hierarchy, the two establishments were about as dissimilar as two public houses could be.

The Iron Duke had been rough – really, really rough. Perched on the corner of one of Leicester's less salubrious estates, it was what might euphemistically be referred to as a locals' pub. By which it was meant that nobody in their right mind would walk past any other pub to seek out The Iron Duke. But it was profitable. The locals were thirsty. And they employed a definition of disposable income that would have puzzled many economists. If they had it, they spent it on beer. As soon as possible. Running the Iron Duke was not like running The Old Volunteer. There were no quiz nights at the Duke, no pensioners' specials, no horse brasses on the wall or prints of hunting scenes.

Running The Iron Duke had been hard work. George had had to keep a very close eye on the staff, the stock and the young men who regarded the gents as a retail outlet for recreational pharmaceuticals.

George had had to decide how much of that he was willing to tolerate, how large he was willing to allow the stakes to rise on the games of three card brag and how many car radios being passed under tables to which he was willing to turn a blind eye.

It was more than any one man could do alone, but fortunately he hadn't had to. Linda, his wife, had been by his side. Always ready and able to calm an emotional customer, to remember the faces of punters barred months earlier and to charm the brewery reps, the weights and measures people and the council's licensing officers. Never the VAT people, though. God, they were humourless bastards! It needed all George's experience to keep one step ahead of them. He'd throw them a bone now and then. Make them think they had caught him out. Kept them happy. Kept them from looking for something bigger.

Fourteen years they had spent running The Duke. They had done well, made a few quid and they were discussing moving to somewhere a little more genteel when Linda had received the diagnosis. George knew he couldn't run The Duke on his own and, anyway, he didn't want to. Linda had helped him choose The

Old Volunteer, but by the time the lease was transferred, she was gone.

The Old Volunteer was an entirely new sort of challenge. It was on the corner of an estate, too, but this one was owned by a Duke or Earl or something and comprised a hundred thousand acres of bucolic Rutland countryside.

Leighton Parva might have shared a fire brigade with Leicester, but that was where the commonality ended. It had a population of maybe two hundred and fifty and at least half of those were of pensionable age. Villages like Leighton Parva had been losing their pubs for years. A combination of cheap supermarket booze, satellite television and a more zealous enforcement of drink-driving rules had proved too punishing a combination for most.

But George Bowman knew what he was doing. He wasn't greedy, didn't need to make a healthy living. The Old Volunteer was more of a retirement project or a hobby, not that George would have admitted that – even to himself.

The proceeds of The Iron Duke had provided him with a nest egg. A nest egg he now didn't really need. Linda and he had discussed taking cruises on their retirement, seeing the world, maybe buying a little place on one of the Costas for the winter months. George didn't really want to do any of that without her.

He was happy just being a publican. But his pride wouldn't allow him to make a loss. That would be contrary to his personal code. So, he used every trick he had learned over a lifetime spent in the trade. He had three sets of books: one for the brewery, one for the VAT man and one for his eyes only, which reflected the true trading position. The last one showed that he just about broke even.

Even this modest goal required him to be on his toes. The Thursday pub quiz was an important element of his business plan. On a good week, he might get thirty or forty customers. And so, writing the questions had to take priority over topping up the Bacardi bottle with Tesco's rum, emptying all the slops into a barrel that would be returned to brewery as being off and all the other

4

little tricks of the trade that, while mostly illegal, were absolutely permitted, in fact practically mandatory, under George's code.

There had been a time last year when George had been considering whether he needed to 'put his thumb on the scales' when compiling the questions. For months on end, the same team, captained by the bumptious and vain Peter Roberts, had won almost every week. For most of the competitors, the result was unimportant, but Peter was such an ungracious winner that George was seriously worried that his pompous self-congratulation might lead to numbers dwindling.

George would never actually cheat or allow others to do so – that was against the code – but he was ready and willing to slant some of the questions towards others' specialist subjects. Not too much, just a little. It wouldn't do to make it too obvious. He couldn't, for example, give Ron Godsmark's team a whole round on crown green bowls.

However, since the New Year, the problem seemed to have solved itself. Curiously, Peter's team seemed to have come second each week for the past five months. More curiously still, a different team won each week. George was enjoying the sight of Peter getting more and more frustrated, but he didn't understand the reason for this new, most welcome, and very amusing, phenomenon. The only thing that had changed was Bernard's new teammates.

Bernard Taylor, widely known in the village as 'The Major', was pushing eighty and therefore only slightly above the average age of The Old Volunteer's customers. He had been in the army for years and years and had spent a lot of time in Germany. George didn't know if he had actually been a major or not.

At The Iron Duke, there had been a regular, who insisted upon being called 'Digger' and claimed to have been a Sergeant Major in the SAS. When, one day, it was revealed, quite by chance, that he had actually been a Lance Corporal in the Pay Corps, he couldn't live it down and was never seen again. So, George always called 'The Major', Bernard. He didn't seem to mind.

Bernard had had a German wife, a lovely woman – Karin, she had been called. Bernard and Karin had always formed their own two-person team. She had died last summer; very sad. Since Christmas, Bernard had formed a new team with Ron Godsmark and Frank McBride, who had recently moved into the village. The creation of this new team had coincided with the downturn in Peter's fortunes. But that had to be nothing more than a coincidence, hadn't it?

George spent an hour on the quiz, six rounds of ten questions each and a couple of tie-breakers just in case. He put the questions in a buff folder and put them under the bar. He made up the floats for the bar's two tills and put ten five-pound notes in his waistcoat pocket. He had a little bit of business to do with young Leo and that required cash and no paperwork.

He spent the next hour bottling up, fetching bottles of light ale, lager and soft drinks up from the cellar and making sure that the fridge and cold shelf were both fully stocked. He took the empty bottles round to the yard at the back where they would remain until his next delivery, which would be on Tuesday. He was still in the yard when he heard Leo arriving. More accurately, he heard Leo's car.

Leo would have referred to his personal transportation as 'a classic', particularly if he had been trying to sell it. Others would probably have called it 'an old banger'. It was noisy, smelly and unreliable (a bit like Leo) and its advent usually promised a frustrating or disappointing time for someone. Some say that owners start to resemble their dogs. With Leo, it was his car.

Leo Davidson had been born and raised in the village – one of the very youngest to have been so. He had left for university about ten years ago to study for a degree that he had never finished. He would return every couple of years, usually unannounced and a few steps ahead of various creditors. If asked, and he rarely was, he would say that he was still studying or starting a business, or on the brink of launching a career in music, theatre or writing. He was halfway to being a charming rogue. He probably considered himself to be a free spirit, a bohemian and a restless soul. Everyone else considered him to be a bum.

Leo had been good-looking once, but now his hair was thinning, his paunch was growing and the skull-and-crossbones earring was less a symbol of an untamed rebel as an ageing adolescent who needed to grow up and get a proper job. George had employed him briefly at The Old Volunteer one winter but that had not gone well. During his latest spell at his long-suffering parents' home, he was working 'up at the hall'.

Leighton Hall was a stately pile that sat atop the hill that separated the villages of Leighton Parva and the paradoxically slightly smaller Leighton Magna. It had been built by some returning nabob a couple of centuries earlier. A combination of death duties and world wars had seen off the family's descendants and it was now owned by a Swiss couple, Joe and Hanna Keller, who were running it as a sort of hotel and wedding venue.

Leo was 'up at the hall' working as a waiter/barman/bottlewasher and mopper of floors. Being an enterprising, if somewhat light-fingered, youth, he had found a few ways of supplementing his fairly meagre hourly rate. And this was why his ancient Volkswagen Beetle was even now trundling down Leighton Parva's main street, making a noise like two pounds of broken clock parts in a tumble dryer.

The Beetle, last taxed when Margaret Thatcher had been prime minister, clattered, wheezed and gurgled its way into The Old Volunteer car park. Leo turned off the ignition and leapt out. A few seconds later, the engine finally stopped. Leo ostentatiously looked left and right like a pantomime villain invoking boos and hisses from a crowd of seven year olds. He couldn't have looked or acted more suspiciously if he had been wearing a stripy shirt and was carrying a sack marked 'swag'.

He swung forward the driver's seat, retrieved a largish cardboard box and trotted over towards George, his face contorted in a conspiratorial leer. He handed George the box and returned to his car to repeat the performance.

"Two cases of the very finest vintage cava all the way from Champagne! To you, a mere fifty quid."

George knew that Champagne was in France. George knew that cava was from Spain. George knew that there was no such thing as vintage cava. And George knew Leo. He opened the first box. It had been sealed. Twelve bottles. He opened the second box – it wasn't, and there were only ten. He looked quizzically at Leo. Leo shrugged.

"I'll accept forty-five," he said, without the slightest hint of shame.

"I'll give you forty or you can take the whole lot away and good luck trying to put it back where you 'found it'." The quotation marks hung in the air like a pair of tarantulas hanging from their threads.

"Forty, it is! A pleasure doing business with you."

George took the cash from his waistcoat pocket, his eyes never leaving Leo's, peeled off eight five-pound notes and handed them over.

"Tonic water, napkins and dishwasher soap. Just if you happen to find any."

Leo grinned, nodded and returned to his car. Thirty seconds later, the clattering sound was receding in the distance and George was waving away the acrid black smoke that had spumed forth from the Volkswagen's exhaust.

TWO

Frank was lacing up his brown brogues. They were the first pair of brown shoes that he could remember owning. They were certainly the first pair of brogues. His tweed jacket was his first, too, and all those check shirts. Frank was a metropolitan man. Apart from his national service and a few months spent in Nottingham, he had never lived anywhere smaller than Glasgow. Now he was in Leighton Parva and adjusting, slowly and not without occasional mishap, to the life of a country-dwelling retiree. The proletarian in Frank – he still considered himself a proletarian – was slightly embarrassed by how quickly he had adapted and by how much he was enjoying his new life.

The clock on the mantlepiece struck to indicate that it was eight o'clock. It wasn't. Frank had set it five minutes fast so that it would serve as a sort of alarm. Michelle left at eight to take Maisie and Frankie Junior to school. Frankie was five now and in 'big school'. He had returned one afternoon a month ago and announced that he now wished to be known as 'Francis'. Frank thought this was just adorable.

He thought that everything that Maisie and Frankie said and everything that they did was adorable. As the eighth chime was still echoing, he opened his door and went and stood in the small area between his home and Michelle's that had once been a farmyard. He liked to see the kids off, to give them a whiskery kiss and slip a chocolate biscuit into their blazer pocket when Michelle wasn't watching.

Frank was very well aware that he would have won no prizes as a parent, but he was doing his absolute best to be an Olympic-standard grandparent. He had even bought them both England football shirts and that had hurt. But he bought them Scotland ones, too.

Frankie was first out of the kitchen door, his schoolbag clutched in his right hand, both arms raised above his head in triumph. "*Shearer*! Shearer scores for England!"

Frankie felt a momentary stab.

"And Scotland; Shearer scores for Scotland, too!" he shouted, upon catching sight of his grandfather's expression. He completed two laps of his mother's car, arms outstretched, screaming, "*Goooaaaallll*."

Maisie was far less preoccupied with that month's World Cup. She raced out of the kitchen door a few seconds behind her little brother and made a beeline, not for her grandfather, but for Rocky. Maisie simply loved Rocky. And Rocky loved Maisie and Frankie Junior. But most of all, Rocky loved Frank.

Rocky, like Frank, had actually retired when he was at the top of his game. But somebody, somewhere had decided that sniffer dogs had to retire at the age of eight. Rocky's handler, who had had first refusal, couldn't or didn't want to take him and so Michelle, somehow, had pulled strings and twisted arms in an organisation of which she had never been a part. It had been frustratingly difficult at first and she was on the point of surrendering to the exasperating bureaucracy when she had stumbled on the magic words, "It's for Frank McBride."

Michelle knew what her father had done for a living. If she had thought about it, she might have considered that he was well thought of. *If* she had thought of it. For Michelle, Customs and Excise was the reason she had grown up mostly without a father. She didn't understand its culture, its language or its folklore. In particular, she didn't realise the place that Frank McBride held in the organisation's pantheon of heroes or, at least, characters.

"Maisie! Don't let that dog lick your face! Dad, you shouldn't let him do that!" Michelle hurried to extricate her daughter. "Come on! We're going to be late."

Maisie reluctantly parted from Rocky and rushed to kiss her grandfather. She felt the Penguin biscuit slip into her pocket. She knew where they came from. To Frankie, it was still a bit of a mystery. It took three full minutes to get both children into the car and Rocky out of it. And then out of it again, because he had rushed around to the other side and leapt in through an open window. It was five past eight when Michelle pulled out of the drive. Frank stood and waved until they were out of sight.

Rocky nudged Frank's right hand. He was almost sure that he had him properly trained, but it couldn't hurt just to remind him gently that the next order of business was his walk. Frank hadn't forgotten. He went back inside to collect Rocky's lead and to fetch his cap. Yes, he had a flat cap, too, but, to be fair, this was not the first that he had owned. First tweed one, though.

It was Monday, and on Mondays Frank and Rocky headed out of the village on the Oakham Road before mounting a stile that led to the bridlepath. Well, Frank mounted it, somewhat creakily. Rocky cleared it with a single bound. Frank returned Rocky's lead to his pocket. He always carried it as they walked through the village, but he couldn't remember the last time that he had actually attached it. Rocky set off up Beacon Hill at a happy gallop. Frank followed behind, somewhat more slowly, but equally happily.

Frank would have denied it, assuming that anybody had been brave enough to pose the question, but the truth was that retirement actually suited him. He was walking miles every day.

He had lost weight, was smoking less and sleeping properly for the first time in about thirty years.

He still missed 'the job'. He still missed the mental challenge, the battle of wits, the low cunning and mendacious skulduggery. These days, his only outlet for mischief was the weekly pub quiz. Although he did enjoy that – in particular, the expression of dismay and fury on Peter Roberts' face each week. Frank was not an evil man, but sometimes it amused him to do evil things.

Rocky was barking. He had reached the top of the hill and, from the excited yelps, it was clear that he had found Ron Godsmark waiting for him.

Ron was a lot older than Frank, but a lot fitter. He was the type of person that is usually described as spry. He walked five miles every day before breakfast and was almost at the end of his route when he lingered, as he did each day, to meet Frank beside the beacon.

The local history society claimed that Saxons of Laegess Tunn had lighted beacons on this hill to warn of Danish invasion. Frank wasn't so sure. But somebody had deemed it a sufficiently good excuse to mount a twenty-foot-high pole with a small brazier on its top. There was a small plaque at the bottom giving thanks to the (unstated and unexplained) efforts of Peter Roberts, Chairman of the Parish Council.

Frank was slightly out of breath when he reached the beacon and was glad of the few minutes afforded to him to recover while Ron played with Rocky. When he was ready, Frank considered, and then rejected, the idea of lighting his pipe. Instead, Ron and he set off down the far side of the hill on the path that would eventually lead to Leighton Magna and Ron's kitchen where a restorative cup of tea was sure to be found.

Ron was a man of few words and those he did utter were broadcast in an utterly impenetrable Rutland accent that rendered them mostly incomprehensible. This suited Frank very well. He enjoyed the companionable silence. For twenty minutes, neither man said anything at all, unless you counted Frank's occasional imprecations to Rocky to: "Leave that alone."

Frank had spent a lifetime learning to give accurate descriptions of people based upon a minute or two's acquaintance or sometimes on merely a momentary glance. But he might have struggled to describe Ron. He was just Ron.

His companion was about seventy or so, Frank supposed. Medium height, medium build. His hair, which was worn a little long, had once been brown, but was now one shade greyer than snow white and mostly concealed beneath a flat cap that Ron wore a little low over the left eye. In his summer garb, he wore a pair of grey flannel trousers and a grey open-neck shirt. His sleeves were rolled up, but this exposed neither distinguishing tattoos or a pair of forearms that Popeye might envy.

He was just Ron.

It was the first day of June, the first day of summer. Even at this early hour, Frank could feel the sun warming the back of his neck. On the far side of Beacon Hill, a few dozen lambs were gambolling. Frank had never seen lambs gambolling before he came to Leighton Parva – never seen a lamb doing anything except emerging from an oven and sitting on a plate. Over to the north, a tractor – a John Deere; Frank could now identify different makes of tractor – was gathering the year's first cut into large round bales of hay. Overhead, a light aircraft was beginning its descent towards the Rutland Aero Club.

The two reached the back of Leighton Hall and then set off diagonally on a path that ran across the grounds. The owners had erected signs declaring the land to be private property and threatening all manner of legal consequences for trespassers. But Ron had assured him that the path was a right of way since time immemorial, at least he thought that was what he had said. And so, Frank called Rocky to heel and made the journey anyway. At the point where they passed nearest to the hall, Frank could see a navy van parked on the gravel drive that led to the rear of the building. 'Bolus & Bartsch – Painters and Decorators', it said on the side.

"Big job painting that place," offered Frank. He knew that Ron had been a painter himself once.

"Arr!" said Ron, apparently in agreement. "Done it meself twice!"

"Did you? Really?"

"Arr, weren't no fancy hotel then, though."

And that appeared to be all that Ron had wanted to say on the subject. And nothing further was said for twenty minutes until the two very dissimilar pensioners found themselves outside Ron's cottage in Leighton Magna.

Ron's cottage was half of a pair and had been built in 1912 – or if it hadn't, it was some sick builder's weird idea of a joke. Anyway, it had '1912' carved into an escutcheon on the first floor where the two semi-detached homes met.

It was, or had been, an estate cottage, built to house the many agricultural workers who tended the earl's many farms. There were several more like it in Leighton Magna and in other surrounding villages, mostly built at the same time. But the number of young men from the earl's estate in 1919 had not been the number there had been in 1914. And farms had no longer required as many strong backs and men skilled in driving a pair of plough horses. Ron had been living there since 1946. He had carried his wife over its threshold in 1949 and her coffin over it, in the opposite direction, in 1992.

"Cuppa tea?"

Frank gratefully accepted and followed Ron into his kitchen. Rocky, who had run three times as far as the two men had walked, threw himself down in a corner with a weary sigh. Frank absent-mindedly fondled his ears as he sat in the nearest chair.

"So, how long has the hall been a hotel?"

"Well, now…" Ron continued to potter about with kettle, teapot and caddy. "Let's see… about three years, I'd say. Four, if you count the renovation."

"Renovation?"

"Arr, that took about a year. Place had been derelict mebbe ten, twelve years before that."

"So when did you paint it? What was it then?"

"Well, I painted it twice, see. Once as a young man, once as an old 'un. T'was a school, sort of. An approved school, sort of a borstal, for naughty lads, like. Biscuit?"

Frank pondered how much time and how much money it must have taken to convert a derelict borstal into the luxury hotel that the hall was now.

"Owned by a Swiss couple now, isn't it?"

"Arr!" said Ron, apparently in assent. He put two biscuits on Frank's saucer, then took one back, broke it into two and gave the larger half to Rocky.

It was difficult to estimate Ron's age, not least because he was supremely fit. However, from various dates and life events mentioned, Frank was able to piece together that he was probably born in the mid-twenties and was therefore in his early to mid-seventies now. About the same age as Bernard, Frank's other friend in the village – perhaps a few years younger. They looked similar, too: the same smoke-grey eyes, the same Roman nose. It had taken months to piece together the tiny fragments of information to deduce Ron's approximate age. It wasn't that Ron was secretive. He just didn't say very much. To anyone. About anything.

For reasons of his own, Ron liked to affect the role of the simple countryman. But Frank suspected that this was, at least in part, an act and that Ron was actually far shrewder than he liked to pretend. He had been surprised to see a copy of the Concise Oxford Dictionary in the kitchen on an earlier visit. On a later occasion, he found a completed *Times* cryptic crossword. Finally, a month or so later, he had found a number of sheets of paper that contained blank crossword grids, without clues. These had puzzled Frank for a while until he found the final clue, a partially completed grid with handwritten clues underneath. Eventually, having considered and rejected every other explanation he could think of, and despite its inherent unlikelihood, he was left with only one. Ron was a professional crossword compiler.

Most people would have considered it very rude to look through their host's possessions, seeking clues as to their hobbies, pastimes and activities, and deep down Frank knew that it was. But he simply couldn't help it. Any mystery, any secret – whether deliberately concealed or not – cried out to him for investigation.

He did it all the time, piecing together theories from scraps of evidence, testing those theories, seeking confirmation or refutation. He had spent decades seeking and interpreting pieces of evidence and the habit had become too ingrained to cease.

Twenty minutes later, Frank and Rocky were sufficiently rested and restored to complete their journey back to Leighton Parva. Together, they left Ron's cottage – the second or the second last, depending on your point of view, house in Leighton Magna. They passed what had once been the village school, but was now a private dwelling, and what had once been the post office. The only remaining example of community life was the Bowls Club where Ron spent so many of his summer hours. Where the road forked, Frank and Rocky turned right and followed the lane down the hill until they reached the junction on the edge of Leighton Parva, where the road changed its name from Stamford Road to Main Street.

From there, it was only five minutes to home, past The Old Volunteer and Bernard's house. Except they didn't get that far.

Frank was mentally planning the rest of his day when he heard the scream. Technically, he heard only the first half of the scream as it rose in volume and pitch. Rocky heard it all. Frank paused for a moment and then started to run towards the sound of the horror. Some people are like that. That is the sort of thing they do. Frank was one of those people.

As he reached the side door of The Old Volunteer, he was met by Bridget. From her complexion, it was obvious that she had been the source of the scream and it appeared to have winded her. She was bright red, obviously distressed and temporarily robbed of the capacity of speech. She pointed behind herself and then bent almost double in an effort to regain her breath. Frank hurried inside, slightly breathless himself. It had been a long time since he had run twenty-five yards. He had been sufficiently senior in Customs to have others do the running for him.

Inside the pub seemed exactly as normal – or at least exactly as one would expect to see it on a Monday morning. In the middle of the room was a large, industrial-type vacuum cleaner of indeterminate age. Stools and chairs were upended and resting on tables or on the banquette that ran alongside one wall to facilitate cleaning. There was no evidence of damage and nobody to be seen. Frank halted. A second or two later, he was joined by Bridget, who had recovered herself just sufficiently to point behind the bar. "The cellar!"

Frank looked at his watch. That is what customs investigators did. Any event, any anticipated event, anything that might at some point give rise to the question, 'At what time?', customs officers looked at their watches. Eleven minutes past ten.

The entrance to the cellar was via a trapdoor in a little passageway behind the bar. There were steep steps leading down and at the bottom of the steps was George Bowman. Frank had to take three steps down to reach the light switch that illuminated the cellar. He could see straightaway that George was dead. He was surrounded by broken bottles and his legs were soaked in what looked a lot like blood, but the biggest clue was his face. Live people didn't look like that.

Frank returned immediately to the bar where Bridget was sitting on the banquette, bent forward with her face in her hands. Rocky had his chin on her knee as if he were trying to comfort her. She looked up at Frank, her face a blend of horror and inquiry. "Is he... is he?"

Frank nodded. He looked beneath the bar. He was sure that there was a telephone here somewhere. He had seen George retrieve it on occasion. He found it among a pile of invoices and delivery notes. He put the receiver on the bar, lifted the handset and pushed nine three times. Bridget had begun to sob quietly. Rocky was making soft whimpering sounds.

"Emergency. Which service do you require?"

Frank paused for a moment. He had had to switch on the light. *Why would George be in the cellar with the light off?*

"Police, please."

Bridget looked up and gave a little gasp.

THREE

Frank knew that it would be some time before the police and the ambulance arrived. In his mind, the cellar was a crime scene and therefore he should leave it alone. Whether anybody else was prepared to consider it a crime scene was entirely another matter.

Nevertheless, Frank did what he had done hundreds of times before. He wrote up his notebook. Of course, he didn't actually have an officially issued notebook anymore. He was retired. But he knew the value of contemporaneous notes. He had spent too long standing in too many witness boxes not to know that. He found a spiral-bound notebook on a shelf below the bar and wrote down all that he had done and seen since hearing Bridget's scream. He checked it through twice and signed it, 'FD McBride. 1/VI/98. 10:26 hrs'. He tore the two pages he had used from the notebook, folded them and put them in his pocket.

Strictly speaking, he should have done nothing more. But he couldn't help himself. Bridget was still sitting on the banquette, muttering something about brandy being reputedly good for shock. Frank was sorely tempted to give her a glass, but Bridget was likely to be a poor witness anyway and with a brandy or two inside, she was likely to tell the police a story involving sea monsters, aliens and the ghost of Winston Churchill. He decided to ignore her ever-broader hints. Instead, he turned his attention to the notebook.

To most casual readers, the book contained a mixture of notes, reminders and seemingly incomprehensible figures and sums. But Frank had seen books like this before. He had spent most of his Customs career investigating drug smuggling, but he had spent a few years on a VAT fraud investigation team and he knew an 'off book' when he saw one.

To the trained eye, the book revealed how George Bowman had reduced his VAT liability. Frank was not shocked. The pub was largely a cash business and cash businesses almost always kept a little revenue aside, away from the VAT man. The trick was to disguise it sufficiently well to survive a visit from the VAT inspector. Even after a few minutes' examination, Frank could tell that George had known what he was doing.

But Frank was no longer paid to care about such things. He was retired. And in any event, how much VAT could George realistically be fiddling? The Old Volunteer didn't have a great many customers. How could it in a place like Leighton Parva? The fact that it was surviving at all was testament to George's skills as a publican. And if those skills included a talent for false accounting, and they obviously did, well, that was probably what kept the place afloat. Frank had only lived in the village for less than six months, but he didn't want the pub to fail. He replaced the book on the shelf.

The police, the ambulance and the chef all arrived within a few minutes of each other just before eleven o'clock. Even before the police officer had made it halfway across the car park, Frank had already formed an opinion. Some would have called it prejudice. And they would be right.

Frank would have called it something else. Intuition layered upon experience, a close reading of body language, an instinct informed by years and years dealing with coppers. But Frank would have been wrong. It was prejudice. Of course, just because Frank had leapt to a conclusion based upon prejudice didn't mean that he wouldn't be proved one hundred per cent correct.

Frank thought that he knew the type. Young. Probably been in CID for a year or two. Already thought himself too good, too special for that. Anxious to secure a berth at the National Crime Squad or a transfer to the Met. Vain. Arrogant. Not interested in doing the hard work. Not interested in gradually acquiring experience, honing skills, developing himself as a detective or even a human being. Just a brash, flash, arrogant little git! And he didn't like his tie either.

Frank introduced himself. The copper's name was Vaughan and he was a detective constable. Frank gave his account of the morning's events and placed particular emphasis on the fact that the cellar light had been switched off.

It was clear from the outset that Vaughan did not share Frank's view of the suspicious nature of George's death. He listened to his account, but he took no notes. He seemed more interested in the pub itself. He looked around, examining the pictures on the wall and nodding approvingly at the labels on the beer pumps.

When he eventually decided to examine the cellar, he spent less than a minute looking around and then returned to the bar area. Frank was still there, standing as if he was expecting a report. Normally Vaughan wouldn't bother explaining himself to a member of the public, but there was something about this man that seemed to demand it. He decided to give it in the quasi-legal, semi-medico language that coppers use when they are trying to intimidate others with their knowledge of matters too technical for the layman to understand.

"Preliminary examination of the locus indicates, ipso facto and prima facie, the deceased appears to have fallen down the cellar steps with a load of bottles and either sustained a fatal fracture of an upper vertebrae or multiple or singular lacerations caused by broken glass and death by er... loss of blood."

"In the dark. The cellar light was off. Why would he go down into the cellar in the dark?"

Vaughan had an answer for this. "Perhaps he couldn't turn the light on because he was carrying bottles. Listen, sir, I know you mean well, but this is my job. I do this all the time. You were quite right to alert us, but this is not a suspicious death."

Vaughan turned and nodded at the ambulance crew, who began the tricky process of manoeuvring George's body up the cellar steps. He retrieved a mobile phone from his pocket, presumably to call the police station and report his findings. He left through the side doors to make his call from the car park, where his candid and less-than-complimentary assessment of Frank's representations would not be overheard.

Frank turned his attention to the ambulance crew, one man and one woman, who were having a short rest, having moved George's body onto the floor behind the bar.

"Did he break his neck?"

"I don't think so. Wouldn't have mattered anyway. Got a piece of broken bottle in his femoral artery. He would have bled out in minutes. Terrible luck. Million-to-one chance, really. Didn't stand a chance."

The woman pointed to half a bottle, the neck half, which was lying on the stretcher beside George. It was brown, a half-pint bottle judging by the look of it. It had a pale blue label, probably light ale.

Frank nodded sadly. He had been raised in Glasgow and, in his younger days, he had seen for himself what the business end of a broken bottle could do. Faintly, very faintly, in the back of his mind, something didn't seem quite right, but he couldn't bring the nagging doubt forward. He went and stood over the entrance of the cellar.

Perhaps the young pup had been right. It was necessary, as Frank had discovered himself, to walk down two of three of the cellar steps to turn on the light. Perhaps George had simply not bothered nor been able to with his hands full of bottles. Or had they been in a crate? If they were in a crate, he could have walked down backwards. The steps were so steep he would probably have done that anyway – Frank had. It would have been very easy to rest the crate on a step and flick the light switch. Even without a crate, it might have been possible to flick the switch with a spare finger or thumb.

Frank peered down into the cellar. He couldn't see a crate. He wanted to investigate further. He stood, paralysed by the equal and opposite urges to follow his investigative instinct and just mind his own business. Without choosing either course, he walked back into the lounge bar from where he could see Vaughan, standing in the car park. He almost felt sorry for him.

Vaughan was talking to Peter Roberts, the chairman of the Parish Council. Frank was not an avid student of local government civics, but he was fairly confident that the parish council was a mostly pointless and powerless talking shop and that being its chairman conveyed no more real authority than when Frankie Junior had been made the milk monitor in primary school.

However, he was equally sure that Peter considered the position to occupy the level of prestige and influence somewhere between Alexander the Great and Napoleon. Frank couldn't hear what was being said, but he could all too easily imagine that Peter was behaving like a cross between an examining magistrate and the king fish of some corrupt Mississippi backwater.

Frank returned to the cellar. This time, he did not hesitate. He turned on the light and descended. The cellar had a bare brick floor with a narrow gutter running diagonally across it. Even in the poor light of the single bulb, Frank could see the evidence that blood – quite a lot of blood – had flowed through it. The bricks beneath where poor George had lain were sticky. Frank squatted amid the broken bottles – one remained complete – and sniffed. He smelt damp and the faint trace of stale beer. Only a faint trace. Perhaps the bottles had been empty.

Frank looked about. He couldn't see any bottle tops. Then, he remembered. The bottle from the stretcher hadn't had a bottle top either. And if the bottles had been full, surely there would have been a lot of beer alongside the blood. There wasn't. He picked up the one whole bottle. It was empty and had no crown top. So, George had been either taking empty bottles out of the cellar or moving empty bottles into it. But why?

Frank decided that, even though the conversation was likely to be futile and aggravating, he had to bring this to the attention of the police. He climbed the steps from the cellar and back into the bar area. The ambulance crew had now picked up the stretcher bearing George and were carrying him through the lounge bar to the main doors. Vaughan was still in conversation with Peter Roberts in the car park. Peter was becoming more exasperated and shrill. Vaughan was seeking to disengage and return to his car. If Frank didn't intercede now, he would be gone and Frank was not confident that a phone call, however well reasoned or persuasive, would induce him to return to the scene of the crime. He hurried over.

"Bottles!"

That was enough to gain their attention and, critically, to stop them talking.

"The bottles at the bottom of the cellar steps, including the one that killed George, they're empty."

Vaughan rolled his eyes.

"He had no business moving empty bottles into or out of the cellar. Empty bottles go into the bin and then to the back for collection. They never go in or out of the cellar. And the light was off. And the ambulance woman; she said that piercing the femoral artery was a million-to-one shot. Please come back and take a second look."

Vaughan paused. He appeared to be thinking. This was a very positive development because, from Frank's point of view, it was the first time the young detective had done so since arriving on the scene. Surely he could see the logic; that moving empty bottles into or out of a cellar was improbable and therefore needed explaining. Frank could see the slow passage of understanding navigating its way across Vaughan's face… and then Peter intervened.

"Well, I'm sure that we're both very grateful for your theories, Frank, however fanciful, but there are larger issues at stake here. Now, Constable…" he turned again to Vaughan, "as the competent civil authority here, I am entitled to be kept abreast of any and all developments promptly, and in writing."

The moment was gone. Frank saw the expression of mulish stupidity return to Vaughan's face. He turned on his heel and fifteen seconds later, his car was out of the car park, sending a modest spray of gravel behind him.

"That young man has made a very grievous mistake," began Peter. "My brother-in-law plays golf with the deputy chief constable…"

But Frank was no longer listening. He had turned and was walking back to the pub, but now his pipe was clenched between his teeth and he was emitting rapid little puffs of smoke like a submachine gun in the hands of an expert.

The first person he saw was Bridget. She was in the process of helping herself to a brandy from the optic. She caught Frank's eye. "For the shock. George wouldn't have minded."

Frank looked at her. She put down the glass. "Well," she said, "I need to be going anyway." She hurried towards the door to the car park.

"Not that way!" Frank indicated the road to the street.

"Well?"

Frank had forgotten about the chef. He was sitting on a stool at the end of the bar. An empty glass in front of him.

"Well, I suppose you're in charge, unless you can think of anybody else," said Frank.

"Not me, mate. I'll be back tomorrow week for my wages." He put on his jacket and headed for the car park, leaving a set of keys on the table nearest the door. Frank was alone.

Any second now, Peter Roberts will be in here commandeering the place on behalf of the citizens of Leighton Parva! thought Frank. He picked up the keys and locked both doors. He returned behind the bar where he improvised two signs, one for each door. '*Closed today, sorry for the inconvenience.*' He had better call the brewery and let them know, he supposed. The number had to be around here somewhere.

The clock struck twelve. Frank opened the side door, the one that led to the car park, and attached his sign. Then, he went to the door that led to the street and opened it to do the same. Standing outside was what looked like the result of an experiment whereby somebody attempted to recreate the letters section of *The Daily Telegraph* in human form. He was clad head to foot, or so it seemed, in tweed, corduroy, a love of cricket, gardening, wet Labradors and the shipping forecast. Silvery hair, a military bearing, a military moustache even, Bernard Taylor was the epitome of a retired Rutland citizen.

"Hello, Bernard."

"Hello, Frank. Want to tell me what's been going on?"

FOUR

There is something horrible and empty about a closed pub when it ought to be open. There is no gentle murmur of voices, no chink of glasses and the dust mites illuminated by the sunlight slicing through the gap in the curtains take on a sinister, alien air. Even so, a closed pub is one that is scheduled to be an open pub. There is hope and promise. Here, there was no hope, but rather the broken promise of conviviality, the vacuum where social interaction and community ought to be. Oh, and the death – that, too.

Bernard was sitting at a table in the bar. Frank was fighting with the coffee machine and losing. He was growing ever more exasperated; his language was getting worse and his Glaswegian accent stronger. In the end, he gave up and instead pulled two pints of Guinness, and took them both over to the table where Bernard was stroking Rocky as he lay with his head in his lap.

Frank and Bernard were an unlikely couple, even unlikelier friends. Frank was a Glaswegian, proud of his proletarian roots. His politics had been forged in the Clydeside Shipyards. His father had been a Marxist trade union leader and, if the cards had fallen slightly differently, Frank might have become one, too. For the first six decades of his life, he would have viewed somebody like Bernard with a mixture of suspicion and hostility.

Bernard had been born into moderate wealth and qualified privilege. He had spent the better part of his life engaged in a covert war against Marxism-Leninism. On paper, the two ought to have been implacable enemies. And for a while, they were – sort of. A few months ago, Frank had been trying to arrest Bernard and send him to prison for a very long time.

Frank's last investigation – he would have called it an operation – had been targeting a small gang of drug smugglers based in Lincoln. As far as gangs went, they were far from being first division – not a criminal mastermind among them. But for reasons that Frank still did not understand, Bernard had somehow become involved. He had used the skills he had acquired over a lifetime to lead Frank and his team a merry dance. Two merry dances, actually; the first to enable the gang to evade detection, the second to land them right in Frank's lap with enough evidence to send them all to prison for double-figure sentences, while keeping his own fingers spotlessly clean. Frank knew what Bernard had done. Bernard knew that Frank knew. They had just reached an unspoken agreement that neither would ever mention the subject.

Similarly, Bernard remained mute when Frank described himself as a retired civil servant. It was technically true, and Bernard was not going to add any depth or detail to the description. Partly, this was for self-interest because Frank knew that Bernard had been a brigadier and not a major, as he allowed people to think. Frank also knew that he had been head of Military Intelligence in West Berlin for many years and suspected that Bernard still had a digit or two in one or more intelligence pies.

Bernard indicated, without saying anything, that he was ready to receive his briefing.

"You're going to think me a silly old fool!"

"Never."

"You will; you are going to think 'Poor old Frank, can't let go, can't accept he's retired, looking for crimes and mysteries everywhere.'"

"I assure you, I won't. Why don't you just tell me?" Bernard took a long draft of his pint, finishing almost half of it. He smacked his lips, either in appreciation of the beer or anticipation of Frank's explanation. It was hard to tell.

And so, Frank told him. He started with the facts: Bridget's scream, the sight of George at the bottom of the steps, the fact that the lights in the cellar had been switched off. Then, he told him of his conversation with DC Vaughan, his examination of the cellar, the broken bottles, empty and without caps. The bottle on the stretcher and what the ambulance crew had said. Then, he recounted his final conversations with Vaughan and Peter Roberts.

Bernard sat silent throughout, sipping his Guinness, nodding occasionally. "I suppose that the brewery will have to be told."

"I was just going to call them."

"And they, I imagine, will tell you to secure the premises, retain the keys and wait to be contacted by one of their people."

"I expect so. Something like that."

"Which gives us a very narrow window in which to examine the scene of the crime." Bernard finished his Guinness in a single long swallow. He smacked his lips again. It wasn't because of the beer. "Shall we?"

Frank could think of a hundred objections. Technically, they were probably trespassing. Technically, they were probably interfering with a crime scene, although the chances of DC Vaughan returning with a tape measure and fingerprint powder seemed remote in the extreme. That didn't bother Frank so much. He was more concerned that he was being ridiculous. Was he playing at being an investigator one last time? He was trying to decide which of these to make the spearhead of his objection, when Bernard rose and, taking a torch from his pocket, headed for the bar. Frank shrugged and followed him, wondering if

Bernard always carried a torch – and if he didn't, what did this signify?

The trapdoor was still open, but the passageway was narrow and only one man could stand there at once. Bernard shone the torch down the steps. He allowed the beam to play over the light switch. Then, he turned and gingerly descended, switching on the light as he reached the third step. Frank followed him.

Bernard considered squatting to examine the broken glass at close quarters, but he was seventy-seven. He decided to explore further into the cellar. There were three bare light bulbs hanging by short cords from the ceiling, but only the first, the one at the bottom of the stairs, was working. The back of the cellar was therefore rather gloomy, even with the benefit of Bernard's torch. He ventured slowly in, stooping slightly, but he didn't really know what he was looking for. Frank was a little more certain. In the furthest and darkest corner, he gave a small grunt of satisfaction.

"Found something?"

"Only what I expected. Tesco's cheapest blended scotch, likewise vodka, gin, rum. Peanuts from the cash and carry. Beer barrels from the brewery. Bottles – some from the brewery, some from the cash and carry. Wine, likewise."

Bernard approached, panning his torch beam to and fro across the floor. "There's more here. Champagne, I think."

Frank glanced over. There was what looked like a dozen bottles on the floor. Beside them was a cardboard box.

"It's probably just cava."

"You may be right. The labels on the bottle are a bit small and the box is damaged."

Frank looked a little closer. "What happened to the other box? There's a dozen bottles on the floor and ten more in this one. Where's the other box?" He looked again at the damaged box.

Just then, both men heard the sound of someone knocking – no, pounding – on the pub doors. Rocky was giving excited little barks upstairs.

"A pound says that's Peter Roberts."

"Sure to be. Anyway, I've seen enough."

It took a full fifteen minutes to persuade Peter that the situation was under control and that he neither needed to declare martial law or take The Old Volunteer into protective custody. He really was a very tiresome man. Bernard wondered whether it wasn't time for some sort of coup on the parish council. He hadn't personally organised any coups himself, but he knew one or two people from the old days who had. In the end, it had been Frank's entirely imaginary conversation on the phone with an entirely fictitious representative of the brewery that persuaded Peter he had no business there. When he'd left, Frank decided it was time to make the genuine call.

*

Frank put down the phone. He had explained the situation to the brewery and, as he had expected, he was asked to secure the premises. Somebody from the brewery would be along a little later to collect the keys.

Frank spent the next half hour riffling through the invoices, bills and purchases he had found in George's tiny office and on the shelf below the bar. As he worked, he murmured a half commentary to himself. Bernard was feeding Rocky with some cheese crackers he had found behind the bar. Both men were on their second pint of Guinness.

"There's no purchase order, delivery note or invoice for that cava," said Frank.

"No?"

"No. It's one of George's off-record lines."

"Well, that's to be expected, isn't it?"

"Of course, but I was particularly interested in that cava."

"For why?"

"Two reasons. First, why would anyone unpack a full case of

31

twelve and then discard the box, when it would be easier to just take some from the already open box with ten bottles in it?"

"Perhaps he needed exactly twelve or, more likely, wanted the box."

"No. If he needed twelve, why discard the box? If he needed the box, why open the second one?"

Bernard shrugged. "That one was damaged. You mentioned a second reason."

"The box we did find. It had diagonal slashes in the sides. Have you ever seen anyone do that to a box? And don't tell me it was an accident. There was an identical diagonal slash on every side. Can you think of a reason somebody might do that?"

"No. No, actually, I can't."

"Yes, well, I can. Let me show you."

Frank disappeared back into the cellar. He emerged a few minutes later with the empty box that had contained ten bottles of cava. He put it in the table in front of Bernard and then returned behind the bar. He rooted around beneath the counter for a second or two, and then returned.

"Now, look at the cardboard that makes up the side of the box. You see that there is a thin skin on each side and the space between is filled with a further strip that sort of zigzags to and fro to provide the bulk."

Bernard nodded.

"And in between the zig and the zag, there is a little gap." Frank picked up the straw that he had found beneath the bar and slid it into the gap within the two skins of the cardboard.

Bernard nodded again. "And that straw could be filled with, what? Drugs? Money? Gold dust?"

"Yes, any of those things. It's a popular method of smuggling. But what's important is this. If you are a busy customs officer, or anyone else in a hurry who wants to check if a cardboard box has been used to…"

Bernard was already there. "You simply slash the sides with

a knife and see if white powder falls out. Are you suggesting that George Bowman was at the centre of a narcotics ring and that somebody murdered him because of it?"

"It doesn't sound very likely, does it?" Frank conceded. "But combined with everything else; the missing box, George moving empty bottles in or out of a cellar, in the dark, the million-to-one shot of a bottle piercing his femoral artery. It's just too many unexplained things. I just wish I knew who had supplied him with that bubbly. That's why I was looking for the invoice."

"So, your theory is that someone was looking for whatever they had hidden in a cava box, slashed this one, found nothing, found what they were looking for in the second box, emptied it of bottles, took it away and at some point in this enterprise murdered George, in a way that probably required specialised medical knowledge, then faked the scene to make it look like an accident?"

"It does seem a bit far-fetched when you put it that way, doesn't it?"

"I don't know. It seems eminently plausible to me. Anyway, there is a way we could check."

"I don't really feel like crawling around on a cellar floor with a magnifying glass, looking for traces of cocaine, if that's what you have in mind."

"Oh, Francis! Francis, Francis, Francis! You were doing so well up to that point. We've got a bloody sniffer dog!"

FIVE

Frank had looked everywhere that he could think of, but he couldn't find any peppermints anywhere. He was sure that he'd had half a packet of polos in a coat pocket somewhere, but he couldn't find them. In the end, he settled for brushing his teeth four times. It was absurd. And a little embarrassing. And completely the wrong way around. Here he was at sixty years of age, trying to disguise the smell of alcohol on his breath from his own daughter.

It should have been the other way around. It should have been Michelle, fifteen years old, giggling, back from a night out with her friends, desperately chugging Tic Tacs as she staggered up the front path. But Frank hadn't been there when Michelle was fifteen. He had been in a darkened shed in Felixstowe, binoculars trained on an abandoned lorry, or sitting in a parked car waiting for the order to go and break down someone's door. More likely than either of these is that he would have been in a pub somewhere surrounded by ten others just like him, substituting an investigation team for a real family.

Anyway, he had completely forgotten that he was supposed to be babysitting for Michelle and Simon tonight and so he was trying to remove all traces of the Guinness he had drunk that afternoon. Now that he had remembered, he was looking forward to the evening. He had rented a video of *Home Alone 3*, which he was confident Maisie and Frankie Junior, sorry, Francis, would love.

It was slightly odd that Michelle and Simon were going out on a Monday, which was part of the reason why it had slipped his mind. Perhaps it was some sort of special occasion or anniversary. Young people these days seemed to feel the need to commemorate all sorts of dates that seemed utterly insignificant. He had just enough self-knowledge to recognise that if he took such things a little more seriously himself, perhaps he wouldn't have been married three times, divorced twice, widowed once.

At a quarter to seven – Frank would still have called it eighteen forty-five; some habits were hard to break – he walked across what had once been the farmyard. VHS cassette in one hand, Rocky trotting at his heels.

Frankie Junior was delighted to see him. Maisie was delighted to see Rocky. Michelle was coming down the stairs, fixing an earring as she came.

"Oh, hello, Dad. What have you got there?"

"It's *Home Alone 3*," said Frankie Junior, whose reading skills were developing rapidly. "It's got a parrot in it. And a rat."

"Well, put in on quickly. I don't want them up too late."

"Grandad smells of Polos," said Frankie Junior.

"He's probably been to the pub," Maisie offered, without looking up from the game of tug of war she was having with Rocky over one of her shoes. Frank didn't know whether to be embarrassed at being exposed or proud of the little investigation team his daughter was raising.

"In bed by half past eight. I mean it. They have school tomorrow."

*

Frank had become something of a connoisseur of children's films in the past few years and, in his opinion, *Home Alone 3* was not of first-division standard. His mind started to drift to the events of the day.

He was conscious that deep within himself there was a desire to investigate something and so he forced himself to approach the known facts in a cynical fashion. George had died from what the paramedic had called a one-in-a-million chance. A broken bottle piercing the femoral artery. But was it really one in a million? That was just a figure of speech, surely – shorthand for 'very unlikely'. Well, very unlikely things happened every day. Even million-to-one events occurred surprisingly often. And what was the alternative?

Well, there were two: the first was that George had been deliberately murdered by someone who was able to use a broken bottle as a weapon and knowledgeable enough to know how to pierce a key artery. Wasn't that even more unlikely? That suggested either a homicidal medic or a professional assassin. Frank thought that professional assassins were probably fairly scarce in Rutland. The second possibility was that it had been a blend of malice and bad luck. A struggle followed by the unlikely – one might even say, freak – piece of luck that led to George's death. This didn't seem likely either, but it was likelier than 'the Jackal' being in Leighton Parva on a Sunday night.

So, what about the other elements? The light being off. Well, perhaps George had been too lazy, with his hands full, to switch on the light. This would likely have contributed to him losing his footing. Or perhaps he had slipped while reaching for the switch. The issue of the light, which had first aroused Frank's suspicions, seemed less significant now. Maybe he had even fallen against the light switch on his way down. Wasn't impossible – likelier than a million to one, at any rate.

This left the bottles. The bottles were definitely wrong. Full bottles – that is to say, bottles with their crown caps still attached – were delivered by the brewery lorry to the little yard at the back of the pub. From there, they were taken, with the bottle tops still attached, down into the cellar. They were taken upstairs, as and when required, still with bottle tops, up to the bar where they were either put in the fridge or on the cold shelf. When a customer ordered a bottle, it would be taken from the shelf, the cap removed, and either handed to the customer or poured into a glass. In either event, once emptied it would end up in the little blue bin on wheels that fitted under the bar counter. When full, this bin would be wheeled – Frank had seen George do it – to the area at the back where the bottles were put in the crate for return to the brewery.

Frank examined this chronology again and again looking for flaws. There were none. He could think of no circumstances whereby George or anyone else would have any reason to move empty bottles up or down the cellar steps. So, if the bottles were wrong, the issues of the million-to-one wound and the light switch needed to be re-evaluated in the light of this one fixed point.

And then there were the drugs. Okay, the slashes in the side of the cava box were highly circumstantial, to say the least, but Rocky had given an indication. At least Frank had thought he had. Frank had never been a dog handler himself, but he must have seen a dog being put over a suspect cargo on at least a dozen occasions. He had urged Rocky to "Go find it! Go find it!" in what he thought was the right tone. He had used a blend of: 'this is an order', 'this is a game' and 'be a good boy'.

Rocky had bounded happily down the alarmingly steep cellar steps with ease and begun his work. Frank stood by and Bernard observed from the top of the steps. Rocky had examined everything in what appeared – to Frank, at least – a business-like and professional manner. Frank caught himself holding his breath as Rocky approached the collection of cava bottles with no box in one corner. He had almost been angry with himself for being so childishly apprehensive. Rocky circled the area, just as he had circled everywhere else two times. And then a third, and then a fourth. And then he had sat down and fixed Frank with a gaze that normally meant 'I have done well – reward me.'

"Bernard, Bernard! Can you come down here a second?"

It had, in fact, taken Bernard considerably longer than a second to make it down the steps.

"Go find it! Go find it!"

Rocky got up – reluctantly, it seemed to Frank – then had a perfunctory sniff around before returning to his spot next to the cava bottles and sitting down. He had fixed Frank with the same 'reward me' stare.

"I think," began Frank, "I think that's a positive indication."

"I think so, too," said Bernard. "I mean, I've only seen bomb detector dogs, but I assume it's the same principle."

Both men had stood in silence for a second or two. Then Bernard had reached into his pocket and extracted a small packet of Mini Cheddars and handed it to Frank. "Reward."

So, empty bottles, light switch, unlikely wound, popular concealment, missing cava box and Rocky's indication. Frank decided that he was not imagining it. There was something wrong. And Bernard had thought so, too. Of course, Bernard had spent years in military intelligence. They were always leaping to conclusions, imagining things that weren't there and concocting elaborate, far-fetched theories. In Frank's world, you were right or wrong. The target was convicted or acquitted. In Bernard's world, it was a game when nobody ever knew who had won or lost.

*

Home Alone 3 wasn't as good a film as its predecessors. As well as failing to hold Frank's attention, it had failed to grip Maisie or Frankie Junior's either. Maisie had turned her attention to a colouring book. Frankie was writing and rewriting his name on a pad of paper. He was concentrating intently, his tongue sticking out of the corner of his mouth, and he was leaning hard as he traced each letter: 'Francis Anthony Nicholson'.

It was already half past eight and, for once, Frank was determined to stick to the Michelle-mandated bedtime. It took him fourteen minutes to get Maisie and Frankie Junior to bed, beating his previous record by seven minutes. He put the kettle on and, while it boiled, he picked up Maisie's colouring book and pencils, as well as Frankie's pen and the pad upon which he had been writing. He had leaned so hard on the tip of his pen that the impression of 'Francis Anthony Nicholson' could still be seen several pages below. Smiling, Frank took the topmost sheet, folded it and put it in his pocket.

Michelle and Simon arrived home about ten. Frank had managed to stay awake and was watching a programme previewing the forthcoming World Cup. The opening match was going to be between Brazil, the reigning champions, and Scotland. Now, that really was a million-to-one chance. Michelle and Simon sat side by side on the settee directly opposite him. They were holding hands. Frank ran his own hand over his snow-white beard. Too short to be Santa Claus; too similar to Captain Birds Eye for comfort.

"Dad…"

"So, you're getting hitched, are you? Have you told your mother?"

"Dad! You're supposed to let us tell you."

"Oh, yes, sorry. Well, have you?"

"No. We… I wanted you to be the first to know. How did you know, by the way? No! Don't tell me. I don't want to know. Bloody investigators! You're supposed to be retired."

"You'd better phone your mother."

Michelle left to do exactly that, leaving Frank and Simon smiling at each other.

"I'll do my best to make her happy."

"I know you will."

"Can I… can I call you Dad?"

"What do you think?"

"Grandpa Frank?"

"Much better."

Frank rose. "I'll leave you to the rest of your evening. Congratulations!" And with that, he left, Rocky at his heels.

For over twenty years, almost every evening of Frank McBride's life had ended with a glass of whiskey. Whiskey, not whisky. Proud Scotsman though he was, he just preferred Jack Daniel's. Frank smiled to himself at this memory as he reached to the cupboard and took down the tin of cocoa. He filled the kettle and reached into his jacket pocket for his pipe. He was smoking less than ever, too. Who was this sober, abstemious Frank McBride who walked miles every day and whose greatest pleasure was watching bad films with his grandchildren?

As he withdrew his pipe, a piece of paper came with it. It was the one on which Frankie Junior had been, what? Practising his signature? Frank smiled at the deep trenches gouged in the paper by the pencil's point. He thought for a second. From another pocket, he took the two pieces of paper upon which he had written his 'notebook' earlier that day. He laid them flat on the table, writing side down and gently ran his hand over them. It was possible that his pages had been directly below the last thing that George Bowman had ever written. And if they were, was it possible that there might be a tiny impression left behind? A few months ago, he would simply have sent the pages to the Laboratory of the Government Chemist and asked them to carry out an ESDA test. The Electro Static Device Analysis test would reveal any impressions, however faint. But this wasn't a few months ago. He was a retired civil servant in Rutland. He would have to do it the old-fashioned way.

Frank hunted in various kitchen drawers looking for a pencil. Eventually, he found one of Maisie's colouring pencils. It was purple. It didn't matter. Turning the paper over onto the unused side, he lightly – very, very lightly – swept the pencil to and fro,

just grazing the surface of the paper. It was faint – very, very, faint
– but he could just make out the impressions of the last thing
written on the pad. The page above the one where Frank had made
his notes.

Dear Jo   m,
Someone   s deliv   me of y   Ca   t me
It is clea   a very s   ivery
I am sure that y   t have it re   to y u
I would be happy to r   to you in ex   f   t
Sum of £3,
George B
The Old V
Leighton Pa

SIX

Frank decided to visit Bernard to see if he had had any further thoughts or insights overnight. The old brigadier was sitting in his kitchen with a teapot in front of him and a coffee maker on the stove. He had clearly been expecting him.

Frank knew better than to interrupt Bernard while he prepared the beverages. He was of a generation who made tea only in a pot and according to a formula and ritual that he would not compromise in any circumstances. Similarly, he abhorred instant coffee. It was a full five minutes before each man had a cup, not a mug, sitting on a saucer before them.

"I have had one further thought," said Bernard. "George died on Sunday night or Monday morning. He didn't work on Sunday nights. Lunchtimes, yes, but never evenings. It was his one time of the week to be on the other side of the bar. And so, it is even more unlikely that he was moving bottles into or out of the cellar on Sunday night. And given how much he used to drink, it also seems highly improbable that he was up early on a Monday morning doing so either."

Frank nodded. Bernard had been in the village far longer than he and doubtless knew the various villagers' routines far better. He passed Bernard the shaded piece of paper with the partially legible message upon it.

"What's this?"

"The imprint of something written on the spiral notebook I found underneath the bar."

Bernard studied it for a moment, then, rising, held it up to the light at the window. He put it back on the kitchen table and left the room. When he returned a minute later, he was carrying a pad of squared paper and a pair of pencils. Slowly, he transcribed such parts of the message as could be read. He wrote one letter in each square and left blank squares corresponding to the missing letters.

"Of course, I am guessing how many letters are missing. I could easily be wrong."

Frank nodded. He drew the paper and pad across the table and repeated the exercise two times.

"Master copy," he said and folded one sheet of squared paper and put it in his pocket with the original page from the notebook. Both men sat in silence looking at their puzzles, trying to guess what the missing letters might be and therefore what the message had been. Some parts were easy – the last lines were obviously: George Bowman, The Old Volunteer, Leighton Parva.

Other parts were trickier. After half an hour, and quite a lot of rubbing out, Frank leaned back. "I can't do it."

"Neither can I. I was never much of a hand at crossword puzzles."

"Nor me. But I know a man who is."

*

Ron Godsmark played bowls on a Tuesday, at least during the summer, and so Frank had to wait until the following morning. His plan was to wait until they reached Ron's house before broaching the subject of his little word puzzle. So, for the first thirty minutes of their walk together, Frank was content to allow

43

Ron to give a blow-by-blow account of the previous day's match. Bowls was the only subject upon which Frank had ever known Ron incline towards the loquacious. It was not a game that Frank knew well, but he was able to follow well enough, despite Ron's accent becoming stronger still at the description of what were obviously the most dramatic moments, to understand that Leighton Magna had pulled off a famous victory.

Since the subject was a sporting one, and since Ron's account appeared to have been completed, Frank turned the subject to the World Cup being held in France and starting in just over a week's time.

"Ever been to France, Ron?"

"Arr. Twice. Once a couple of years back. Once fifty year before that."

Frank did the sums. The arithmetic was suggestive. He was going to press him further on this, but Rocky returned from some ditch with a rabbit – or three-quarters of what had once been a rabbit – in his mouth. It took some time to persuade him to give up his prize and by the time he had, Ron had returned to his default setting of silence.

This continued until the pair, and Rocky, reached the back of the hall. There was a sand-coloured Volkswagen Beetle parked at the rear, next to a lorry that was delivering fruit and vegetables.

"I haven't seen one of those in years," said Frank.

"Arr. That'll be Light-fingered Leo's. They want to keep a close eye on those vegetables or half of them'll be in the back of his car."

Frank was about to remind Ron that the back of a Beetle was where the engine was when something else occurred to him.

*

By the time they had reached Ron's cottage, Frank still hadn't thought of a way of casually introducing the subjects of crosswords and puzzles, so instead he just came out with it. Ron admitted readily that he was a keen cruciverbalist and Frank showed him the partially revealed message from George Bowman's notebook. He wondered whether he ought to impress upon Ron the need for discretion, even secrecy, but ultimately decided that it wasn't necessary and might risk offending him.

"Arr!" said Ron, taking the piece of squared paper that Bernard had prepared. He studied it for a few moments and said, "Arr!" again. Then, he took the paper to his little kitchen table and studied it in more depth.

"Arr, ahh, arr!" he said and then took up a pencil. Frank sipped his tea while Ron set to work, frowning and with his tongue sticking out of the corner of his mouth, just like Frankie Junior. After ten minutes, he sat back.

"Not difficult," he said. "Apart from that first bit. Has me stumped, that has."

He pushed the paper towards Frank.

> *Dear Jo m,*
> *Someone has delivered some of your <u>cats/caps/cars/cash</u> to*
>
> *me*
>
> *It is clearly a very <u>special/small/strong</u> delivery*
> *I am sure that you want to have it returned to you*
> *I would be happy to return it to you in exchange for the*
> *Sum of <u>£3,000 / £3,000,000</u>*
> *George Bowman*
> *The Old Volunteer*
> *Leighton Parva*

"I underlined my guesses."

"Arr!" said Frank. "I mean, thanks. Thank you very much."

"Arr."

*

Bernard had even laid out a plate of biscuits when Frank arrived. It was extraordinary the way that he was able to predict Frank's movements. Or perhaps it wasn't. Perhaps the old man just knew Frank's routine. Or perhaps he kept watch on all the comings and goings in the village. Bernard's house, The Old Vicarage, was well situated for that.

Frank waited until both had taken their first sip of tea and their first nibble of biscuit before taking Ron's effort from his pocket. He slid it across the table, a slight smirk on his face. Bernard raised an eyebrow and drew the piece of paper towards him. He read it through twice.

"Well, it's cava, isn't it? Has to be. It's not cats or cash."

"Yes, basically it's a ransom note. George found the drugs – or whatever it was, probably drugs – and ransomed it for three grand. Whoever received that note either decided to pay him off and then there was an argument or just flat out decided to murder him. Pretty ruthless."

"Ruthless and expert. If it was a premediated killing, it was somebody who really knew what he was doing. Single stab. Improvised weapon. No signs of a struggle. And then the plausible explanation of falling down the cellar steps."

"Or it was an argument and a freak fatal injury."

"Do you really think that, Frank?"

"Not for a second."

"Nor do I."

"The only problem is that we don't know who the note was addressed to. Jay Oh. John? Joseph?"

"Joanne? Josephine?"

"Joshua? Jocelyn? Not very helpful, really. And what about that stray M? Is it part of the word beginning J O? Or part of a second word?"

Both men sat in silence for a few minutes. Bernard pulled the sheet of squared paper towards him. Using a pencil, he tapped out the spaces between o and m. Then, he did it again.

Wordlessly, he held out his hand. Frank drew the original piece of paper from his pocket and handed it over. As Bernard studied it, Frank pondered on the fact that each man had completely understood the other without speaking. Frank wasn't entirely sure how he felt about that. Bernard tapped out the spaces with a pencil again. While he did so, Frank pulled a pipe from his pocket. It was one of his favourites – a retirement gift from one of his colleagues. He slowly filled it with tobacco, his eyes never leaving Bernard.

"Joachim."

"Joachim?"

"Joachim. As in Joachim von Ribbentrop. Father of Mary. Jesus' grandfather. Joachim."

Frank nodded. He was ready to consider Joachim as a viable theory, but he was not yet ready to accept it as the definitive answer. "Could be, could be. Could also be John Smith, of course."

"Yes, but John Smith doesn't own and manage Leighton Hall. Joachim Keller does."

Frank lit his pipe and leaned back. It simply never occurred to him to ask Bernard if he minded. And it never would have occurred to Bernard to object.

"Ah! And Leighton Hall is a wedding venue. Just the sort of place that might have cava."

"Exactly! And it's not impossible that a case or two was delivered to the pub rather than the hall by mistake."

Frank puffed at his pipe. "No, no. I don't think that's it. Do you know a local known as Light-fingered Leo?"

"Oh yes, Leo Davidson. Phillip and Audrey's boy. Terrible thorn in the side of his long-suffering parents. Why do you ask?"

"And does this lad have a reputation for being a bit light-fingered?"

"It wouldn't surprise me, why?"

"Because I saw his car parked at the back of the hall this morning."

"He's probably working there. Every now and then, he runs short of funds wherever he is, comes back here, eats his parents out of house and home, steals the housekeeping money and disappears again. Perhaps he's got a bit of casual work at the bar. He used to work at The Old Volunteer until George kicked him out. Maybe he saw a chance to pinch some booze and tried to sell it to George."

"It seems very plausible. George would certainly have been in the market for any stock that came at a bargain price and without any paperwork."

Bernard rose and filled the kettle. Both men sat in silence while it boiled.

"So, what do we think?" began Bernard. "Leo pinches some cava, with drugs concealed in the box, and sells it to George. George discovers the drugs and sends a ransom note to Joachim. And Joachim visits George on Sunday night. They argue and George ends up at the bottom of the cellar steps, dead."

"And Joachim empties the drug-filled box of the cava and takes it away."

"Yes, but we still have the question of whether this was a tragic accident following a struggle or cold-blooded murder."

"Does Joachim Keller strike you as a man capable of cold-blooded murder?"

"I don't know. I've never met him. I only know his name. He doesn't visit the village, as far as I know. Might go to Leighton Magna, I suppose. I've never had any occasion to go up to the hall, after all. I'm not getting married."

"Ah! But I am!"

"What?"

"Well, not me, obviously – my daughter. Michelle got engaged last night."

"Congratulations!"

"And as the father of the bride…"

"You will naturally want to inspect various potential locations for the wedding breakfast."

"Nobody calls it that anymore, but yes. I have the perfect excuse to go and inspect the hall, meet the proprietors and generally do a bit of reconnaissance."

"And Michelle will be alright with that, will she?"

Well, no, obviously she wouldn't. Frank could all too easily imagine the hurt, the outrage, the reminder that he was retired and not supposed to be investigating, let alone using his new status as father of the bride as a pretext for going undercover. So, he decided not to tell her.

*

Leighton Hall sat on the hill slightly north-east of Leighton Parva and slightly north-west of the nearer, and somewhat smaller, Leighton Magna. It was approached by a long, curving gravel drive that began between two pillars, upon which were perched the stone heads of two elephants, then ascended the hill in a meandering fashion that gave the guests a view of the rolling parkland and the house itself.

Bought with the sweat and blood of the labouring classes and exploited native peoples, thought Frank.

Frank's political opinions had been forged among the working people of Glasgow and had changed very little since. It was only through sheer good fortune that he had had the career he did.

Had he not lost that postal order, if he had not been called up for National Service, if he hadn't been foolish enough to entrust his pay packet to some useless nag highly recommended to him by Tam Clarke, he would certainly have joined the Communist Party. And that would have prevented him ever passing security vetting. Instead, he was a respectable retired civil servant and an Officer of the Order of the British Empire. He snorted in disgust at himself. Bourgeois affectation!

The house itself was from that period in the eighteenth century when every parvenu who had returned from Bengal with a chest full of cash wanted a huge white cube with a neo-classical porch. A porch beneath which a young woman appeared to be collecting confetti with a dustpan and brush.

Frank parked a little to the side. From there, he could see that the original building had been substantially extended at the back. The newer wing – people who owned houses like this always called extensions 'wings' – was almost double the size of the original house. There were also other buildings. They might have been stables or coach houses or something. They were brick-built, too, but not recently.

There was a small sign indicating that the offices were to be found at the rear. Frank straightened his tie and marched in the direction indicated. He hadn't mentioned to Michelle that he was using her upcoming nuptials as a pretext for checking out the lay of the land at Leighton Hall. He didn't feel the least guilty about that. If there was mischief up at the hall, then it was his duty, his paternal duty, to investigate and satisfy himself that a potential location was above board. Yes, that would do. Parental duty. Michelle wouldn't buy it for a second, of course. But he didn't need to fool Michelle, only himself.

There was a door, slightly ajar and painted an alarming shade of purple. This must be it. Frank pushed it open, but there was nobody there. Frank looked for a bell or some means of indicating his presence, but he couldn't see one. He decided to sit and wait and to examine his surroundings.

This was the room where blushing young brides were presumably expected to come and discuss their dream wedding. Here, there would be intense conversations about bouquets and napkins and rubber chicken in nondescript sauces. It was hardly conducive to imagining a fairy-tale day. It was more like a waiting room for a driving test examiner or the tourist office of a nondescript town trying to conjure up some enthusiasm, because it was the birthplace of an eighteenth-century scientist. Frank had paid speeding tickets in more glamourous locations.

In one corner was a desk. It had one of those little Toblerone-shaped nameplates. Madeline Clements – Events Organiser. There was no sign of Madeline, so Frank sat down on an armchair that properly belonged in a much larger room. After a few moments, he picked up one of the glossy brochures from a rack inside the door. On the front was somebody's idea of a dream wedding. A coach pulled by a pair of white horses beneath the portico he had seen earlier. The bride was beautiful, glowing, beaming and generally looking like the happiest person on earth. Frank snorted.

"Oh! May I help you?"

The line was delivered in a tone that indicated that the desired answer was 'No'. And was there the hint of an accent? Frank rose, even Glaswegian communists have manners.

Opposite him was a woman of about forty. She was not beautiful, but she was – what was the word? Handsome? Impressive? Striking? Yes, striking. She was a striking woman. She was dressed in a business suit that might have been expensive. Frank wasn't an expert. It might easily have been expensive. And she carried herself with the sort of confidence one usually associates with maître d's or football hooligans, or head girls at particularly barbaric schools for young ladies.

"Yes, my daughter has just got engaged and we live in the village. Leighton Parva, actually," he added for clarification, lest it be thought he was from Leighton Magna. " I…"

The woman, who did not introduce herself, appeared to be appraising Frank. It lasted an uncomfortably long time. "I see. I shall see if Madeline, the events organiser, is available."

Definitely an accent. Might have been Swiss.

*

Frank and Bernard were sitting at Bernard's kitchen table.

"It's no good. The place is enormous. There's very little I could learn from wandering about pretending to be interested in bouquets and bandstands. We would need to have someone properly on the inside."

Bernard steepled his fingers and leant back in his chair. "I might – *might* – just be able to help there."

SEVEN

The great bell of Tom Tower was sounding 'four'. Emma knew that this indicated that it was exactly five minutes and two seconds past four. Christ Church College kept 'Oxford Time', not British Summer Time. Emma was amazed that she remembered this because she could remember very little else.

She had been at the Pembroke College May Ball, at least she thought she had. It was her third ball that week, or possibly her fourth. She couldn't remember. But she remembered that Christ Church was five minutes slow. And she remembered that May balls took place in the first week in June. Further evidence that Oxford was absurd.

Her feet hurt. She decided that she would remove her shoes. That was difficult. She frowned in puzzlement. How was a woman supposed to remove a pair of silver sandals when she was holding a bottle of champagne in each hand? After a moment or two, she hit upon a solution. She should discard the bottle containing the least remaining alcohol. She weighed each, a little uncertainly. Then, she leant against a lamp post and tried again. The bottle in her left hand might be empty. She peered unsteadily into it. Yep, empty. There might be a little in the other bottle. She held it to her lips.

Now that was empty, too. She could safely discard them both. But why did she want to? Oh yes, shoes.

It was only three-quarters of a mile from Christ Church to New College, but it was almost five by the time Emma arrived. Exams were over. Term was over, good as, but somewhere in the back of her mind, there was a nagging feeling that there was something she had to do tomorrow, or rather today. It was very puzzling, as perplexing a mystery in its own way as the empty champagne bottles. She made it to her room, vaguely aware that it might be a good idea to have a glass or two of water before she went to bed.

In the bathroom, she remembered what she had to do. It was the mirror that told her. At first, she didn't know who was in her bathroom mirror. She looked familiar except for the vivid purple hair. That was different. Then, she remembered. Ah yes! Job interview!

Emma was a law student. She liked studying law and she was very good at it. And she came from a long line of lawyers. Her father was a partner at a big city firm; between Emma's talent and his connections, a glittering career was hers for the asking. Unfortunately, she wasn't asking.

Emma did not want to be a lawyer, for a number of reasons. Firstly, she was an anarchist. Well, possibly not an anarchist per se, but she was certainly anarchy proximate. She was a radical. And a rebel. She wasn't always exactly sure what she was rebelling against, but often she was. Her parents, for example. She was definitely rebelling against them.

Attending Oxford rather than Cambridge might not sound like the sort of thing that Che Guevara would have listed among his greatest rebellions, but in the Butcher family it was pretty strong stuff. And the year that she had spent as an au pair. That was a kind of rebellion, too. But the big one, the greatest rebellion of all, was that she was not going to go into the law.

Unfortunately, she hadn't organised any other way of spending her summer and her father had arranged for her to interview for a place as an intern at a city law firm. Not his own, of course – the network of nepotism and privilege was subtler than that. Doubtless some spotty young scion of Stewart, Poole & DeQuidt's senior partner would be interning at her father's firm as a quid pro quo.

Emma despised the back-scratching, the old school tie and the ethos of 'people like us'. And she wasn't going to go along with it. No. She was not. But neither was she going to stand up to her parents. That was too exhausting and emotionally damaging. No, she was simply going to ensure that she failed the interview. Hence the purple hair. It was a brilliant idea. At least it had seemed like a brilliant idea a day or two ago after the Oriel College ball, possibly, or Brasenose.

To be twenty is to be able to drink champagne until four in the morning (or five minutes and two seconds past four) and still be able to catch the 10:40 from Oxford to Paddington. Emma arrived in Chancery Lane in good time and walked smartly up the steps to the front door of Stewart, Poole & DeQuidt at a minute before two.

The interview, from Emma's point of view, did not go well. She had intended to be surly and uncommunicative. But she was too well raised. She was going to light a cigarette, but her nerve failed her at the last moment. She was going to swear, but somehow she couldn't bring herself to. The two men interviewing her tricked her. They asked an intriguing question about Caparo Industries v Dickman and she couldn't help herself. She spoke fluently and persuasively for fifteen solid minutes, demonstrating a level of understanding and scholarship that a first-year law student had no right to possess. It was all going very badly. If she didn't pull something out of the hat soon, she was going to spend the next few months scurrying between Chancery Lane and The Strand with armfuls of legal documents bound in pink ribbon.

"Well, yes, jolly good," said one of the men. He might have been the one called Jeremy. Or possibly both of them were called Jeremy. They looked like Jeremys. "There is just one thing…"

Jeremy One tailed off. He looked at Jeremy Two. Jeremy Two looked faintly embarrassed.

"Err, yes," said Jeremy Two. Actually, he might have been Julian. One Jeremy and One Julian. Emma wasn't sure which was which.

"It's, err, it's, well, you see. The firm has a sort of dress code…"

"More of an appearance code, actually," contributed Jeremy/Julian One.

"Yes, appearance, and your hair…"

Emma dug deep. This was it. The whole game was on the line. "What's wrong with my hair?" She stuck out her chin and glared at the two Js.

"Err, nothing, nothing at all. No, nothing." Jeremy looked at Julian (or the other way round).

"Nothing whatsoever. Well, I think we have all we need. It was lovely meeting you, Miss Butcher. We shall be in touch."

The two men rose. Emma did the same. Only then did she trouble to read the two business cards that had been on the table in front of her the whole time. They were both called Justin. And neither of them offered her the job.

*

It was Saturday. Emma was dreading her journey home. Her father would doubtless have learned by now of her unsuccessful interview, the interview for which he had doubtless pulled strings, scratched backs and schmoozed shysters. And doubtless, too, she was going to hear all about it all the way back home to Sussex.

She had spent over four hours the previous day trying to remove all traces of purple dye from her hair. In certain lights, she appeared to have been successful; in others, less so. Outside on Holywell Street and up the Mansfield Road, Jaguars and Range Rovers were parked illegally, waiting to take her fellow students home. The average rolling value of the street reduced considerably when Michael's Ford Focus drew up. But Emma was relieved to see him. Relieved and pleased. Relieved, because it postponed her interview with her father for a couple of hours. Pleased, because, despite everything, she loved her brother.

Emma and Michael had spent their entire lives in an uneasy competition. Both would have denied it. Both would have struggled even to admit it to themselves, but it was true. Everything from school sports days to A level results had been the subject of silent, introspective comparison. Emma's A levels had been slightly better, but Michael had a full blue for cricket from Cambridge. Emma had only a half blue, for water polo. By every measure of their lives, they had been effectively neck and neck. If one had exceeded the other in some field, the other would equal or surpass them almost immediately. All this they refused to acknowledge, much less mention.

The current scoreboard in Emma's head showed Michael with a slight lead. This scoreboard could not have existed anywhere except in Emma's head. It would have made no sense to anybody else. Points were awarded for achievement, for acts of rebellion, for artful deceit and generally thwarting their parents' will while pursuing their own goals.

Emma had awarded Michael ten points (a record) for his latest coup. Michael had somehow escaped the world of law. She wasn't exactly sure how he had done it. He suddenly and unexpectedly announced that he had found himself a job and was now working for the Foreign Office. Emma had no idea how he had pulled this off, but she did enjoy the consternation that it had provoked at home. Her mother, somewhat puzzlingly, had blamed her own father. Emma couldn't imagine how her grandfather, an elderly man whom she knew only slightly, could possibly have been responsible.

At first, she had admired Michael's escape and cheered his victory against their common foe. Then, she realised that it only increased the pressure upon her. One child had slipped away and so her parents, in particular her father, would be determined that she would be frogmarched to the bar, or the Supreme Court – wherever it was that reluctant lawyers were frogmarched. The fact that she was studying law gave her even less room for manoeuvre.

"Come on, Em! I'm parked on about eleven yellow lines! What a bloody hole this town is!"

"It's a city! And it's a hundred times better than that windswept piece of marshland you call a seat of learning!"

Michael grinned. Emma grinned. They hugged.

"Seriously, though. We should get a move on."

Together, they carried Emma's luggage down three sets of stairs. Emma returned her room key and followed her brother to the car. It took over half an hour through the busy streets to reach the A40. Only then did Emma raise the subject that she had been dreading.

"Have you spoken to Dad?"

"Sort of. Listen, Em, he's not best pleased, but it's possible that you may have a way out."

"What do you mean?"

And so, Michael explained. Their father was, predictably, very unhappy. Their mother, even worse, and in a fit of vindictiveness had arranged for Emma to work at a restaurant owned by their aunt. Emma began to protest, but Michael silenced her.

"There is an alternative," he began, "but it comes with a health warning. There is a job at a place near Grandpa's. You could stay with him."

"Where is that again?"

"Rutland."

Michael's eyes never left the road, but he sensed Emma's expression.

"Some sort of country house hotel or something up there, and since you are going to be waitressing anyway…"

"So, what's the catch?"

"Grandpa."

"Really? I mean, I don't know him very well – hardly at all, really – but he seems such a sweet old man."

"Oh, I know. Tweed suit, pocket full of Werther's Originals – kindly old Grandpa! Don't be fooled. Our grandfather is a devious, duplicitous, dishonest and totally amoral rogue! You cannot trust a word he says. He hasn't found you a waitressing job out of the goodness of his heart. He has an agenda. I don't know what it is and neither will you until it's too late, and possibly not even then."

"Oh, come on! He must be about a hundred years old. I haven't seen him since I was twelve and he was positively ancient then."

"I'm telling you, Em, the man is an absolute snake."

"But you stayed with him last summer."

"That's how I know."

"And Mum blames him for getting you that Foreign Office job. I don't know how she thinks he's done that."

"Well, actually, she's right about that. You've got to understand, Em; he's not what he seems. He's not what he seems at all."

"I'd have thought if he was the one who saved you from a lifetime of legal lunches and snazzy cufflinks designed to show what a zany character you are, you'd be more grateful."

"I am. I totally am. But... look, I can't tell you. I just don't want him to use and manipulate you the way he did me."

"It's a waitressing job. How could he manipulate me? Is he going to want me to steal the cutlery?"

"It wouldn't surprise me in the least. I don't know what he's up to. It'll be skulduggery and mischief of some sort."

"Skull what?"

"It's what he calls it."

"Is this because he got you a job in the Secret Intelligence Service?"

"Who told you that?" Michael looked shocked, angry and perhaps just a little frightened.

"You just did, Michael. You just did!" Emma had clawed back one point on her private scoreboard.

Michael laughed. "Oh, go on then. You're just like him. You'll get on fine; just don't come complaining to me when he has you pinching the Magna Carta or smuggling microfilm into Albania. Look, M25, five miles, are we going home or to Rutland?"

"Rutland; we're going to Rutland for a summer of deceit and subterfuge."

Michael chuckled. He had done his best. He had warned her. Privately, he was quite pleased. He loved his little sister and he knew that whatever his grandfather had planned, she would have the time of her life. He hoped one day he would hear all about it. Personally. He certainly didn't want to learn about it professionally.

"I just have one question."

"Hmm?"

"Where the fuck is Rutland?"

EIGHT

Rutland, specifically Leighton Parva, is 90 miles from Oxford. It was a little after one when Michael pulled off the A1 and began the last leg of the journey through chocolate-box villages filled with *Famous Five* cottages of honey-coloured stone. Emma was familiar with rural Sussex, but this was on a different level. It was as if the locals had had a vote and agreed that 1956 was perfectly fine and there was no point in evolving further. Even the road signs were of that cast-iron circle design that you normally only saw in Ealing comedies or in television programmes about country vets or eccentric detectives.

"This place is..." Words failed Emma, so she tried approaching the subject again from a different angle. "Why didn't I know about this place?"

"Almost nobody does. The locals like it that way."

"It's like a time capsule. Do the police ride around in pairs on bicycles?"

"I seriously doubt you'll ever see one. Of course, that might depend on whatever Grandpa is up to."

"You make him sound like some sort of scheming super villain. Oh, look! Leighton Magna. Are we there?"

"Almost, next village."

Emma was still shaking her head in disbelief at Rutland when they reached Leighton Parva.

"Well, at least it's got a pub."

"Ah, yes, I should probably warn you about the pub quizzes."

But Michael never did because they had arrived. The gravel crunched beneath his tyres as he drew into The Old Vicarage, signalling that Rutland had ceased to be a drive-through amusement – a sort of John Major safari park for clotted cream and thatched cottages – and was now Emma's actual environment.

"Still time to back out."

"Right, because it looks so terrifying!" Emma pulled down the sun visor. It was one of those with a little vanity mirror set into the back. The purple was definitely still visible. She got out of the car and began smoothing herself down. The way her parents had insisted she did when visiting aged relatives as a small child. This was absurd. Her grandfather, whom she hardly knew, had found her a waitressing job. If she didn't like it, or couldn't stand living in the sort of place that looked like a jigsaw puzzle sold in aid of the Women's Institute, she could just go home.

Michael led her to the kitchen door at the back of the house. Through the window, she could see an old man, older even than she remembered, with his back to her, apparently making tea. Michael knocked smartly three times and, without waiting for a response, opened the door. The old man turned round.

Emma's first thought was: *Colonel Mustard, in the library with the lead piping.* Her grandfather appeared to have come directly from central casting. "Send me a retired colonel please!". Emma knew nothing of military ranks.

He wasn't a tall man, but he was – and Emma had to stop herself giggling – erect. Perpendicular, upright, like a man who had spent his life standing to attention. Despite the warm weather, he was wearing a tweed jacket over a yellow moleskin waistcoat. He probably would have called it a 'weskit'. He wore a tie in some combination of colours so hideous that it could only have signified a club or regiment or something, and his shoes, brown brogues, were highly polished. For the first half second, he appeared watchful, alert, stern even, but when he recognised his visitors, his face creased into a warm smile.

"Hello, Mikey, nice to see you. Have you brought… ah, yes, Emma. My, how you've grown. What a fine young woman you've become! And the hair! I approve. A slight suffragette hue, very fetching. You must be hungry."

"Hello, Grandpa!" Emma sensed that he wasn't the sort of grandfather one hugged or much less kissed. And, in any event, she hadn't seen him for eight years. She didn't really know him. Of one thing, she was confident. This kindly old man was not some sort of rural Machiavelli. Michael had clearly been teasing her.

"I've laid out a sort of high tea. I hope that's alright. It's in the dining room."

The Old Vicarage was like Rutland in microcosm. Honey-coloured stone? Check. Tweed-clad resident? Check. Oak-panelled dining room? Check. There was a barometer on the wall just inside the front door. A barometer! Opposite this was a grandfather clock that ticked gravely and tocked sombrely. An umbrella stand, with two, no three, umbrellas.

The dining room table, which could have comfortably seated ten, was laden with food that might feed at least twice that number. The only thing that slightly jarred with the whole image of Englishness was what appeared to be three different varieties of sauerkraut. Emma remembered that her grandfather, while as English in appearance and mannerism as John Gielgud in a union jack bowler hat, had spent most of his life in Germany.

*

Frank was slightly embarrassed that his reconnaissance mission to Leighton Hall had accomplished so little. And he was somewhat sceptical about Bernard's ability to whistle up an undercover agent at a moment's notice. "We don't even know if there's a vacancy for a waitress," he had pointed out. But, in fact, a vacancy had already arisen. Light-fingered Leo Davidson had left. Not given his notice, just left. His didn't arrive for his shift. His Volkswagen was no longer outside The Olde Forge, his parents' home. He was just gone.

This was not an unusual or an unexpected development. Those who knew Leo – and that seemed to be just about everyone in the village – were used to his unexplained appearances and disappearances. Frank wondered whether this departure might be linked to George's death, but there was no way of knowing now.

In order to make up for his failure at the hall, Frank was conducting a second reconnaissance. This time, in more familiar circumstances – the saloon bar of The Old Volunteer. Frank wasn't seeing the place for the first time, of course, but he tried to force himself to see it through fresh eyes.

The Old Volunteer still had two bars. When Frank had started his drinking career some forty-five years ago, most pubs had had two bars. Usually, one was slightly grander than the other and the price of the drinks was marginally higher. While there was always a differential, the exact nature of the two bars varied according to the nature of the pub. In the pubs that Frank had frequented in Glasgow in the early fifties, the bar with a linoleum floor had been the posh one.

In Leighton Parva, there appeared to be little or no distinction in terms of décor – both had upholstered seating and good-quality carpet – or pricing; Frank had checked. Both bars were liberally decorated with prints of hunting scenes, horse brasses and sepia photographs of the village. A photograph of Bernard's house, probably taken in the twenties or thirties, was mounted between one of the post office and another of an Eastern Counties bus, both of similar vintage.

The difference between the bars was more in terms of utility and, by extension, clientele. The larger bar – the sign on the door called it the lounge bar – was largely given over to dining. The smaller bar, where Frank had taken a position of maximum vantage beneath a photograph of a smiling farmer on a pre-war Fordson tractor, was the saloon bar. It catered – or, at any rate, was used – for customers who were solely there to drink. If there had been a dartboard or a bar billiards table (there was neither), they would have been in the saloon bar.

Frank was sure that George Bowman had been pulling every trick in the book to keep the pub as a viable business. And he was also of the opinion that he had been, perhaps, the only man alive who could have done so. Without George, the Old Volunteer was sure to fail and it probably wouldn't take very long for the brewery to come to the same conclusion.

The temporary manager, who had arrived two days after George's death, appeared to know his business and it probably would take him no more than a month to report his findings. After that, the pub would close. There would be a few months of scaffolding and then there would be a handsome five-bedroom property on the market that no local could afford to buy. This time next year, it would probably be the second home of some parasitic capitalist – sorry, city-dwelling titan of business, same thing in Frank's book – who only used it a few days each year.

So, Frank had decided to see how things were and to see if there was anything that he might be able to do to make the pub look a little healthier as a business proposition. And to enjoy a pint there while he still could.

Sometimes it seems as if every man who has ever stood at a bar and ordered a pint thinks that he can run a pub. A small number of them actually get to test this and a surprisingly high proportion learn the hard way that there is more to running a boozer than emptying the ashtrays and changing the barrels.

Frank was not such a man. If standing at bars and ordering pints were the sole qualification, he would be Landlord of the Year – though he knew it wasn't. But Frank had been born and raised in a pub. Literally. Frank's father had died in Spain a couple of months before he had been born and his mother had moved in with her sister, whose husband ran Hennessy's Bar in Glasgow's East End. Frank had learned his arithmetic playing cribbage and his dialectics by carrying in drinks to the meetings in the pub's back room. He knew how a pub worked. Not as much as George Bowman, but a great deal more than the average customer.

Frank also had the advantage of having conducted quite a lengthy VAT fraud investigation into a bookkeeper who had been fiddling the VAT for a number of pubs. It had served as a useful refresher course in pub financial management.

Frank rarely visited The Old Volunteer pub on a Saturday lunchtime. He was usually on duty ferrying Frankie Junior or Maisie to or from some social engagement or improving activity. Maisie had ballet and was a member of some sort of junior paramilitary organisation called Rainbows. Frankie Junior attended football. Frank wouldn't put it any higher than 'attended'. He had never seen Frankie participate in anything that might be called a game. Most of the time, there wasn't even a ball involved, just a couple of dozen five-year-olds milling about and making a noise like feeding time at the hyena enclosure. He seemed to enjoy it anyway. He had been wearing his Scotland shirt that morning.

Anyway, it meant that Frank wasn't in a position to judge whether today was an unusually quiet day at The Old Volunteer. It certainly wasn't an unusually busy one. Aside from himself, there were five customers. Frank did a few sums in his head. Six customers, two drinks each, a couple of packets of crisps, revenue maybe twenty-five pounds. Say a gross mark up of about fifty to sixty per cent (Frank knew these things), maybe fifteen pounds gross profit. Take off bar staff costs, lighting, wastage, sundry overheads. Basically, the pub was losing money on this session.

Frank decided to test his evaluation by interviewing the temporary manager, Gary. Gary didn't know he was being interviewed, of course. He was just grateful to have somebody to talk with in the long periods between customers ordering drinks.

Yes, he had worked for the brewery for about five years. Yes, he had served as a temporary manager many times. This was the first time that he had actually stepped into a vacancy created by a death. Usually, he was covering for a publican's holiday or more rarely an illness. He reported weekly takings to the brewery. He reported to the area manager, who would probably visit each week. Thursday, probably – why did he ask? Oh, no reason.

Yes, it was very quiet. Yes, a lot of these village pubs weren't able to survive. Where they did, it was usually because there was a reliable core of regulars. A darts team or, better yet, a football team who could be relied upon to cover the fixed costs. Without that, the overheads and the competition elsewhere usually combined to make a pub less than viable.

Gary mentioned two pubs that had recently closed. Frank hadn't heard of either, but that was to be expected. A year ago, he couldn't have even pointed to Rutland on a map, much less Leighton Parva.

NINE

It wasn't exactly dawn, as that had been an hour earlier, but it was still very early. Bernard didn't seem to be able to sleep for more than a few hours these days. Yet another symptom of old age, he supposed. In deference to Emma, whom he assumed was still sleeping the deep and dreamless sleep of a carefree twenty-year-old, he had sought to be especially quiet as he made his first cup of tea.

Now he stood in his front room, which he called the drawing room, surveying the sleeping stillness of Leighton Parva. He couldn't quite see the whole village, but his panorama, from left to right, took in the lychgate of St Cuthbert's, The Old Volunteer, the village's telephone kiosk – its pillar box outside what had once been the post office – the war memorial and the fork in the road where one branch ran south to Barnsdale and the other west towards Oakham and the entrance to the cricket club.

It is often said that every town, village and hamlet has, somewhere, a war memorial paying tribute to the local dead of two world wars. This is not strictly true. There are a few, a very few, villages with no memorial. These places, known as doubly thankful villages, sent just as many young men to the trenches of

Flanders, to the deserts of North Africa, the jungles of Burma or the skies above the Ruhr, but, somehow, they all came home.

Leighton Magna was just such a place. It had sent fourteen to the first war, eight to the second, but there was no memorial there. They all came home. Somehow, Bernard had not known this and he probably would never have known it if he hadn't been standing at this same window twenty-four hours earlier.

Ron Godsmark had approached from the East. He always walked briskly, but this time his gait was ever so slightly different. It took Bernard a moment to recognise it, but when he did, he was sure. It was a quick march past The Old Vicarage, Ron's eyes firmly to the front. If he saw Bernard, he gave no indication. He halted in front of the Leighton Parva war memorial. He didn't stop. He halted. And stood to attention. Bernard felt himself standing to attention, too. Silly.

After a minute or two, Ron's hand went to his left jacket pocket. Bernard thought he knew what was coming, but he couldn't have told you how. He stepped back a pace from the window a split second before Ron looked about himself. Bernard was confident he hadn't been seen. Ron's left hand emerged from his pocket. There was the slight flash of sunlight on medals, then he donned the old and slightly faded beret, and saluted. He held the salute for a few seconds and then he about-turned.

Almost faster than the eye could see, the beret was back in his pocket, the medals had gone. Ron started back up the road to Leighton Magna. This time he was walking, but a little slower than usual and with his head held just a little lower. But Bernard had seen it. At least he thought he had. Anyway, he knew how to check.

Bernard had spent a lifetime seeing old soldiers performing some version of this private little ceremony. But it had usually been on Remembrance Sunday, not on the 6th June. He could check that, too.

Emma thought that she had made a special effort by coming down for breakfast at half past eight. It was a Sunday, after all, but Michael was already tucking into a plate of bacon and eggs. Michael had definitely gained a pound or two in the past year. Whatever he was doing at MI6, it wasn't being James Bond. Her grandfather was reading some sort of glossy leaflet. He peered over the top of his glasses and gestured towards a dish laden with bacon, sausages and mushrooms. "I could do you a fried egg, if you like."

Emma had yet to see any evidence that her grandfather was at the centre of some web of intrigue and that at any moment he was going to suggest that she apply for a North Korean visa under a false name. The previous evening had been spent, very pleasantly, bringing her grandfather up to date on various pieces of family news. He, in turn, had been happy to hear about her adventures at Oxford and was particularly interested in her water polo career. In short, a model grandfather.

The subject of Leighton Hall hadn't been mentioned at all the previous evening, but Emma now noticed that it was the subject of the glossy leaflet that the old man had been reading. When she had finished her second slice of toast, Bernard pushed it across the table towards her.

"We shall have a proper briefing a little later, but you may as well take a look at this now."

Briefing? Briefing! Emma looked at Michael. His expression was somewhere between 'Told you so' and 'Don't blame me'. Emma poked out her tongue at him.

"My friend, Frank, will be over in a little while. He's actually seen the place, unlike me, and, well, it will become clear when he gets here – which will be quite soon, Michael, so if you don't want to be here when he arrives…"

Michael clearly didn't. With no more than a longing half

glance at the last remaining sausage, he rose and went upstairs to gather his things.

"Does Michael not like Frank?" asked Emma.

"Oh, they've never met. It's a long story, actually. Suffice to say that Michael is following the wise old dictum that a temporary withdrawal is often the wisest action to pursue."

Emma considered whether this conversation had earned Michael a point and decided that it did not. He had warned her and she had pushed ahead anyway, thus frustrating her Father's ire and revenge. If anything, she thought, she deserved a point herself. Or if not a point, she at least deserved the last sausage.

Michael reappeared a minute or so later clutching his overnight bag. "Right! I'm off back to the smoke. I might pop up again in a week or two, all things permitting. Cheerio!"

He's actually fleeing! thought Emma. "Grandpa, who exactly is this Frank that has sent Michael scurrying off?"

"He's a friend of mine. Just a retired old codger like me."

Emma considered this for a moment. "So, what is he retired from exactly? The SAS? The Mounties? A lifetime spent as a professional assassin?"

"Oh, far worse than any of those – far, far worse."

*

The twin bells of St Cuthbert's were calling the faithful to the ten-thirty service. There were only a couple of services a month these days. Leighton Parva shared its vicar, a rather breathless and earnest middle-aged woman called Jennifer, with half a dozen other villages. Jennifer was based over at Ashcombe, where she lived in a modest, modern house that, while technically a vicarage, did not in any way resemble Bernard's home. Ashcombe's actual old vicarage was doubtless also a private home now.

Frank arrived just as the peals stopped. Bernard had just finished making a pot of tea when her grandfather's friend arrived at the kitchen door with a liver-and-white springer spaniel at his heels. He ushered the dog to what appeared to be 'his' corner of the kitchen and sat at the table removing a check cap. This gave Emma an opportunity to size him up.

Emma was twenty, and when you are twenty, the ages from forty to seventy-five are all one. Frank appeared to fit somewhere within this range. He was dressed in what Emma had started to call retired Rutland chic: tweed jacket, checked shirt, brown shoes. But Frank seemed to wear them less easily than her grandfather. He didn't seem to be born to the garb of the country-dwelling retiree. It may have been the beard. He had a full snow-white beard – well, snow-white except for the faint yellowing that told of a fondness for nicotine. The broken capillaries on his nose suggested that he was not unfamiliar with a bottle, too. His hair, thinning somewhat, betrayed that it had once been a sandy colour. He wore no rings and an inexpensive wristwatch that might have been bought in any high-street retail jewellers. He was unremarkable. Sherlock Holmes might have been able to guess his erstwhile profession, but Emma couldn't.

Bernard put a plate of biscuits on the kitchen table, immediately picked one up and tossed it in the direction of the corner. There was a slight snap as Rocky plucked it from the air as easily as an expert wicket keeper taking a routine catch.

"Emma, this is Frank. Frank, this is my granddaughter, Emma. She is ready for her briefing."

Emma had never been briefed before and never expected to be. She wasn't exactly sure what she was supposed to do. Should she take notes? Should she sit up straight? Ask questions? Would the whole bizarre event begin with taking an oath of secrecy or signing some disclaimer? She certainly wasn't going to do that. She was that much of a lawyer.

In the event, it was pretty unremarkable. Frank, it turned out, was a Scotsman. Perhaps that is why the Rutland thing didn't really work for him. Perhaps he would have been happier in a kilt. Probably not. He didn't seem like the type of man who would need to draw attention to himself. He spoke in a calm and measured way. Everything he said followed logically. He was honest about the gaps in his knowledge, and clear and concise about what he wanted Emma to do. Even to Emma's untutored ear, it was clear that this was not the first briefing that Frank had given.

"So, you just want me to work as a waitress and keep my eyes and ears open?"

Frank nodded.

"And generally suss out how everything works. Who does what and when. What everybody's job is, that sort of thing."

Frank nodded again.

"And in particular the roles played by Mr and Mrs Keller, what happens to stock being received, who does the paperwork, that sort of thing?"

Frank nodded again. He was not one of those people who felt the need to say something just to fill the air.

Emma was a little disappointed. She had fantasised that she was going to be asked to do something dangerous or illegal, ideally both. Michael had led her to believe that her grandfather was going to lure her into some perilous caper. This all seemed rather tame and rather dull.

"Your grandfather tells me that you speak a little German."

How had he known that? Perhaps her mother had told her grandfather her A level results. Actually, she was bound to have done so; she seldom passed up an opportunity to boast, even to the extent where she would deliberately talk to her father.

Emma nodded.

"Well, keep that to yourself. You may learn more that way."

That was more like it!

*

Michael had told Emma that her grandfather had got her a job, but that wasn't quite true. He had actually got her an interview for a job. Emma had little experience of this. Au pairing didn't count, as her mother would have said – somewhat sniffily, probably. And interviews that you are trying to fail like the one at Stewart, Poole & DeQuidt probably didn't count either.

With that in mind, she had decided that she needed to try to return her hair to its natural fair colour. Unsurprisingly, her grandfather hadn't a bathroom cabinet full of Clairol or Schwarzkopf products and so she was improvising with a couple of lemons that she had found on the drinks cabinet. It occurred to her that they were probably considered an indispensable element of a gin and tonic and that she would need to replace them quite soon, but if she couldn't pinch a couple of lemons, then she wasn't going to be much good as a secret agent, was she?

Then, it occurred to her; she had been in her grandfather's company for a little over twenty-four hours and she was already contemplating committing theft, not exactly grand larceny it was true, but theft nevertheless. Was this what Michael had meant when he had said that their grandfather had a peculiar way of corrupting people?

She looked in the bathroom mirror and examined the results of her citrus-based efforts. It didn't look too bad. No trace of purple, although some strands of her hair were a lot blonder than others. Put that down to sun bleaching.

Was the face squinting back at her the face of a top undercover operative? Maybe. I mean, what did they look like? Her brother was a spy, or something similar. He worked with spies, certainly. And her grandfather… Mum had always been quite circumspect about exactly what he had done. He was a soldier, sort of, but there was more to it than that.

Anyway, if she didn't know what a spy looked like, how could a couple who ran a wedding venue? And she was posing as a student, utterly devoid of any useful or marketable skills, earning a little holiday money. And that was exactly what she was. It wasn't exactly a difficult pose to pull off.

TEN

The June sun beamed down on the rolling hills of Rutland, promising a beautiful summer's day. It easily permeated the thin cotton of the curtains in Emma's room, but even as it rose above her window ledge, it did not wake her. The bloody birds had already done that. Dawn chorus? Dawn cacophony, more like. Emma vowed that wherever her life took her, whatever dreams she pursued or banality she settled for, she was never going to live in the middle of the bloody country. She had been awake since four-thirty; it was now seven and was that a tractor starting its engine? It bloody was!

Her grandfather was already sitting at the kitchen table when she came downstairs. He appeared to be reading, or perhaps consulting, a simply enormous book. Something military, by the look of it. A regimental history, perhaps. He closed it when his granddaughter entered and looked up, beaming. "Ready for your first day?"

"It's just an interview today, Grandad."

"It's just an interview for your job as a waitress, but it's your first day as an agent in the field. And one of the most important. You're brand new. You know nothing. You can ask questions. You are expected to ask questions and you are so new, you cannot be expected to know what questions you are not supposed to ask. Do you see?"

Emma nodded.

"Cloak yourself in the mantle of ignorance and naivety, my dear. It will serve as excellent camouflage."

Emma sometimes wondered whether her grandfather was just a bit potty. But if he was playing 'Let's pretend', why shouldn't she, too? More fun than working at her aunt's restaurant in Eastbourne.

*

Her name was Madeline and she said that she was the events co-ordinator. No, that's wrong. She announced that she was The Events Co-Ordinator, in much the same tone in which you might announce that you were the Admiral of the Fleet or the Archbishop of Canterbury. Then she paused, possibly for applause, or for a curtsey, or perhaps she was just waiting for Emma to appear impressed.

Emma hoped it was the last of these and hoped that she had faked her response sufficiently well. Madeline then went to explain for about thirty minutes how very important she was and by implication how utterly unimportant everybody else within her sphere of command was.

The interview, if a thirty-minute monologue punctuated by a handful of questions could be called an interview, was delivered while Madeline strode about Leighton Hall being demonstratively dissatisfied with things. The napkins were folded incorrectly. The continued presence of yesterday's flowers was a disgrace. The speed with which a young man was carrying a cardboard box of cava was simultaneously too slow and dangerously hurried. Emma followed at what she hoped was a respectful distance, fantasising that Madeline was the centre of some evil enterprise for which she would one day be imprisoned for life.

When they had returned to Madeline's office, which was surprisingly small for someone who clearly had the most important and significant job in the country, if not the world, she fixed Emma with an expression that seemed to say, 'Why are you still here?'. Emma met this with an expression of polite inquiry.

"You start tomorrow. Go and see Terry in the kitchen. He'll tell you the rest."

This time, the expression definitely said, 'Why are you still here?'

Emma nodded and headed for the door. Madeline began typing on her computer like somebody trying to kill the world's fly population one digit at a time. Despite having spent half an hour marching all over the hall, Emma had never actually been shown the kitchen. Therefore, she had the perfect excuse to explore a little. If she was challenged, she could simply ask to be directed.

Leighton Hall had originally been built in 1799. Since then, it had more than trebled in size. There were twenty-nine bedrooms, including the bridal suite, almost all of them located in the East Wing – a two-floor extension added, perhaps, a hundred years ago. What had once been the main house now comprised the entrance hall; two large rooms, where civil ceremonies were performed; the large ballroom, for weddings with a hundred guests or more; a smaller, but similar room for smaller events; and an enormous staircase. Finally, there were a few small rooms, including Madeline's office, opening off the entrance hall.

The entrance hall and both ballrooms were double height. Emma didn't think that she could convincingly claim to be seeking the kitchen upstairs and so she was forced to find it. There was only one door left. The door to the South Wing looked just as grand as all the others, but beyond it was like a different world. Where the main house had been grand, opulent and mainly silent, beyond the door Emma was met with a wall of sound, smells and steam. Immediately to her left were a pair of stainless steel double doors with circular windows, the kind you only ever found in hospitals or commercial kitchens.

Again, Emma could hardly walk past them and claim to be looking for a kitchen. She was reconciled to the fact that she would have to enter, when one of the doors swung open and the young man she had seen carrying cava earlier emerged carrying a stack of bread trays that was at least two too high for him to see where he was going. Accordingly, he was navigating the corridor in a series of half pirouettes as he shuffled sideways, half turned, glanced over his shoulder to get his bearings and then returned to his crab-like progress. In the course of one of these manoeuvres, he found himself face to face with Emma. He seemed to like it. Emma definitely did. He was really rather good-looking.

After an hour or two, or perhaps it was a second, Emma finally managed to stammer, "Err, I'm looking for Terry."

"I think he's in his office." The young man tried to indicate exactly where that might be found, but that's a tricky thing to do when you are carrying nine bread trays and hopelessly in love. He tried to jerk his head in the direction he meant, but it could have indicated anything.

Emma thanked him and took this as her cue to explore the corridor in front of her, which had three or four doors down the left-hand side and a staircase at the end. Dare she try the staircase and claim that she thought that was what she had been told? Damn right she could dare. Or could she? It would be difficult to explain why she had been fired for snooping before her first day. She compromised and decided to try only the ground-floor rooms.

Now, which door looked the least likely to contain someone called Terry? She put her ear to the first door and listened. Nothing. Or was that the sound of a very suspicious person working silently at a desk? Impossible to tell. Emma looked left and right, took a deep breath and tried the door handle. What an anticlimax! The bloody thing was locked. Okay, second door, repeat the process.

Silence again. This time, Emma didn't bother with what she decided could only be interpreted as furtive glancing and just turned the handle. It opened.

This was a slightly different type of anticlimax. It was a sort of store room or, perhaps more accurately, a delivery room. There was a desk in one corner, but it wasn't the type of desk assigned to a single person and used for many hours each day. It was more like one of those desks that whoever happened to be performing whatever task occurred in that type of room – which certainly wasn't an office – might sit at for thirty seconds or so while they did whatever it was one did in a room like that.

Alongside two walls were sets of racking upon which were catering-size boxes of napkins, dishwasher tablets and cleaning fluids. There were great big bales of sheets, pillowcases and that sort of thing. In the corner opposite the desk was a door that probably led into the locked room Emma had tried a few seconds earlier. On the desk itself was a notepad, a couple of biros, one of those claw things you use to remove staples and a few pieces of paper.

Emma scurried over and glanced at them. There were delivery notes for toilet rolls and imitation flowers, joints of ham and prawns. Emma was very aware that while she could justify looking into a room in her search for Terry, she could hardly claim to have been expecting him to be among paperwork for the laundry. She decided that she had spent enough time in the room. She exited cautiously. The corridor was still empty, so she decided to try one more door.

The third room was smaller. It was full of clothes – chefs' whites, aprons, something that Emma supposed was a chambermaid's uniform. As she stood in the doorway, Emma felt a presence behind her. She turned quickly. In front of her was a slightly harassed man in early middle age.

"I'm looking for Terry."

"You've found him. Are you the girl Madeline was talking about?"

"I expect so."

"Okay, follow me."

Terry led Emma to the last door on the corridor, the one at the end. It was a genuine office, with a computer and family photographs and a Leicester City Football Club calendar on the wall. Terry sat down behind what was obviously his desk and waved Emma to a chair.

"I'm sure Madeline's… err… I mean… Okay, let's begin at the start. Have you done any waitressing before?"

"A little."

"So, I'm going to assume that means next to none. Doesn't matter. It's not exactly hard; smile at the punters and try to keep your thumb out of the gravy. Done any bar work?"

"No." Emma decided that she may as well be entirely frank.

"Can you open a champagne bottle without taking someone's eye out or covering the ceiling in expensive suds?"

"Yes." Emma could definitely do that. It was quite nice to discover that she had a useful skill.

"Know how to make a martini?"

"Yes."

"Cosmopolitan?"

"Yes."

"Moscow Mule?"

"Yes."

"What's the difference between a Mimosa and a Bucks Fizz?"

"They're the same."

"Right. You're qualified to do waitressing and bar work. Can you start tomorrow?"

"Yes, what time?"

"Eleven. No, make it half past ten, that will give me time to show you the ropes. Have you got a black skirt and a white shirt?"

Emma had. For reasons that had never been explained to her, Oxford required its undergraduates to take examinations in a peculiarly understated form of fancy dress known as 'sub fusc'.

"You'll need to find yourself a purple tie and an apron next door. I'll need your full name, address, local address, a number I can reach you on and your National Insurance number. Okay?"

It was definitely okay. Very much okay. Emma had successfully penetrated the criminal organisation. Or got a job handing out lukewarm Mimosas, depending on your point of view.

"Just one last thing. I don't care, but Mrs Keller can be a bit funny. You missed a bit."

Emma looked blank.

"Behind your right ear, bit of purple – like I say, I don't mind, but Mrs Keller…"

"She's the owner, isn't she?"

"Part owner, alongside Mr Keller."

"Am I likely to see them much?"

"Mr Keller, no, he's more of a back-office type of man. Started off as an accountant, I believe. His office is immediately above us here, but I doubt you'll see much of him. Mrs Keller, her office is on the first floor of the main house, but she could turn up anywhere at any time."

"What's she like?"

Terry paused. Then paused a little more. "I think it's safe to say that she has high standards. If you know what I mean?"

"You mean she's absolutely terrifying?"

"That's exactly what I mean. I think she strangles kittens to unwind."

*

Emma had never been debriefed before. [Don't smirk! You know what I mean.] And if she had ever thought about it, she wouldn't have expected it to happen around a kitchen table in an old vicarage in Rutland. And she wouldn't have expected to be debriefed by two men with a combined age of nearly a hundred and forty. She didn't have any idea how undercover agents were debriefed, but she had a funny feeling, location and ages aside, that it was probably a lot like this.

But it was quite hard to put those things aside. Her grandfather's kitchen was just so... cosy? Quaint? Well, it was those things, but it was much more, too. It was like you had asked an interior designer to describe *The Archers* through the medium of kitchenware.

There was a pewter-grey Aga – well, of course there was – and a smaller, barely more modern electric cooker. There was a copper kettle of a type that Emma thought didn't exist outside of tearooms specialising in separating tourists from unfamiliar bank notes. There was an enamel bread bin and several jars of jam bearing labels that indicated they came from Fortnum & Mason's. The whole effect looked like a Hollywood producer's idea of an English kitchen. There was even a tea cosy.

And then there were her – what were they – handlers? Her grandfather, who looked like a minor character from a seventies sitcom about a hotel in Torquay, and Frank, who looked and sounded like the sort of person who used to give her mother nightmares during general election campaigns.

Frank began by asking her to hand over everything she had been given, including the apron and tie, and every note that she had made. As instructed, she had made none. She had passed that test, at least.

Then, the two men took her through the events of the day minute by minute. Frank made notes. Bernard didn't. Emma did her best to recount everything in chronological order, but it was harder than she had expected. She was very good, however, at differentiating between actual facts and her impressions and perceptions. When she had finished, Frank passed over a sheet of A4 paper and a pencil and asked her to draw a floor plan. Emma had seen less than a quarter of the hall, but she did her best.

"Should we give people code names?" she asked. "I thought that Mrs Keller could be 'Liz' and Mr Keller, 'Phil'."

"No code names. And no thinking you're Jane Bond either. Just keep your ears and eyes open for now. We'll let you know when we want a deep penetration." [I warned you. Stop smirking.]

Frank was stern, a bit grumpy. Emma looked at her grandfather, hoping for an encouraging smile or some positive feedback. If anything, he was worse.

"Just one last thing; the boy, do not take him into your confidence. It is as important, more important, that you deceive him than anybody else. Got it?"

Emma felt her face redden slightly. She hated herself for that.

ELEVEN

The Old Volunteer was doomed, Frank was pretty sure. Pretty sure that only George Bowman or somebody very like him could make the place break even. Leighton Parva was just too small. And the demographics were all wrong. It was full of people who, if they visited the pub at all, would only stay for a half of bitter and a small Amontillado.

It was a little better in the summer as Leighton Parva had a cricket team. And a couple of dozen young – well, mostly young – men who had spent a few hours in the sun made for ideal customers. The problem was that there were just too few of them and the cricket season didn't last long enough. Leighton Parva had no football club. In any case, it wasn't that sort of place. Cricket can be played by men in their fifties. Football really can't. And even if the demographics had been right in terms of age profile, Leighton Parva was not a football town.

Football was the game of the urban proletariat. It was Frank's game and that is why on Wednesday 10th June 1998, he knew that The Old Volunteer was doomed. Its fate lay in the report made by Gary, the temporary manager installed by the brewery, and much more importantly by the profit and loss account while he was there. And Gary did not understand Leighton Parva.

He had installed a television so that customers could watch the World Cup, which was beginning that day. In Frank's view, this was a serious misjudgement of his clientele. And he had opened early in order to be able to show the tournament's first game, Brazil against Scotland, which was kicking off at four-thirty.

Frank had arrived at twenty-five past. He was the only customer. Frank noted that Gary had decorated the whole pub, not just the bar with the television in it, with bunting in the flags of the thirty-two competing nations. What had he been thinking? If the regular customers had been forced, absolutely forced, to accept any change to the décor of The Old Volunteer, they might, just might, have grudgingly accepted another horse brass or two. But a small triangular flag depicting the national colours of Cameroon? Really?

It seemed to Frank, from the expression on Gary's face, that he was starting to appreciate his misjudgement, when he made another. "Afternoon, Jock, what'll it be?"

If Gary had really wanted, he could have paid somebody to remove all his internal organs with a rusty scythe, liquidise them, douse them with the worst kind of rotgut whiskey, burn them in front of him and then trample on the ashes. But instead, he chose to call Frank McBride 'Jock'. Frank gave him a look. The effect was much the same. He retreated to the other bar and was actually considering hiding in the cellar when, after five minutes (five minutes!), Brazil scored. Frank momentarily forgot that he was in a country inn in Rutland. For a second, he was back in Hennessy's bar and he responded accordingly.

By the fifteen-minute mark, Frank needed a second pint. By the thirty-eighth minute, his glass was empty again. Gary had noticed and was summoning up the courage to approach him when it happened. "Penalty! Penalty, I tell yeez! Yon fella has cut doon poor wee Kevin Gallacher. Ya cheatin' swine! Tha's a penalty right enough!"

And then a second later, "Gary! Another pint here, big mon!"

Gary began pouring. Any skilled barman will tell you that Guinness must be poured slowly, with a short pause at the two thirds stage to allow it to settle. The whole process takes just over a minute. Or, if you want a more precise timing, it takes exactly the amount of time for ten Brazilians to leave the penalty area and a Scotsman to place the ball and retreat a few paces and gather himself.

"Get in! Ya wee beauty! Get in! C'moan, Scotland!"

Gary wiped himself down, selected another glass and began the process again. By now, there was no doubt in his mind. Opening the pub for the World Cup had been a terrible mistake. The softly spoken old man with the white beard and the tweed jacket had been transformed into Hampden Park personified and, frankly, it was frightening.

It was one-all at half-time and Frank had started to regain his composure. He didn't care much for the analysis provided by washed-up old pros on the television and didn't pay it much attention. He noticed for the first time that Gary seemed to have taken a bath in Guinness and wondered why. He ordered another pint and promised Gary he would keep an eye on things while he went upstairs and changed.

In the seventy-second minute, the Brazilian right back broke down the wing and cut inside. Frank was muttering ever more urgent curses under his breath. Forced to shoot with his weaker left foot, his shot lacked power but it struck the goalkeeper in the face and would have rebounded to safety were it not for the Scottish number three racing back to defend his goal. He had no time to react. The ball bounced off him and into the Scottish net.

In Rio de Janeiro, somebody doubtless screamed, "Gooooaalll!"

Frank's reaction was more guttural. He watched the rest of the game with clenched teeth. He didn't utter a word. When the final whistle sounded, he drained his pint.

"When's the first England game?"

Gary knew that it was the following Monday at lunchtime. The television would definitely be gone by then.

*

Ron Godsmark had also been watching the match. At least he had had the television on in the corner of the room. He wasn't particularly interested, but he thought that he ought to at least know what had happened in the game in case Frank wanted to discuss it the following day on their morning walk. That didn't seem very likely now. He switched off the television and turned his attention once again to his album of wedding photographs.

Today was the sixth anniversary of Phyllis' death. People had assured him that as time passed, the pain would lessen. They had lied. All that had changed was that people remembered less, visited less often, called him less often. They had lied about that, too. She had died on their wedding anniversary. One last way of trying to make him remember. He had been terrible about dates. He remembered 10th June, though.

Ron put down his wedding album and picked up his scrapbook. There was a picture of him as a very small child. It might have been his first day at the village school, when Leighton Magna had had a village school. There was another, with his sister; he would have been about fifteen. He had left school by then. There were two of him in his Home Guard uniform, the forage cap low over the left eye. One with him and his Uncle Jim, who had been the platoon Sergeant. They were standing outside Leighton Hall. They had been used as extra guards occasionally.

The next page was given over to his first year in the army. He had spent a lot of it training in Scotland. There he was, fresh-faced, smiling, surrounded by his mates. The same faces featured on the next page: Sid Harris, Bob Fletcher, Archie MacLeish – the little Scotsman who had joined the Lincolnshire Regiment apparently by mistake – and Ted Cullen. Ted was in all the photographs. They had been inseparable. The city boy from Lincoln and Rutland Ron.

Ted was the reason there was no war memorial in Leighton Magna.

"Duck!" he had said. And Ron had ducked. But Ted didn't. At least, not quickly enough.

They probably wouldn't have put a war memorial up just for Ron anyway. A war memorial with just one name on it. It would have been ostentatious. His mother wouldn't have allowed it and in Leighton Magna, what Mrs Godsmark didn't allow very seldom happened.

There were other photographs: Normandy, back in England, the Ardennes and Germany. Ted wasn't in those. And the other faces were not so fresh anymore. Neither was Ron's. He flicked back a couple of pages and then forward again. What those eleven months had done to him! The last few photographs were taken after the war. They were group photographs mostly. The men with the careworn faces and the suspicious eyes all had medal ribbons. The young, unafraid soldiers didn't.

The final page, the final photograph. Ron remembered this being taken. The last day before his demobilisation. Standing to attention with a sad sort of half-smile. You could see the single stripe on his sleeve quite clearly. The medal ribbons were blurred. Ron's medals were in a tin box on the top shelf with his paybook and his beret. He didn't bother to fetch them down. He knew what he had.

Nobody else did. Ron didn't attend Remembrance Day parades. He never wore his medals, except when he went to the war memorial to salute Ted. He had taken them with him when he had visited Normandy four years ago on the fiftieth anniversary of D-Day. But he didn't want to wear them. He couldn't. He felt such a terrible fraud. He wasn't a war hero. He wasn't even particularly brave. He had just been a heartbroken and angry young man who had lost his best friend.

In the end, Archie MacLeish had persuaded him, for Ted's sake. Standing on the spot where it had happened. Or somewhere nearby. So much had changed. It was so long ago.

It had been a mistake. He thought that he had checked, but his eyes had not been what they were. Somebody had had a camera. It was on the front page of the regimental magazine the following month: 'Lance Corporal Ron Godsmark outside the chateau at Lion-sur-Mer, the scene of his famous action'.

TWELVE

Emma, as she had been instructed, kept her eyes open on her first day. And her eyes had indeed been opened. There is nothing like pulling a few shifts in a wedding venue to make you question the whole concept of marriage as an institution and weddings, in particular. It was the same every day. June was a popular month for weddings and there were four or five each week. Each one had more drama than an *Eastenders* Christmas special. Even without knowing anything about the cast of characters, Emma overheard enough while serving the starters to know how each occasion was going to pan out.

It was easy to identify the ringleaders, too. Or, rather, they identified themselves. Tart observations about the venue, the bridesmaids' dresses, the choice of hymns or, as was increasingly common, the choice of a secular rather than a religious service. Even the weather provided an opportunity to limber up in terms of arch comments. It was extraordinary.

Emma was astounded. She had attended very few weddings herself and hadn't appreciated how often and how quickly they could turn into some sort of festival of score-settling, backstabbing and general bitching. It was all rather fun, from the point of view of the anonymous spectator.

The entertainment value was increased still further by the attitude of her co-workers, mostly people of her own age who regarded the whole thing as a sort of pantomime laid on for their amusement.

"The one in the pink hat at table five is going to kick off any minute."

"I'll bet you a pound to a piece of tripe that the bald bloke with the silly tie is having or has had an affair with the woman opposite. You should see the looks his wife is giving him."

"I'll give it about five minutes before someone slaps one of those twins. If it hasn't happened in ten, I'll probably do it myself."

The work was hard. Hour after hour on your feet and it wasn't long before the welcoming smile became a rictus grin. It was amazing how many people, when confronted with linen tableware, suddenly thought that they were Marie Antoinette.

"The tea? Does anyone know if it's Ceylon? The woman at table four wants to know."

"I think it's PG Tips, isn't it?"

"Tell her it's what the duchess drinks."

"What duchess?"

"I don't know. Make something up."

But it was fun. And the time passed quickly. Emma spent most of her time so busy that she had less and less new information to report at her regular debriefing sessions. She had never even seen Mr Keller. The most information that she could provide was that he lived in Ashcombe and arrived at five minutes to eight each morning in a silver Mercedes. He left, she had been told, at five minutes past five each day, but if Emma was there at that time, she was probably topping up glasses to toast the bridesmaid or cutting the cake into takeaway portions.

She had at least seen Mrs Keller once or twice. She arrived by Mercedes, too, but hers was a bright yellow convertible. And her comings and goings were far less predictable. Whenever Emma had seen her, she seemed to be hurrying without hurrying. She covered ground at an impressive speed, but never seemed to be rushing. She moved like an athlete or a dancer, or a special forces PT instructor. She was confident, professional and – was elegant the word? Not quite, but something similar.

Once, she had seen her going up the stairs at the end of the kitchen corridor to the first floor where Mr Keller's office was supposed to be. She briefly thought about following her and trying to listen at the door, but before she had gathered the nerve, Oliver had come out of the kitchen and asked her to hurry to the ballroom with a mop and bucket. A pair of young guests had amused themselves by shaking up all the cava bottles with entertaining but messy results.

Emma liked Oliver. It was his second summer working 'up at the hall', as everyone seemed to call it. He was a local. He lived in Warhurst about three miles away. He was studying art somewhere in London. He wouldn't say exactly where. After a few days of gently probing, discreet inquiries and generally employing the sort of tactics that she was supposed to be using on behalf of her grandfather, she established that Oliver was single. Now all she had to do was make him fall in love with her.

This was proving more difficult than it ought because Oliver appeared to be terribly, painfully shy. She thought that he liked her. He looked at her as if he liked her – until he caught her looking. Then, he would turn away bashfully. Emma thought that that was rather sweet. She thought most things about Oliver were rather sweet: his fair hair, his sideways half-smile, his hazel eyes. But because they were so busy all the time, the opportunities for shared shy glances were all too rare.

Because it was Oliver's second summer up at the hall, he had a very slight and very unofficial senior status. He could change the Guinness barrel, for example, and that could be quite tricky. He knew where things were, even the rarely used things, and he had actually seen Joachim Keller.

Because Keller was so rarely seen, it didn't feel unnatural to Emma to express a slight curiosity about him. Unfortunately, most of those to whom she spoke either hadn't seen him or gave a vague description of a very unremarkable man.

"He looks like a bank manager or an accountant."

"I heard he was an accountant."

"Well, there you are then."

Emma would have liked to ask about his age, appearance, any distinguishing features, but to have done so would have seemed very odd. She began to worry that she was not a very good undercover agent, but then she got an opportunity to put herself to the test.

She had arrived at work early, not too early – she was there at a quarter to ten for a shift that started on the hour. She had been hoping that she might see Oliver arrive and walk from the car park to the hall with him. In fact, Oliver had been even earlier. His Mini Metro was already in the staff car park when she arrived. He was also the first person she saw when she walked into the kitchen. He was making coffee using the big machine and small china cups.

"Oh, hi, Emma. Would you mind taking these up to Mr and Mrs Keller? They're in his office on the first floor."

This was her chance. She could see Mr Keller in the flesh for a start. She sensed that her grandfather was starting to become a little exasperated at her lack of progress. Perhaps she could linger outside the door and overhear something. It was worth a try anyway. She put on her apron, checked her reflection in the stainless steel door of one of the fridges and took the tray from Oliver. Besides the two cups of coffee, there was a plate with a pair of doughnuts on it. Emma raised an eyebrow.

"Mrs Keller brought them in." Oliver shrugged.

Emma walked boldly down the corridor and up the stairs. It was the first time she had been on this floor. Directly in front of her was the closed door that she assumed belonged to Mr Keller's office. She took a deep breath and knocked.

"Come in, please."

Emma knew that she had, at best, just a few seconds to size up the place and its occupants. It was a large office and her first impression was how very orderly it was. There were cupboards along one wall, but every door was closed. There was a single, rather large, desk, but Mr Keller was not sitting at it. He and Mrs Keller were seated in armchairs either side of a small coffee table. Emma put the tray down and resisted the urge to say '*Kaffee und kuchen.*' She wasn't supposed to reveal her knowledge of German. If she had not known, she would not have guessed that the Kellers were married. Even though they were sitting together, there was no evidence of mutual warmth. Mrs Keller was sitting so upright she could have passed for a sculptor's model or one of those soldiers outside Buckingham Palace that never seem to blink. She looked a bit like Grace Kelly, but in her Princess of Monaco phase, not her *High Society* phase.

Mr Keller's attractions obviously ran deeper because he certainly was no matinee idol. If you had been forced to construct an accountant – and a Swiss accountant at that – out of a tailor's dummy, steel-rimmed spectacles and repressed sexuality, you would have come up with something like Mr Keller.

He was between fifty and sixty, probably. It's difficult to judge how tall someone is when sitting, but Emma thought he was probably of average height – of average everything, really. He certainly wasn't handsome, but neither was he 'attractively ugly' in a sort of Humphrey Bogart way. He was just… unremarkable.

Having delivered the coffee and doughnuts, Emma had no reason to linger further. She glanced round one last time and left, pulling the door closed behind her. It was only three paces to the top of the stairs, from where she could see that the corridor below was completely empty. This was it. She crept back to the door and listened.

The pair were talking in German and didn't appear to be making any special effort to keep their voices down. Probably because it was a pretty dull conversation. They appeared to be talking about bookings and cash flow and suppliers' discounts.

After a minute or two, Emma started to become aware that her absence might be noticed downstairs, that she was hearing almost nothing of any evidential value and that one of the Kellers might emerge from the office at any moment and find her lurking – there was no other word for it, really – outside the door. She glanced at her watch. It was a minute to ten. She had to get downstairs or she would be late for her shift, and that would be noticed.

*

Emma was quite pleased to able to report some progress to her grandfather and to Frank. In the kitchen of The Old Vicarage, she set out the events of the day, her early arrival, going upstairs to Mr Keller's office, her description of it and of Mr and Mrs Keller, and finally what she was able to recall of what she had overheard listening at the door. She wanted to get this over with quickly, but past experience had taught her that the more she tried to hurry or to gloss over details she considered unimportant, the longer the whole process took. The old Scotsman was meticulous, thorough and – what was the word? – annoying.

Frank usually did most of the talking. Today was no exception, although he seemed more than usually grumpy. Emma suspected that she knew why. Scotland had only drawn with Norway that afternoon and although Emma didn't follow football closely, she had been able to pick up from the general discussion in the kitchen that this was an unsatisfactory result. Scotland's continued participation in the tournament hung in the balance.

Frank took a blank piece of A4 paper and passed it over. He invited her to draw a plan of Mr Keller's office and then another of the floor plan of the first floor. The second was not all that useful. So far as Emma could tell, the first floor replicated the ground floor in terms of layout. Mr Keller's office was the first door at the top of the stairs, immediately above Terry's office. It therefore followed that there were probably three other rooms corresponding to what Emma called the uniform room, the delivery room and the kitchen below. Emma couldn't be sure and she had absolutely no idea what might lie behind those three doors, if there were actually three. And she hadn't checked if they were locked. But she knew they were there. She could go back another time when the Kellers were elsewhere and explore further.

"Can you describe them both?"

"Well, Mr Keller is... I don't really know how to describe him... he's sort of grey."

"Age?"

"Mid-fifties, I suppose. Grey hair cut quite short, glasses."

"What type?"

"Ordinary glasses. Silver frames. He was wearing a suit and tie. Green tie. White shirt, sort of a light-grey suit. I can't remember his shoes."

"Any jewellery? Distinctive watch?"

Emma shook her head. She couldn't remember.

"What about Mrs Keller?"

"Oh, she's younger. Probably ten years younger. And she dresses sort of in a power style. Businesswoman, with just a touch of Cruella de Vil. Fair hair, sort of a bob. Not her natural colour, I'd say." Emma felt herself blushing again. "She had a briefcase. One of those silver metal ones, but quite slim."

"What did they say?"

"Well, I couldn't hear everything clearly and I'm not used to the Swiss accent, but it mostly seemed pretty routine stuff – bookings, deliveries, staff numbers."

"Swiss accent?"

"Well, I assume so. They're supposed to be Swiss. They say 'Ich' like 'Icke' instead of 'itch'."

"Do they?" This was the first time her grandfather had spoken.

The debriefings were usually conducted mostly by Frank and this was no exception.

"Can you think of any other unusual pronunciation?"

Emma thought. "No, not really, but they used a few words I didn't understand. Like '*Abschreibung*'."

"That's 'depreciation'. It's an accounting term. Anything else?"

"They said, '*Alles paletti*'. Is that a sort of Swiss Italian thing?"

Her grandfather shrugged. He looked at Frank, indicating that his intervention was over.

Frank asked a few more questions about Mr Keller's office. Was there a computer? Was there any sign of a safe? What was the lock on the door like? Emma privately found it quite amusing that she was asked these things. Were these two old men going to break in and download files off a computer? It seemed so improbable as to be absurd.

*

Emma had left the kitchen and gone upstairs.

"Go on then."

"What?"

"What is it?"

"Frank, you can be exasperatingly oblique sometimes."

"You know what I mean. What did she say that set your synapses snapping?"

"Ah! You noticed, did you?"

"I used to do this stuff for a living."

"Hmm, yes, well, I don't think that the Kellers are Swiss."

"Because?"

"Because they pronounce '*Ich*' the way only Berliners do and '*Alles paletti*' is uniquely Berlin vernacular. Damn! I should have asked her about the doughnuts!"

"You suspect a Berlin delicacy?"

"I do. And if the Kellers are German, not Swiss, are they even the Kellers?"

The two pensioners sat in silence for a few minutes.

"I can think of no advantage in a German pretending to be Swiss. Switzerland isn't in the EU; the bureaucracy would be a nuisance. Why pretend?"

"There is still some hostility to the Germans here or perhaps they thought there was. After all, nobody really has a grudge against the Swiss. They're so neutral, so inoffensive."

"So, there could be an innocent explanation?"

"Could be."

The two sat in silence for another minute.

"I think I'd like to see Herr Keller for myself."

Frank leaned back in his chair and half closed his eyes. He even steepled his fingers, like clever and wise people do in films. But it was no good. That was not how Frank McBride did his thinking. He reached into his left-hand pocket and fished out his pipe. His Tuesday pipe. The one that Joe Lake had given him as a retirement gift. It was a meerschaum, but not one of those silly ones like the smoker's equivalent of a Toby jug. Frank would never have smoked one of those in public and probably not in private either.

It was a standard billiard smooth with a bent fishtail stem. A proper pipe for people who took such things seriously. From the other pocket, he took his pouch of McLintock's Black Cherry and a box of matches. He had had a proper pipe lighter once, a gift from his second wife, but he had lost it in an after-hours drinking club in New Fetter Lane.

It was only when he had filled the pipe to his satisfaction and tamped it down to the correct consistency that he looked at Bernard. "What do you mean exactly?"

The phosphorous met the sandpaper with a melodic rasp and he made eye contact through a plume of smoke.

THIRTEEN

Emma didn't waste too much time lingering on the image she had of her grandfather scaling the walls of Leighton Hall clad all in black with a torch between his teeth. She had a date. After almost a week, she had managed to bully – no, that was not quite the right word. Coerce? Not exactly. Cajoled, goaded, persuaded – something like that. Anyway, Oliver was taking her out for dinner in Oakham. He had promised to come and collect her at half past seven and it was almost that time already.

She cast clothes in every direction as she tried to decide what to wear. It was important, she thought, that she avoided a sort of 'Oh, we're just getting a pizza together as friends' look. And she didn't want to appear to be throwing herself at him either. *That* dress was definitely out. It was unequivocally a third-date dress. But it was important that Oliver recognised that this was a date. He was so painfully shy. It was very sweet actually, but Emma didn't want him to think that this was to be platonic. But neither did she wish to rush him, to frighten him off. She eventually settled on a pair of jeans that were just the right side of tight and a T-shirt that was just the wrong side.

She heard a car pull up outside and rushed to the window.

Not Oliver. Oliver drove a white Mini Metro that he shared with his mother. The car outside was a BMW and of considerably more recent vintage. But that was Oliver getting out. And he was wearing a jacket. A proper jacket. Emma rushed back to her wardrobe. She was underdressed. A shirt, that's it, a proper shirt – not white, though; that meant work. She could hear him coming up the path as she surveyed herself one last time in the mirror. One more button undone? No. Yes. No.

"Play it cool," she muttered, as she forced herself to come down the stairs like a princess attending a ball, not a fireman attending a disaster. Oliver was standing in the hall. Her grandfather had opened the door to him. He was holding a bunch of flowers and looking like one of those awkward American teenagers attending a high school prom in the movies. Emma thought he was sweet.

"Nice car! Where did you steal it?"

"It's Dad's. I have to have it back by midnight or it will turn into a pumpkin."

Emma absent-mindedly undid a button and wondered whether BMWs had reclining seats.

*

Oakham is the capital of Rutland and, by far, its largest... err... conurbation? Let's face it, it's a small town. You could even make a case for it being a big village. But it was surprisingly well served for places selling pizza. Oliver and Emma drove past two before he steered the BMW, somewhat cautiously and far from expertly, into the public car park on Church Street. The parking itself was equally painful. Oliver clearly wasn't used to an automatic and was so frightened of denting his father's car that he spent three full minutes edging forwards and backwards an inch at a time before he was satisfied that he had parked perfectly, or his sense of shame just wouldn't let him continue further.

"You know, I wouldn't have minded if we'd come in your Mini."

Oliver looked slightly hurt. "I wanted to make a special effort. I'm... I'm not very good with girls. Short on experience, you see."

He blushed a little, which made him cross with himself. He rushed out of the car, failing to shut the driver's door properly so that he could open Emma's door for her. The impression of courteous gallantry was somewhat undermined by the fact that he had to return to the other side of the car to close his own door. Then, he hurried back to stand beside Emma. It was only about a hundred yards to Gino's Trattoria, but even that short journey provided Oliver with a dilemma. Should he walk alongside her? Should he try to hold hands? To link arms? He was pretty sure he shouldn't put his arm around her. Not on a first date. A thought suddenly filled him with horror. Did Emma regard this as a date? Had he made a terrible error by turning up in a jacket, in a BMW? And the flowers – how corny was that? Oliver stood paralysed by indecision. Emma slipped her arm through his. "Come on! I'm starving."

Even Oliver's choice of Gino's had been an agony for him. Oliver considered himself a bit of a connoisseur where pizzas were concerned, and a lifetime spent in Rutland had armed him with an in-depth knowledge and understanding of all the places they might be obtained. Gino's had the second-best pizzas in Rutland. The best were at Cantina Augusto in Uppingham, an even smaller town ten minutes to the south. But Gino's had red-and-white tablecloths and candles in those funny bottles with the raffia around the base – what were they called? Oh, yes, fiascos. Not a good omen. But it seemed more romantic. Was he overdoing it again? Flowers? Candlelit dinner? He risked a glance at Emma. She seemed to be wearing a contented smile. Or was it an amused smirk?

Gino showed them both to a table in a quiet and dimly lit corner. He gave Oliver a conspiratorial wink. Might have been a leer, actually. Oliver was on the verge of panic. While Emma examined the menu, he tried to calm himself by taking a few deep breaths. That didn't work. Now he was starting to worry that he was actually panting. If he was panting, or almost, was he also sweating? He casually drew a finger across his brow. No, no perspiration… yet. Gino coughed gently. He raised an eyebrow, just one – he was good at that, like a Neapolitan Roger Moore. Oh! Drinks.

Emma looked up at this point. "Oh, just a sparkling water for me, thanks."

Oliver nodded and Gino disappeared.

"It all looks so good," said Emma. And it seemed to be sincere.

"I always have the Napoli." Oliver was back on firmer ground, almost his specialist subject.

"Ooh! Is that the one with capers and anchovies?"

Oliver was horrified. Had he committed some terrible faux pas?

"I'll have the same." Emma closed her menu and smiled at him. Maybe it wasn't going so badly, after all.

*

Perhaps Gino had sensed the importance of the occasion and pulled out all the stops, but the pizzas were excellent. Oliver started to relax and the conversation started to flow. Emma told her about her studies and how she was trying to wriggle free of her parents' ambitions for a career in law. From time to time, she would sweep her hair back behind her right ear with her fingers and he could still see the very slight magenta traces of her self-sabotage of her interview.

Of course, Emma had no idea of the agony through which Oliver had gone to choose this venue. Nevertheless, she approved. Gino's was cosy. It was intimate and if it was a little old-fashioned, so what? She was rather taken with the candlelit ambience. She wondered if it was a regular venue for Oliver to take dates. On balance, that seemed unlikely.

Most of the other customers were twice Emma's age. She was struck, in particular, by two separate couples. One was a pair who must have been approximately her parents' age. They held hands across the table and bent their heads together in what Emma liked to imagine was a shared intimacy. This must be one of those 'date nights' that long-married couples occasionally had. Some couples. Not her parents. It was impossible to imagine her parents holding hands across a red-checked tablecloth. Or anywhere else actually.

When they went out, it was to a charity ball or a Rotarian event. Her mother would spend an hour choosing the right jewellery, calculated to impress without appearing ostentatious. Her father would be grunting and swearing and failing to knot his bow tie correctly. And, she imagined, they would part a second after crossing the threshold and not speak to each other again for the rest of the evening.

The second couple were far more like Emma's parents. They were casually dressed. At least they would have thought so. Some people can appear casual because they are casual. Others have to work at it and they seldom carry it off. They end up looking like they are posing for a catalogue. The second couple fell into this camp. He was wearing the loafers or boat shoes, whatever they were, that had become popular that year and that a certain type of middle-aged man believed conferred youth. Emma had to bend forward to test her theory. Yep. No socks! Oh dear, oh dear!

And that was just him. She was dressed like a gap-year student who had persuaded themselves that Marrakech was their spiritual home and that a combination of a near-translucent white linen shirt and far too many bangles indicated that they were a free spirit. Emma didn't even need to check to guess the footwear.

But the thing that really struck Emma was that each appeared to be utterly unaware of the other. They hadn't exchanged a word in ten minutes and gave no indication that this was likely to change.

Oliver normally felt intimidated by people who were obviously so intelligent and he almost always felt intimidated by attractive young women. Or unattractive young women, actually, or old women. He was intimidated by women, basically. And if they were attractive and intelligent and self-assured and charming and... actually, why was he not intimidated by Emma anymore?

Eventually, he was lured into talking about himself. He had been born and raised in Rutland. He found school baffling and boring most of the time, and while enthusiastic, he was no great hand at sport either. Like Emma, he had an older brother. And like Emma, he often felt as if he were in his shadow. Timothy, never Tim, at least not at home, was four years older than Oliver. He seemed to have inherited the family's share of brains. He had gone to university and was now working in Birmingham. Something to do with mobile phones. Oliver wasn't exactly sure. Oliver's parents were terribly proud of Timothy. They did their best to appear proud of Oliver, too, but they never really pulled it off. His father would usually introduce him as 'training to be a struggling artist'. And the worst part was that it was probably true.

For as long as he could remember, Oliver had been able to draw and to paint. He could see and replicate patterns of light and shade, depth and lustre. He wasn't sure how. He had just always been able to do it. By the time he was four, his works of art had replaced all his elder brother's on the fridge door. That was the last time he had inched ahead of his brother in his parents' private competition. He had won competitions. Silly little competitions for the county council's literacy campaign poster or designing the flag for the local cub scouts. By the time he was sixteen, he knew that he wanted to be an artist.

"Perhaps you could draw me."

"I'd love to."

"Tomorrow?"

"Why not?"

They lingered over coffee fifteen minutes longer than ordinary customers decently could and five minutes longer than the time Gino normally permitted for young lovers. When the bill eventually arrived, Oliver reached for it, but before he could pick it up, Emma's hand closed over his.

"Halves?"

Oliver turned his palm up and their fingers intertwined. "Okay."

It seemed completely natural that they should hold hands on the way back to the car park, too. Emma had slightly paused under a street light. Yes, Oakham had street lights – it wasn't that small! But Oliver had failed to recognise the significance of this until it was too late. But there was another street light just ahead. He would kiss her there. He would. He wasn't misreading the signals; he wasn't going to make a fool of himself. He was going to kiss Emma under that street light. Except he didn't.

Brazil versus Morocco had finished. Brazil had won three-nil and a dozen young men spilled out of The Wheatsheaf and gathered at the end of Northgate by the entrance of the car park, under the last street light between Oliver and the car.

The young men, as young men will do when they have spent ninety minutes appreciating both the flair and grace of the Brazilian football team and the miraculous combination of hops and barley, offered some unsolicited commentary on the young couple, and made some suggestions and predictions as to what the next stage of Oliver's and Emma's evening might entail.

Emma made a suggestion of her own in response and it was definitely something that you weren't allowed to say in court. The young men took it in good spirits and resumed their earlier debate about the merits and de-merits of a young man named Rivaldo.

By the time Oliver and Emma had reached the car, they were out of sight – if not quite out of earshot. Oliver ideally wouldn't have liked risking making a fool of himself again by opening her door, but, having done it once, he didn't really feel that he could dial back the gallantry at this stage. At all costs, he wanted to avoid creating the impression that he was cooling off with regard to Emma.

He opened the door and turned. Emma was standing very close to him. He kissed her. She kissed him. He ran the back of his fingers gently down the left side of her face and he kissed her again. This was perfect. This was wonderful. Gino, his parents, Rivaldo – they were all insignificant background in the story that was the very epicentre of the universe. The rest of the world might as well not exist. A second later, they were caught in a violent, intense searchlight. The type used by air-sea rescue or the London Palladium. It was a Range Rover manoeuvring in the car park. Bloody Range Rovers. It sometimes seemed like every second car in Rutland was a Range Rover. Why did they need such powerful headlights? The magic – those few precious seconds of blissful magic – was gone.

*

It's not far from Oakham to Leighton Parva and in a little more than five minutes, Oliver's father's BMW was entering the village.

"Turn left here, here."

Oliver did as he was bid. He was a little puzzled because it was fifty yards further to The Old Vicarage.

"But this is the cricket club."

"Yes, I fancied a game of cricket. Park over there, in the darkest corner."

Again, Oliver did as he was bid, but this time he understood why.

*

In the upstairs window of The Old Vicarage, Bernard Taylor looked down over the cricket club car park. He had a set of binoculars at his side, but he didn't touch them. Young people will be young people and Oliver seemed like a nice young man. And if the car park of the Leighton Parva Cricket Club seemed like an unromantic location, it certainly beat a bombsite in Charlottenburg in 1947.

FOURTEEN

Brigadier Sir Bernard George Taylor had been a spy for forty-seven years. Sort of. He hadn't spent half a century snooping around top-secret military installations or crouched in an attic tapping out messages on the morse key of a suitcase radio. He had been an army officer in military intelligence... mostly. And that had been an accident.

He had been sharing a cup of tea with the crew of his Crusader tank on the outskirts of Tunis, when he had been hit by fragments of an anti-tank shell meant for someone else. His wound was just serious enough to take him out of the line, but not serious enough to merit a return to England. After a short spell in hospital, he had been appointed the brigade intelligence officer.

Originally, this had meant buzzing around Tunisia or Italy in a Daimler Dingo Scout Car, trying to guess what was on the other side of the next hill. Then, it had involved doing something similar, but back at Divisional HQ with aerial photographs of Normandy. By the time he had reached Berlin, he was a lieutenant colonel in the Intelligence Corps. He wasn't entirely sure how either of those things had happened.

After that, he had mostly been sitting behind a desk in West

Berlin, engaged in a decades-long battle of wits with an unseen opponent. Actually, it wasn't really a battle of wits. Oscar Wilde would have been a rubbish intelligence officer. A ready wit was not a key skill at all. Dishonesty? Yes. Duplicity? Absolutely. Cynicism? Scepticism? Mistrust? Absolutely de rigueur, old boy. And it turned out – on his good days, Bernard was slightly ashamed of this – that he was rather good at it.

Bernard had been good at it because he was a shameless, deceitful, double-crossing, mistrustful old bastard. He had been hoodwinked a few times, of course. If you spent long enough in the game, that was bound to happen from time to time. But he had successfully pulled a few strokes of his own, too.

And in the twilight of his career, when he was no longer a serving army officer but something else, something that didn't really have a name and certainly didn't have a job description, he had turned his hand to other things. He had become an expert in counter surveillance, for example. His views of fieldcraft were sought and disseminated far and wide. He had even taught Frank McBride, but that was a long time ago.

The point, however, was this, despite almost half a century as a sort of spy, he had never actually conducted surveillance himself. He had never squatted in the back of a van with a telephoto lens. He had never scurried down a side street on a parallel course so that he could observe a target from an unlikely angle. He'd never even followed anyone. Ever.

Frank McBride, by contrast, had spent half a lifetime on surveillance. It had cost him two marriages and earned him an OBE. As a lifelong republican (he had accepted the OBE to please his second wife), he considered this to be a bad bargain. But he did know what he was doing and so Bernard was willing to defer to his former pupil.

They were sitting side by side at Bernard's kitchen table. Frank had just returned from his usual morning walk with Ron Godsmark and Rocky, who was now lying in a corner snoring steadily and breaking wind intermittently.

"There's good news and bad news," began Frank. "The good news is that what we are trying to do isn't especially difficult. We want one good look at a single person, whose movements we know and who probably isn't very surveillance-conscious. And it doesn't matter where or in what circumstances we see him."

"There's a but coming, isn't there?"

"Well, a small one. We don't have a team of trained surveillance officers at our disposal. We don't have any specialist vehicles and we don't even have radios."

"We could buy some."

Frank ignored this and continued, "We know that Keller arrives by car at more or less the same time at Leighton Hall every weekday and we have a description of his vehicle. We could just park in the car park and wait for him or we could easily arrange to walk past at the right time. Ron and I walk quite close to the car park every day."

"But?"

"But Keller would likely get a good look at us, too, and we don't necessarily want that."

"So?"

"So, our next best option is to see him on his way to or from work. Disadvantages with that are numerous. We would probably only get a fleeting glance. Probably wouldn't be an opportunity to take a photograph. It's June. He might be wearing sunglasses to drive. Sun might be reflecting on the windscreen – that's more of a problem if we do it in the morning when he's travelling south."

This last point hadn't occurred to Bernard, but then Frank was a pro.

"Finally, we don't know his address. We don't know exactly where he's going."

"He lives in Ashcombe, doesn't he?"

"So we're told, but that might mean the village itself or it might be somewhere in the middle of nowhere where Ashcombe is just the closest village. He's not in the phone book and being Swiss, or at least posing as a Swiss, he won't be on the electoral roll either. So, we don't know his address, yet. We could check out every house in Ashcombe – there's probably only a couple of hundred. If we exclude the ones we can trace, we should be able to narrow it down to a handful of houses – maybe just one."

Bernard nodded.

"But let's assume for the moment that we can't do that." Frank spread out an Ordnance Survey map on the table and an A-Z of Leicestershire and Rutland. "We can see that there is basically one road from the hall towards Ashcombe for about three miles and then there's this turning to the right and then what amounts to a fork in the road as you reach the village itself. Beyond the village – it's possible Keller lives on the other side of Ashcombe – the road divides again and one branch divides further before you get anywhere that couldn't be described as Ashcombe."

Bernard nodded again, but he was starting to get impatient. Was this all a long preamble to the revelation that the task was impossible? Or was Frank just teasing him prior to revealing his brilliant solution?

"So, what I propose is that we begin by finding out where the Kellers live. We have two options. We can try to eliminate every other house in the village, which might not work, or we can plot up on the hall and follow him until we've housed him. Once we know where he lays his weary head, we can either find an observation point to see him come in and out or, if that's not viable, find a spot on his route to or from the hall."

Bernard nodded. Slightly frustratingly, he could find no flaw in Frank's logic or in his plan.

"So, what I suggest is that we go and take a look at Ashcombe now, get a feel for the place, look for potential pinch points where a car has to slow down and places from which to keep observation – that sort of the thing."

"What time?"

"This afternoon, but we need to be in position to pick up Keller any time after four."

"I thought that he left at five past five each day, regular as clockwork."

"And he almost certainly will today, except…"

"You've got that expression on your face."

"What expression?"

"The one you have when you think you've thought of something that hadn't occurred to me."

"I think that almost all of the time."

"What is it, Frank?"

"Probably a red herring – almost certainly, since you seem to think that Keller is from Berlin – but if he's a German speaker who isn't actually Swiss, there is a chance he's Austrian."

"That's possible. Although I'm pretty sure at least one of them is a Berliner."

"Well, Austria are playing Chile this afternoon. Kicks off at four-thirty. So, if he is Austrian…"

*

Frank went home for lunch, but returned to The Old Vicarage at one in the afternoon, driving his old Ford. Rocky was sitting in the front seat and acting as co-pilot as usual. Bernard was slightly surprised. He hadn't actually thought about which car they would use – his or Frank's – but he had sort of assumed that it would be his. He had also assumed that Rocky would not be part of this mini surveillance team.

"Is Rocky here to raise the average IQ?"

"You'll see later." And to the dog, "Get in the back."

Rocky turned his big brown eyes on Frank in a reproachful manner. Surely the nice old man who gave him Bonios was not senior to him and worthy of a front seat. The big brown eyes met the cold blue ones and the spaniel leapt agilely into the back where he took up a position in the middle of the back seat, from which he had an uninterrupted view through the windscreen. Bernard surveyed the hair-laden seat, sighed inwardly and got in. As he did so, he saw that Rocky had actually been forced to take up the position that he had. There were two child seats on the back seat and he was sitting in the small gap between them. Bernard wondered whether seventy-seven might be a little old to be making his surveillance debut and whether Grandad's taxi, smelling quite powerfully of wet spaniel and something that might have been infant vomit, was the ideal starter vehicle.

Frank headed off down the Stamford Road before turning left up the hill into Leighton Magna. They saw Ron Godsmark walking down the hill, clad all in white except for his navy blazer and carrying what both men assumed was his bowls bag. Leighton Magna were obviously at home this Wednesday.

"Ron told me he's played bowls for Leighton Magna for twenty-five years."

"I don't doubt it."

"How old would you say he was?"

"Oh, I don't know. A little younger than me. A little older than you?"

"I believe he's lived here his whole life."

"Probably."

Bernard's reply had been quite clipped, curt even. Frank stored this away .

"There are two vehicle entrances. One is for guests, one for trade. Keller might use either, but it doesn't matter. Either way, he's going to turn left and head north on the Ashcombe Road. There's nothing else for him to do unless he comes down into Leighton Magna."

Bernard nodded. Frank slowed the car.

"We can't wait for him here. There's no cover. He would spot us for sure."

The road curved a little to the left as it went downhill. There was an entrance to a farm field on the right.

"That's no good."

Bernard hadn't said a word, made a sound even, but Frank could smell the inquiry forming in his mind. "He'd see us as he came down the hill and what convincing excuse have we got for parking in a field? Hang on! This might do."

The road turned sharply right and there was a small brick-built humpback bridge over a stream, or a small river – how wide does it have to be to be a river? Or is that even how you define rivers? It was a humpback bridge over a slow-moving body of water about twelve or fifteen foot wide. But just before that there was a turning and a small patch of gravel just large enough to park two or three cars. Frank had almost passed it and was over the bridge before he saw it. He turned the car around with a degree of skill and speed that you do not associate with Grandad's taxi and crawled slowly over the bridge. From this angle, he could see a small sign that read:

OAKHAM ANGLING SOCIETY
NO DAY TICKETS
NO NIGHT FISHING

Frank manoeuvred his car so that it was almost invisible from the road. Ahead, he could see the bridge, the road that lay beyond as it wound lazily up a shallow hill and the outskirts of what must have been Ashcombe on the brow of the hill.

"We wait here. When he's over the bridge and around that first curve, we follow him. Can you see the road behind us in your door mirror?"

"No, sorry."

"Good."

And that seemed to settle it, at least to Frank's satisfaction, and Bernard didn't feel inclined to argue the point. And yet Frank didn't move, didn't restart the engine. He just sat in silence. And opened the window.

Five minutes later, Bernard heard an engine, then a second as Frank started his. A navy Range Rover – they really were ubiquitous in Rutland – slowly negotiated the bridge, which had been built for narrower and more slow-moving vehicles. Frank started counting aloud. When he reached nine, the Range Rover disappeared around the curve ahead. When he reached fifteen, Frank pulled away and put his foot down. Rocky yapped excitedly from the back seat. Bernard gripped the door handle.

They caught the Range Rover about two hundred yards before the sign that read, 'Ashcombe – Please drive carefully through our village' and followed it through Ashcombe's main street. It had a post office and general store at one end and a pub called The Three Horseshoes at the other. The Range Rover started to accelerate at this point. Its destination was obviously further on, but Frank pulled into the pub car park.

"Reconnaissance on foot."

Bernard nodded, but Frank hadn't been talking to him. "Come on, Rocky!"

Now, it made sense.

There are places, and Frank McBride had spent most of his life in them, where it was possible to wander about, apparently aimlessly, without anybody paying the least attention. If he had been on Deptford High Street or in Leicester or Dundee, McBride could have spent an hour or two examining the geography, the likely hiding places, observation post and routes of access and egress without let or hindrance. You couldn't do that in Ashcombe. There was almost nobody on the streets in the early afternoon on a weekday, but there were plenty just behind the net curtains. All of them wondering who the mysterious stranger was and what they were doing there.

That is, unless they had a dog. If you had a dog, those questions were already answered. Who were they? They were dog walkers – and it helped if you looked like Frank and Bernard. What were they doing? They were walking their dog. No need to contact the Neighbourhood Watch co-ordinator, telephone the police or call in the Household Cavalry. In Rutland, if you had a dog – and if that dog was a springer spaniel, so much the better – you had a license to be anywhere.

Frank and Bernard spent forty-five minutes conducting a full examination of Ashcombe. Well, not a full examination, as that would have involved entering The Three Horseshoes and it didn't open until six. Instead, they returned to Frank's Ford in its car park.

"Well?"

"It's far from ideal. Once in the village, the turnings come thick and fast. We are going to have to be right behind him. Then it gets worse. All these new houses are on curved roads. Same issue. And a lot are cul-de-sacs. Some of them don't have proper pavements. If he lives in one of those, it will be almost impossible to see him to a house. We'd have to come back another day and do it on foot. But the bigger problem is if he lives in one of the older, larger houses with long drives. By the time he gets out of his car, he will be twenty or thirty yards away and some of them have got electronically controlled gates."

Bernard nodded. It was extraordinary that it was so difficult just to get one good look at a man whose car and movements they knew. But everything that Frank had said made sense. He reflected slightly guiltily about how dismissive he had been at the excuses provided by the surveillance teams in Berlin. The whole thing was more difficult than it looked. Was it really worth it? Why did he want to see Keller? Did it make any real difference in the short term?

Bernard knew the answer and it made him cross with himself. The Kellers, or at least one of them, were Berliners and Berlin was his city. The city he knew inside out and upside down. But there were over three million Berliners. He didn't know them all. He was hardly likely to get a quick glance at a middle-aged man and immediately say, "Oh! That's old Klaus who used to work as a barman in the Hotel Adlon." It was ridiculous.

But they had come this far, so Bernard said nothing as Frank drove back to the little fishing spot by the humpback bridge. Four o'clock passed and then four-thirty. So, Keller wasn't Austrian. Or wasn't a football fan. Or couldn't tell the time. But he obviously could, because he left at five past five each day. And that was telling, wasn't it?

Keller and his wife were self-employed business people. Such people usually took the attitude that the day was done when the work was done. But Keller behaved like a clock-watcher. Like a civil servant, he would have said, if he hadn't been sitting next to Frank McBride. Bernard didn't consider himself a coward, but he didn't even dare think that in proximity to Frank. Anyway, if he left at five past five and he drove at a reasonable speed, it was perhaps a mile and a half to where Frank and he were parked – 'plotted up', Frank had called it – say two minutes, perhaps three. Keller should be here now.

The Mercedes was obviously well-tuned and regularly serviced because they didn't hear it. But it was a big, powerful car and it ghosted through the Rutland lanes with little more than a faint purr. They both saw it, negotiating the bridge carefully. Bernard caught a glimpse of a middle-aged man at the wheel. They both started to count to ten, their lips moving, no sound forthcoming, but Frank evidently counted more slowly because Bernard had reached twelve before Frank turned the key in the ignition.

Frank had done this sort of thing a million times and usually without the benefit of studying the terrain – Frank called it 'the plot' – in advance. As the Mercedes reached the outskirts of Ashcombe, had Keller been looking, he would have seen Frank's Ford for the first time in his rear-view mirror. He took the first left into Vicarage Lane. Frank smiled; he passed the church, slowing markedly. Frank started to giggle. The Mercedes swept between two large stone gateposts and up a gravel drive towards a largish nineteenth-century house. By this time, Frank was actually laughing and Bernard couldn't help but join in.

On the right of the two pillars was a slate sign giving the name of the house: 'The Old Vicarage'.

FIFTEEN

Emma had made sure that she arrived at work a little early in the hope that she would again be asked to bring Mr Keller coffee. As a ploy, it wasn't exactly going to make it into the pages of 'Espionage's Greatest Ruses', but it did work. She was carrying a tray of coffee (for one) out of the kitchen just as Oliver arrived for his shift. Emma decided to treat him to a coy and maidenly smile, but she wasn't convinced that she had really pulled it off. It might have been a bit more like a lecherous leer and an invitation for Oliver to join her in the linen cupboard later. If so, that wouldn't necessarily be a bad thing.

"Oh! You're early!" said Oliver. "I normally do that."

The fact that Mr Keller was alone limited the opportunities for intelligence-gathering. Emma decided not to linger at his door, hoping to overhear anything. Unless Keller was talking on the telephone, or to himself, there wouldn't be anything to overhear. And if he couldn't be heard, Emma also couldn't be sure that he was busily engaged, meaning that she would have no warning if he decided to leave his office. Accordingly, she decided that this was not the day to try to learn what was behind the other three doors on the corridor. She did risk trying the first, though, just to see if it was locked. It was.

So, she decided to try the next best thing. She slightly begrudged it, because it was so prosaic and felt a bit like cheating. She would ask Oliver. But she didn't get a chance that morning. She was on what the staff called 'Trouble and Bubbles' duty, greeting guests and dispensing champagne – or Prosecco (more rarely) or cava (more commonly).

Today's wedding, according to the playbill script at the head of the seating plan, was for Alan and Trudy. According to the letter balloons that had suffered somewhat from the mid-June heat and from being a little too near one of the chandeliers, the whole event was A LA RUDY. In some ways, today's wedding was very similar to the four or five at which Emma had already worked. There was the happy couple of course. Alan was in his late thirties and was obviously regretting choosing, or more likely agreeing, to wear a top hat. In fact, he spent most of the time carrying it, forgetting it or swiping it out from beneath the posteriors of elderly aunts who were about to sit on it. The only thing that he hadn't done so far was test its frisbee-like qualities in the general direction of the lake. But it couldn't be long before that happened.

But Alan was not the issue. And the other fifty per cent of the happy couple (unless you apportioned it by weight, in which case it was more like two thirds) was not the issue either. Trudy was having the time of her life. Absolutely everything that she heard or saw was the most hilariously amusing thing that she had ever witnessed. She shrieked with laughter at every excuse and at none.

At one point, Emma wondered whether they might soon learn whether the chandeliers were genuine crystal because Trudy seemed to be trying to replicate that thing that opera singers do with wine glasses. The similarity didn't end there. Trudy was what charitable friends might describe as having been built for comfort rather than speed. And she had rolled off the production line about the same time as the first Spitfires. Her wedding dress resembled the effect that you might achieve if you attempted to make an airship out of crinoline. But she, at least, seemed to be enjoying herself. And that was lovely, wasn't it? Yes. Lovely.

No, the problem was Natasha. Natasha was the daughter of the bride. And Natasha had opinions. Inconsistent, unreasonable, illogical and impossible opinions. And plenty of them. And Natasha was a generous soul. She liked to share and the chief commodity of her munificence was, of course, her opinions.

She shared with Emma her views on the superiority of champagne to Prosecco, and then, when she noticed that she was drinking cava, on cava's inferiority to either. Then she had some insights on the correct way to pour sparkling wine of any terroir and the temperature at which it should be served, before moving on to the scandal of the age, which appeared to be the inability of Moss Bros to provide top hats of the correct size.

Emma was inclined to sympathise with her on this last point. Alan, having exhausted almost every other possibility, had surrendered to the inevitable and put the damn thing on his head. Logic and Archimedes and two or three other clever Greek blokes who liked to dress in bedsheets would probably have said that it was impossible for a top hat to be simultaneously too large and too small for its wearer. And they would, each and every one of them, have been dead wrong. Emma was watching him, torn between pity and amusement, when the first of these two emotions suddenly achieved an insurmountable lead.

"Hubby! Oh, hubbikins! Alan, where are you?"

Emma glanced up at the chandelier.

"Hubbikins, come here. I want you to meet someone!"

Alan, making what many a shrewd onlooker might have called his second calamitous decision of the day, responded to this appalling epithet and trotted over to his bride.

Meanwhile, Natasha had discovered some improbably strongly held and inflexible opinions on the subject of confetti and was questioning Oliver in an increasingly aggressive tone on the subject. The woman was a market researcher's dream. Opinion pollsters must have spoken of Natasha in hushed and awed tones. There was literally no subject upon which she did not hold strong views. She had never ticked a 'Don't know' box in her entire life.

At this point, the toastmaster – yes, they had a toastmaster; a slightly pompous man dressed as a cross between a cinema commissionaire and the man from the Johnnie Walker bottles – announced that the wedding breakfast would shortly be served. This signalled two rushes. The amateurs made for the dining hall. The seasoned veterans for the table where Emma and her colleague, Alex, were still dispensing free booze. Natasha announced, possibly to Emma or possibly to the general throng, that she had to go and inspect the figures on the top of the wedding cake.

There now followed the hardest fifteen minutes of the day. Emma and Alex had to clear away the empty glasses, empty bottles and the serving table. All at pace because even those streetwise guests who had helped themselves to one last glass would be getting thirsty again soon and Madeline insisted that wine bottles be opened at the table. Alex had worked at the hall for longer than Emma and she had calculated a formula for determining how difficult the rest of the day was going to be. It was a simple enough equation: divide the number of empty bottles by the number of guests and then apply to a scale of predicted future raucousness. It was going to be a tough day. Fortunately, Alex and Emma were only working until six. After that, the evening bar staff came on and, by then, no fancy mathematics would be required to forecast how the evening might pan out.

Alan and Trudy – let's face it, Trudy – had ordered the house red and the house white, as had about three-quarters of all guests. Emma did not regard herself as an expert, far less a connoisseur, but she knew the basics. And the house wines, in particular the red, were very basic indeed.

Mrs Keller had insisted that the house wines be French and that the bottles should be corked, rather than sealed with a screw top, a plastic plug or a discarded lump of chewing gum. Chateau

Bousier met these criteria, but almost no others. It was produced by a failing cooperative in Languedoc that had presumably tired of trying to have its produce certified as an authorised defoliant and opted instead to pop it in a 75cl bottle and ship it to Les Rosbifs – one imagines as revenge for Agincourt.

Emma had been thinking of something else – Oliver, actually, since you ask – and had made a terrible error. She was last out of the traps for the wine serving and found herself responsible for the top table. Trudy was still having a terrific time and her day could probably only be improved further by the provision of a slightly larger wine glass, or a jug, or possibly a small bucket.

Alan's face bore the expression of a man who was asking himself exactly how difficult it would be to fake his own death. But at the far end of the table was Natasha. And if Natasha didn't have an opinion about Chateau Bousier, then Emma would be forced to reconsider her whole life, her understanding of the universe and everything.

"White or red?"

Natasha fished a pair of reading spectacles from her handbag and carefully scrutinised both labels. She pursed her lips.

"White, please!"

Emma swiftly uncorked it. It was astonishing how quickly she had become genuinely proficient at this. Natasha held out her hand. *Oh God!* She wanted the cork. She was actually going to sniff the cork. If you were a professional sommelier or a wine merchant or something, or the type of person who had a couple of hundred dusty bottles in a temperature-controlled cellar, you might be permitted to sniff the cork. If it were red wine.

"Yes, yes, very good! I never need to taste it if the cork is good. I'm very lucky like that. It's a blessing and a curse because I can't abide bad wine," she told her neighbour as Emma filled her glass with a Languedoc vin ordinaire, which would probably lose a blind tasting against a lamp oil distilled from stinging nettles and parsnips.

Alex's predicted future raucousness index seemed to be pretty accurate. Emma barely stopped topping up glasses for the next hour. Then, it was back to the kitchen to open the cava for the toasts. And the speeches. Emma had never attended a wedding where the daughter of the bride had quite such a key role, but she wasn't surprised when she learned that, on Alan and Trudy's big day, she would be giving a speech. Quite a long one.

It was the first time that Emma had sat down since ten o'clock. She was exhausted and was sure that it showed on her face. Therefore, she wasn't best pleased that Oliver, also sitting down for the first time, chose that moment to sketch her, as he had promised the previous evening.

"Do you have to? What are you going to call it? Waitress is totally knackered?"

"It's a sketch, not a photograph. But I'll do it from memory, if you prefer."

Oliver turned to the side and carried on. If Emma just leaned a little to her right, she could see the page of his sketchbook. He was good. She supposed he ought to be. He was an art student, after all. But he was really good. It was a head and shoulders portrait, but Emma could identify that Oliver had given her the shirt that she had worn the previous evening. She blushed slightly as she remembered how many buttons had been undone. Oliver clearly remembered, too.

"How do you do that?"

"What?"

"Draw. Like that. Entirely from memory?"

Oliver shrugged. "I don't know. I just can."

"Do another one. Do Natasha."

"Who?"

"Natasha. The daughter of the bride."

Oliver turned over the page of his sketchbook. He closed his eyes for a few moments. Then, he began sketching. Every minute or so, he closed his eyes again, paused for a few seconds and then took up again. After five minutes, he had produced a near-perfect image of Natasha sniffing a cork. Emma laughed.

At that moment, Madeline stuck her head around the kitchen door. "Tables, please! Chop, chop!"

Did anybody really say that these days? Apparently, Madeline did. Emma summoned her energy for one last push to get through the final ninety minutes. Oliver put down his sketchbook and leapt to his feet, powered by young love and the knowledge that his working day would soon be over.

It may have been Natasha's speech or it might have been one of the other speakers, but somebody had badly lost their audience – or a third of them, in any case. Emma found them, by accident, in the bar, which was not yet open, glued to coverage of South Africa versus Denmark – an unexceptional one-all draw that was only enlivened by seven bookings and a red card. It made the task of clearing the tables slightly easier and Emma, Alex, Oliver and the other three staff on the day shift had completed their duties a full ten minutes before six o'clock. Alex and Emma spent these ten minutes pretending to look for a microphone lead. Madeline was perfectly capable of sending them home and cutting their pay accordingly.

Aside from which, Oliver was still busy setting up the bar and Emma wanted him to give her a lift home. It was only a ten-minute walk for her down the hill, but Emma wanted her journey to last much longer than that.

SIXTEEN

Bernard was standing in the hall inspecting his tie knot in the mirror when he heard Emma entering through the kitchen door at the back of the house at about a quarter to eight. It was Thursday and there was to be a quiz at The Old Volunteer. Accordingly, Bernard had discarded the green knitted tie that he had been wearing all day and had selected, after considering and rejecting a number of alternatives, a mauve-and-silver number that he considered to be more formal and therefore more appropriate.

Bernard suspected – in fact, he was sure – that Peter Roberts had pestered Gary until he had agreed to host a quiz. Bernard didn't mind. A quiz was likely to bring a few customers in and, like Frank, Bernard feared that The Old Volunteer was soon going to be revealed as an uneconomic concern and that Leighton Parva would lose its only pub.

Bernard also suspected that Peter Roberts had briefed, or perhaps guided, Gary with respect to the quiz's format and that it would be slanted very much to his and to his team's advantage. Bernard didn't care. Once the pub's future was secured – and he doubted that that could be achieved, quiz or no quiz – he could go back to humiliating and infuriating Peter every week. After all, a man has to have a hobby, doesn't he?

Finally satisfied that his tie was fit for public display, Bernard returned to the kitchen to say hello and goodbye to Emma. She was sitting at the kitchen table and smiling in a slightly self-satisfied fashion.

"You've done your buttons up wrong!"

Her hand went immediately to the front of her work blouse. It was correctly buttoned, but that didn't matter. Her reaction had given her away. Bernard chuckled. It was these tiny victories, won by duplicity and deceit that kept the blood pumping. Emma scowled and indicated two pieces of paper on the kitchen table. He frowned and sat. He still had a minute or two. He picked up the first. "Who is this?"

"That's Mr Keller. Do you recognise him?"

Schneider! Captain Jakob Schneider of the Stasi!

Bernard shook his head. The reaction was just too ingrained. Even in a kitchen in Rutland, even talking to his granddaughter, his first instinct was to lie. Never, ever reveal what you know unless you have to or until that revelation will have maximum utility.

"And it's a good likeness, is it?"

"Yeah, pretty good. I mean, I've only seen him twice and for a few seconds, but I'd say it's a good likeness."

Bernard nodded. "Pretty unremarkable-looking chap, isn't he? Could be an assistant bank manager, deputy head teacher, something inconsequential at the gas board. Could be anything really." He picked up the second piece of paper. "Mrs Keller?"

"Yes and she does look exactly like that. I've seen her a few times."

The woman in the second sketch could not be called 'unremarkable'. She appeared to be about forty, but one of those forty year olds that could pass for thirty. Elegant. With strong features and an impression of hidden, only slightly hidden, fortitude. Bernard nodded again. "Well done! Well done, indeed. I assume we have your young man to thank for these?"

Emma nodded.

"And he has no idea…"

"He doesn't know why I wanted them, if that's what you are going to ask."

Bernard nodded again. He glanced at his watch. His teammates would be waiting.

*

Gary was looking pleased. The Old Volunteer was well populated with twenty-five or thirty people. That was a lot – more than ten per cent of the village's population. More than had voted for Peter Roberts at the Parish Council elections. Ron and Frank were at their usual small table in the corner. Everything was as usual. The same six teams as most weeks, including Peter Roberts and his acolytes.

Somebody – Frank, probably, who had very firm ideas on pub etiquette – had bought him his usual drink: two bottles of pils in a pint glass with three slices of lemon. It was the closest approximation of Berliner Kindl that could be found in Rutland. Frank was sitting amid a wreath of smoke from his pipe, his usual pint of Guinness in front of him.

Ron was sipping from a pint of bitter. Like Bernard, he was wearing a tie, but unlike Bernard he had only two from which to choose. This evening, he had eschewed the green and white of the Leighton Magna Bowls Club and was wearing a navy tie with a thin diagonal red stripe.

Bernard often wondered why anybody would want to be part of Peter's team. Its answers were not arrived at by consensus. If Peter thought he knew, even if he was wrong – in fact, especially if he was wrong – he insisted that his was the team's answer. If he didn't have an answer of his own, he would sometimes reject his teammates' answers, declare that the question was misleading or flawed, and refuse to submit any answer at all. He really was an awful little man and rather gallingly likely to win this week since he would doubtless have stacked the odds in his favour.

It was obvious that Bernard's suspicions were well founded before the first question, when the theme of the first round was announced as 'classic cars' – a particular enthusiasm of Peter's. Bernard had spent fifty years outside the UK. He didn't know a Humber from a Morris and he doubted that this was a field of expertise of Frank's or Ron's either. But unlike Peter, Bernard was able to recognise when he was wrong. Frank knew a surprising amount about Hillmans and Alvises. And Ron's knowledge of post-war British motorcycles was practically encyclopaedic. At the end of the first round, Bernard's team had full marks. As had Peter's. The second round was on sport. It's virtually mandatory for pub quizzes to have a round on sport. Peter's team scored full marks. So did Bernard's.

The third round was on cinema. The fourth on science. At the end of each, the scores were tied at full marks with the other teams having dropped only a couple of points. Gary had misjudged the level of erudition among the citizens of Leighton Parva. Bernard began to appreciate the skill which George had used to compile his quizzes.

The fifth round was on local history. Ron was effectively flying solo for this subject and Bernard's mind started to drift. He tried to remember what he had known about Jakob Schneider.

Born in Pankow, just to the north of Berlin's city centre and just in the Soviet zone in 1950. Schneider was of good proletarian stock. Frank would have approved and so did the authorities in the German Democratic Republic. His father had worked as a lathe operator before being conscripted into the Wehrmacht. He had the good fortune to have been captured by the British in Libya and had spent the second half of the war at a camp in England. His mother's history was less well known. But she had survived post-war Berlin, so it was reasonable to assume that she was tough and resourceful.

Jakob had been a bright boy, who had done well at elementary school. He had joined the party's youth wing and studied first at Humboldt University, where he joined the party and where he was probably identified as a potential future agent. Little was known about his life in the early seventies. There were rumours that he had spent a year studying in the Soviet Union, but these were never confirmed. By the late seventies, however, he had been identified as a Stasi employee.

Even State Security departments need their bean counters and the Stasi was a huge bureaucracy. By the early eighties, he was working in headquarters in the Lichtenburg district – not in the accounts division, but as an accountant attached to the main second division, counter intelligence. That was how he had crossed Bernard's path, although they had never met, of course. Bernard was trying to compare a hastily drawn sketch by a lovestruck young man with his memory of a photograph taken more than ten years ago. And yet, he was sure. He was trying to wrack his memory. Had there been a wife? Girlfriend? Mistress? He couldn't remember.

"Bernard! Bernard, you need to pay attention to this round. It's your field – bourgeois culture."

Bernard knew that meant art and literature and that it was time for him to pull his weight. The scores were tied going into the final round. Bernard knew just enough about art to manage the questions on that topic. It was Ron who contributed to the literature portion. At the end of round six, Peter Robert's team and Bernard's team were both tied on full marks. Gary seemed to think that this was an excellent result. He also seemed to think that the affair was over.

But the customers of The Old Volunteer were bloodthirsty. The wanted a victor and a loser. They wanted to witness the agony of the cup of success dashed from the lips at the final second.

Honourable draws were for effete metropolitan types who read *The Guardian*. In Rutland, it was kill or be killed. They were used to a tie break. But Gary didn't have one.

Possibly Peter had been so confident that six rounds on topics of his choosing (Bernard was absolutely certain that Peter had put his thumb on the scales in this regard – local history, for God's sake!) would deliver him victory that he hadn't bothered to mention this.

Gary began to panic. Then, possibly inspired by the bottle of Budweiser in his hand, an idea struck him. "To determine the winner, both teams will have two minutes to list as many Presidents of the United States as they can."

Two pieces of A4 paper were handed out and Gary, rather theatrically, gave the bell a little 'ting'. Peter Roberts naturally drew his team's piece of paper towards himself and began scribbling without reference to his companions. After thirty seconds, he appeared to run out of inspiration. Still, he would not relinquish control of the answer sheet and became more and more exasperated at suggestions from his teammates.

At the table in the corner, Frank McBride drew his paper towards him and started logically with the most recent and current incumbent, Bill Clinton, and worked backwards. He got as far as William McKinley (1897–1901, in case you were wondering) before leaning back and passing the paper to Bernard. Bernard added a few obvious candidates – Washington, Lincoln, Thomas Jefferson – before passing the sheet to Ron. There was forty seconds left. At the other table, Peter's team had descended into a fractious argument about whether there had ever been a president called 'Hoover'.

Ron wrote steadily. Frank and Bernard were impressed, at first.

"Zachary Taylor? Are you sure?" whispered Bernard.

"Millard Fillmore? Rutherford Hayes? James Polk? You're just making stuff up now."

Ron kept writing.

"You've put Grover Cleveland twice."

"S'right." Ron's eyes never left the page.

"Actually, I think one of them did do it twice."

"S'right."

Ron put down his pen just as Gary 'tinged' the bell again. Frank took the piece of paper to the bar. It had forty-one names on it. One of them twice. Each had a small, circled number against it.

Gary decided that he would mark Peter's answers first.

"Well, I think that's a pretty credible effort. Twenty-two names, although I'm not sure that I can accept 'That one who was shot by an anarchist'."

There was a general chuckle among those patrons who had now been reduced from participants to spectators.

"And I'm afraid that Benjamin Franklin was never a president. So, as I say, twenty-two. And I think that's pretty good. But this week's winner, on a tie-breaker, is Ron, Frank and Bernard, who between them were able to name forty-one presidents. Well done, boys!"

Ron Frank and Bernard had a combined age of 211. It was a long time since they had been described as boys. But it was a popular result with everyone except Peter Roberts. Unlike most weeks, most of the quiz participants remained in the pub until closing time. Only Peter left, which seemed to raise the general mood further.

Within a quarter of an hour, word had spread that it was Ron who had been the linchpin of the victory. People were standing him pints, including Geoff Davidson – Leo's father and a member of Peter's team. Ron was standing, somewhat unsteadily, amid a throng of admirers, appearing increasingly uncomfortable with the plaudits he was receiving, but happy to be talking about the Enfield 350 Bullet.

While Ron was receiving his congratulations, Frank was making calculations on the back of a beer mat. More than £250 in revenue. Bernard glanced at his sums once, briefly. Without either speaking, each knew that they shared the other's conclusions. Not bad for a Thursday, but the Old Volunteer needed those sorts of figures four or five nights a week. Without an arch wheeler and dealer like George Bowman, they were both sure the pub was doomed.

Bernard, too, was not joining in the merry throng. He sat quietly sipping his ersatz Berliner Kindl, apparently deep in thought. What was he to do now that he knew that Joachim Keller, proprietor of Leighton Hall, subject of George Bowman's ransom note, was, in fact, Jakob Schneider – former Stasi accountant and agent? He had two options; one mostly legitimate and the other mostly, but not completely, illegitimate. His preference – his instinct, really – was for the second, but he needed to sleep on it. Perhaps he needed to share what he knew and discuss it with Frank.

Perhaps.

SEVENTEEN

As a special treat, the children were allowed to wear football shirts to school on Friday. Frankie Junior had chosen England. Maisie had chosen Scotland. She was a bright girl, so perhaps she understood why she had two penguin biscuits rather than the usual one that morning.

Frank waved Michelle and his grandchildren off as he did each morning and Rocky went inside to fetch the lead that was never necessary from the peg just inside the door. He brought it to Frank and dropped it at his feet, as Frank expected. And Frank put it directly into his pocket, as Rocky expected.

Frank locked the door, reached into his pocket to ensure that his pipe, tobacco and matches were there. He glanced briefly at the clear blue summer sky, then for slightly longer into Rocky's rich chestnut eyes and set off down the Oakham Road with his faithful companion at his heels. By the time they had reached the stile, Frank had decided that the day was just too perfect not to smoke a pipe, so he leant against the fence and reached into his pocket.

Frank had spent years... no, decades telling colleagues, usually much younger colleagues, that his pipe helped him think. He thought that it was probably true. Perhaps he ought to spend the ten minutes it took him to climb Beacon Hill to test the proposition again.

He had spent yesterday being an investigator. It was no longer his job, but that did not mean that he was not still a professional. Nobody paid him, that was true, and he had no more legal powers than any other member of the public, but that did not make him an amateur.

It wasn't about whether you received a salary or issued an invoice. Professional wasn't a status that could be conferred by a line on a ledger. Frank would be a professional until the day he died, which might be quite soon if he repeated the folly of smoking a pipe while walking up a steep hill.

And just what the hell was he playing at? He thought – no, he believed – that George Bowman had been murdered. And the evidence suggested that George had been blackmailing Joachim Keller or holding him to ransom – the distinction wasn't important at this stage. It seemed highly unlikely that those two events were unconnected. And Bernard was sure that the man claiming to be Swiss was actually a Berliner. But Bernard was seventy-seven and – Frank knew this better than anyone – the sort of man who simply would not permit his mind to ossify, even here in the sleepiest village in the sleepiest county in the land. Did that mean, however, that Bernard was trying just a little too hard to find mystery, inconsistency and grounds for suspicion? And was he, Frank, falling into a similar trap? He needed to go over every fact and theory again, coldly, logically, dispassionately. But first he needed to stop here... and have a little cough.

Ron Godsmark was in an uncharacteristically sombre mood that morning, possibly due to the three-quarters of a gallon of valedictory beer he had consumed the night before, or possibly because he knew he was unlikely ever again to set off down the country lanes on a 650cc Triumph Bonneville. He was even more taciturn than usual. Even Rocky caught the mood. Frank didn't mind that much because now that he was heading downhill towards the hall, his lungs had decided to behave themselves again and he was able to give his mind to the mystery of the dead publican.

Up until a couple of weeks ago, Frank hadn't given the hall a second thought. Since then, Emma had provided him with a great deal of knowledge. It wasn't exactly a hotel. Frank and Ron couldn't have popped in for morning coffee. Neither could they have had their lunch or dinner there, or booked a room. This time of year, it was busy almost all of the time, but for much of the year the place was used no more than once or twice a week. It described itself as a wedding venue, but it was also available for hire for anniversaries, christenings, bar mitzvahs – any sort of largish gathering that required the facilities of a hotel, without actually being a full-time hotel.

And it didn't have full-time staff. Not as such. The Kellers worked there every day, as did Madeline, the events organiser, and Terry, the catering manager, but the rest of the staff, like Emma, were casual. If there was no booking for a week, there would be almost nobody there. The catering was mostly done by outside contractors. At night, Emma had told him, there was usually only one or two people on duty. And they were there mostly for the purposes of insurance or fire regulations or something.

Frank didn't consider himself as someone with any business aptitude. If he'd had, he would have been slightly ashamed, but he understood broadly how these things worked. It seemed to him that Leighton Hall ought to be a successful and profitable business. And if its proprietors both drove Mercedes and lived in an old vicarage, perhaps it was. But the proprietors of successful businesses didn't usually dabble in drug trafficking, whereas it was alarmingly common among the proprietors of unsuccessful or struggling businesses.

One large cash injection to set things back on course. No risk, or minimal risk. 'Just to get us back on our feet' – Frank had heard it many times. And the thing was that all these business people who became drug traffickers had something in common. They appeared to be thriving commercially. They didn't all have Mercedes and vicarages exactly, but it was the same thing – swimming pools and Spanish villas, private schools and skiing holidays. A year ago, Frank could have made a phone call and been looking at the business' VAT returns within an hour. Just one of the handicaps of being – what was he? – a freelance professional.

They had reached the back of the hall now. There was a small building – some sort of generator building or boiler house or something. A couple of youngsters in waiter or waitress garb were standing where they could not be seen, smoking cigarettes.

"Takes me back," said Frank, nodding at the pair. "Smoking behind the bike sheds at school." Not that Frank's school had had bike sheds. What would have been the point? Nobody had a bike.

"Arr," said Ron. "That's where they borstal boys used to go for their fags, too – clever little buggers."

"Clever?"

"Well, they were locked in, weren't they? But they found the old tunnel."

"Tunnel? There was a tunnel?"

"Arr. Well, not exactly a tunnel, more of an escape route – a sort of a passage. Very clever, took 'em years."

"The borstal boys?"

"Narr, the generals."

By the time they had reached Ron's cottage on the edge of Leighton Magna, Frank had heard the whole story – or, at least, as much of it as Ron knew or could remember.

When Ron was growing up in Leighton Magna in the twenties and thirties, the hall had still been occupied by the Longstaff family, but their fortune had been much reduced by a combination of death duties, the Wall Street Crash and Young Mr Longstaff's misplaced faith in the staying ability of various racehorses.

By 1940, when the teenage Ron was joining the local Home Guard, the family had been delighted to sell it to the War Office.

It had been left empty and apparently forgotten for many months. It was only in early 1941 that somebody seemed to remember the place and the army moved in, then out again when they surveyed the state of repair that many seasons of disappointing final furlongs had rendered the place.

Refurbishment had only commenced in earnest in early 1942. For reasons that Ron never understood, and certainly weren't explained, Ron, his Uncle Jim and the rest of Leighton Magna's men of non-military age had spent many a cold night guarding the place until the work was finished and Ron was called up.

When the hall was reopened, it was as a prisoner-of-war camp. Not a muddy field filled with Nissan huts, as most were, but a rather well-appointed – one might even say, luxurious – establishment, designed specifically to accommodate the most senior German and Italian prisoners. Until 1942, there were very few of those, but as the tide of war started to turn, generals and admirals started to trickle in.

By 1945, there were almost fifty high-ranking enemy officers in Leighton Hall. It was these men that found a second, unused dumb waiter that led down to an unused cellar and from there tunnelled through a wall at the back of a cupboard into another cellar, and from there into an outbuilding that, at that time, had mostly housed the gardeners' tools and machines. It was all very ingenious. Ron had been impressed and described it in great detail.

The building of the escape – what shall we call it? – route was ingenious and resourceful. Sadly, for those involved, it was also completely futile. Perhaps it is the hubris and sense of entitlement that comes from having lots of gold braid and medal ribbons on your work clothes. Or perhaps it was just naivety, but none of the generals or admirals ever seemed to pause at any stage and ask themselves: 'Why are we being accommodated in a luxury country house?' or 'Do you think it at all odd that it has obviously been recently redecorated?' or even, 'Isn't it the tiniest bit suspicious that on Saturday and Sunday evenings, the nights upon which we are allowed almost unlimited beer and whisky, that we are always left, unsupervised, in the same two rooms – the smoking room and the billiard room?'

Therefore, it is perhaps unsurprising that none of them also never asked, 'Do you think that there might be hidden microphones all over this place?'

The team from the Royal Corps of Signals listening on headphones in the old coach house had known about the escape almost since its inception. They were primarily there to gather general intelligence about the attitude and thoughts of the enemy, but they also enjoyed listening to excited conversations about the progress of the escape attempt. However, by the time the generals' meticulous preparations had been completed, the war was over, thus denying some honest yeoman a couple of days' work bricking up the various apertures.

It was this route that the no-less-enterprising borstal boys had found in the fifties and sixties. Their objectives had been a quiet smoke, a visit to the village pub or, for the boldest, a trip to a dance or to the cinema in Oakham. Modest aims enough, but at least they had achieved them.

Ron's telling of this tale was the most Frank had ever heard him talk. As he warmed to his theme, his account was punctuated by little chuckles and later by large chuckles and finally by a full-throated (but not full-chested) roar. Ron had a funny laugh. It was part chuckle, part cackle and part wheeze. When he really let himself go, he sounded like a piano accordion had been riddled with machine gun fire, which was actually pretty close to the truth.

"I'm just trying to imagine what you looked like as a teenager in the Home Guard," said Frank, as Ron busied himself with the teapot and kettle.

"Got a photo somewhere. Find it for you in a minute."

Ron disappeared into a room at the back of the cottage. There were a few grunts and then he reappeared clutching a biscuit tin. It was a large one, its lid designed to commemorate the coronation of Elizabeth II. Ron put it on the kitchen table and opened it, keeping the lid between himself and Frank. There was a slight rustle of paper and a metallic chink as he rooted through the tin. Ron took out a passport and put it to one side.

"Arr!" he said, at last producing a small photograph. "Arr!" he said again, producing a slightly larger one.

"That's me," he said, passing over the small photograph. It was a small print, even by the standards of the 1940s – less than three inches by three. It showed a young man who was clearly doing his best to look much older and more warrior-like. In truth, it didn't look a lot like the septuagenarian opposite. If anything, it looked more like a young Bernard, and someone else that Frank had seen, but he couldn't quite remember who. Frank turned it over, 'Ronald, March 1941' was written in a careful, cursive hand.

The second print was larger and featured a group of four men in uniform. Three of them teenagers, by the look of it. They were standing in a pub, clutching glasses of beer. There was a dartboard in the background.

"Is that in the Old Volunteer?"

"Arr, public bar like, ninepence a pint. It was ninepence ha'penny in the lounge bar. That's me." This time, it did look like a young Ron. "That's my Uncle Jim." He indicated a middle-aged man with sergeant's stripes. "He was at Gallipoli, sixth battalion. And that's Tony Addington; he moved to Melton, had a business repairing sewing machines and typewriters and such. He died last year. And that's John Roberts, Peter Roberts' elder brother."

"What became of him?"

"I don't know. Never came back from the war. Didn't die, like, just never came back here."

Frank handed back the photographs and Ron put them and the passport back in the biscuit tin. He got up to make the tea. He mused upon the fact that Ron had probably imparted more information to him in the past half hour than he had in the previous six months. He decided to push on while the going appeared to be favourable.

"So, how do you know so much about American presidents?"

Ron chuckled. "Well, that's how we used to pay for our beer. We'd find some yanks and tell them we knew more about America than they did about England, then we'd bet them that we could name more presidents than they could name English kings. Won every time. Couple of bob, like – more, if they were officers or if they'd only just arrived and hadn't got the hang of the money. I can name all forty-eight states, too."

"There's fifty states now."

"Is there? There was forty-eight then. And I knew them all. Alabama, Arizona, Arkansas, California..." He was counting them off on his fingers. "... West Virginia, Wisconsin and Wyoming!" Ron stood and took his biscuit tin of historical treasures back to the other room.

EIGHTEEN

Bernard frowned. Frank was late. Not late in the sense that he and Bernard had an appointment at an agreed time that had now passed. Frank was late because Bernard expected him to be in the kitchen of The Old Vicarage by now. Frank always arrived at The Old Vicarage between ten o'clock and a quarter past. It was now almost twenty-five past. If he didn't arrive immediately, there was a danger that the tea in the pot would grow cold.

He knew that it was irrational to be this vexed about something so simple, so inconsequential, so harmless. He knew also that it wasn't the imminent dilemma of whether or not to pour himself a cup that had vexed him. It was a different, far greater dilemma. He decided that he would have a cup and Frank could either suffer lukewarm tea or he would make another pot. He went to the kitchen counter where he had laid out two cups, two saucers and a teapot beneath a cosy.

Bernard used to tell gullible guests that the cosy was in his regimental colours – turquoise, mauve and lime green. Telling lies had passed from being his occupation to his hobby. He loved lying. He loved misleading and misdirecting. He loved dissembling and deceiving. And he loved keeping secrets. Now, he was wrestling with a dilemma created by those twin passions coming into conflict. Should he tell Frank that he knew the true identity of the man known to the world – alright, known to Leightons Magna and Parva and possibly Ashcombe, too – as Joachim Keller?

Perhaps Bernard was hoping, subconsciously, or maybe not, that some outside agency would intervene and force a decision upon him. If so, he was in luck.

"Who's this then?"

The outside agency, in the form of Francis Daniel McBride, had let himself in through the back door and was studying the sketch portrait of Keller/Schneider.

"That is the man calling himself Joachim Keller."

Bernard was not quite ready to fully commit himself to a choice yet.

"You mean we were messing about in Ashcombe all afternoon when we had a picture of him?"

"Well, we didn't have one then."

"So?"

"What?"

"So?"

Bernard surrendered himself. "So, it's not Joachim Keller. It's Jakob Schneider."

"Goalkeeper for Bayern Munich?"

"Accountant. For the Stasi."

Frank pursed his lips. "Well, that's a bit of a blow."

"What?"

"Well, up until now, our working proposition has been that this man is an international narcotics trafficker who murdered George Bowman with an assassin's skill and ruthlessness. And now you're telling me he's a fucking accountant."

"For the Stasi. Frank. The Stasi."

"And that makes a difference, does it? That's how they train them, is it? Debit this, credit that, carry the four and here's how you improvise a dagger out of a bottle of milk stout and murder someone with a single blow!"

Bernard was forced to admit that Frank had a point. He wasn't exactly sure how much training Schneider might have had. Was he an agent first, who just specialised in accounting? Or was he an accountant who was just given a badge and gun because that is what everybody working for the Stasi was supposed to have? He used to know this stuff. He used to know it all. But it was ten years ago and he was ten years older.

Bernard poured a second cup and placed it on the table in front of Frank. The Scotsman sat down and fished his pipe out of his pocket. This was a good sign. It meant that Frank planned to do some serious thinking. Bernard needed to do some himself. The two men sat in silence for twenty minutes, until Frank had finished his pipe.

"Okay, so what does this tell us? What does it add to our knowledge? What do you know about this Schneider anyway?"

"Stasi since leaving university. Probably identified earlier. Youth wing, party member at the first opportunity. Divorced, I think. Held the rank of captain, but that's probably more to do with pay grade. He only managed three clerks and a secretary."

"And post-Stasi?"

"I don't know. I retired in 1990. We had lost track of him then, but we had lost track of practically everybody. They weren't wandering down the Ku'damm wearing a T-shirt that read 'I used to be a Stasi officer'."

"Accountant? Opportunity for embezzlement?"

Bernard loved the way that Frank thought. He assumed the worst of absolutely everybody.

"Yes. Potentially."

"Enough to buy Leighton Hall?"

"Potentially, but he didn't buy that until about four years ago."

"Embezzlement. Seed capital. Start small. Grow big. Buy the hall?"

"Money laundering?"

"The hall's not really suited for that. It's not a cash business. Of course, he might have bought it with dirty money."

"But once you've made enough to buy the hall and renovate it, which must have cost millions, why would you bother risking life in prison by smuggling cocaine or whatever it was?"

"I'm betting cocaine."

"Because?"

"Cava. Spain. Historic trade routes with Latin America. Common language. Spain is what we call, used to call, a transit country."

"Ah."

"Well, he's a man with a secret. He could be blackmailed. Does a Stasi accountant accrue – see what I did there? – enough enemies to make it critical to live a new life under a new name in a new country?"

Bernard nodded, thoughtfully. "Or maybe he doesn't own the hall. He's an accountant. Perhaps he's just a place man, a front, managing the place on behalf of the real owner."

"Still begs the question, why smuggle drugs?"

Bernard shook his head. "I'll make some inquiries."

Frank was studying the second portrait. "Who's this? The wife?"

Bernard nodded.

"What do we know about her?"

"Nothing."

"Well, we need to. Is she genuinely Swiss? Does she know who Schneider really is? Is she Stasi, too? Is she his secretary, for example?"

"No. No, she's definitely not his secretary."

"Which of them used the Berlin slang? The *'paletti'* thing?"

Bernard shook his head. He couldn't remember. Had Emma even told them?

*

Frank had left. Emma had gone to work and Bernard was alone again with his dilemma. He could either use his contacts at MI6, including his grandson, Michael, to see what the files said about Jakob Schneider and perhaps any woman with whom he may have teamed up. He wouldn't be allowed access to the files, of course. It would be a lunch in a Pall Mall club, a few well-chosen words – oblique, deniable, informative.

Or he could take the other route. He could go back to his old network of spies and informers in Berlin. If they still existed and if they had any useful information, they wouldn't be found in a button-backed leather armchair. Or perhaps they would. One or two of them were unscrupulous chancers back in the day and may well be wealthy entrepreneurs by now. Listen to him. He was starting to sound like Frank McBride! But he couldn't just pick up his phone and call Berlin. He was pretty sure that even after all these years, his phone was still tapped. He would have to go there. And he'd need a full wallet.

Why not do both? He went to his study and picked up his phone. The phone in the kitchen was okay for most types of calls, but business calls ought to be made at a desk. Bernard was not of the modern generation.

"Hello, Michael. How are you? It's your grandfather."

The voice at the other end went from surprised to pleased to cautious to suspicious in about three syllables.

"How about popping up here for the weekend? Germany are playing Yugoslavia on Sunday. And your sister has the day off."

That ought to do it. Michael knew that his grandfather paid absolutely no attention to the game he called 'soccer'. Not even forty-five years in Berlin had changed that.

"Good, that's settled then. What? Oh yes, last night. We won actually. Yes, it turned out that Ron Godsmark knew the name of every US president. Yes, I shouldn't have thought so either. Well, excellent. See you Sunday."

With phase one successfully set in motion, Bernard felt more positive. He picked up his car keys and decided that he would set off for Uppingham. There was a good butchers there and he had never used the telephone kiosk in the town square before. It ought to be clean.

It was only twelve miles to Uppingham, but on Rutland roads and with Bernard's driving, that meant almost half an hour. And since it was a nice day, he thought he may as well pop in to the Exeter Arms and enjoy a pint of beer and a ploughman's lunch.

Accordingly, it was almost three o'clock when he entered the telephone kiosk outside The Falcon Hotel with a bag of fifty-pence pieces and a slip of paper with a long number on it. The number of Erich's bar in the Nikolaiviertel district. It was a long shot. The place was probably a stop now for the coachloads of tourists buying miscellaneous pieces of rubble in the belief (hope?) that it was a part of the wall, but he had to start somewhere.

"Hello, is Erich there? It's Bernd."

Bernard's German was a little rusty, but he found himself falling into the Berlin accent almost immediately.

"Hello, I'm looking for Berti the Limp... I need him to do a job for me... It's Bernd... Yes, from the old days.... Okay. I'll call back at nine."

Bernard replaced the receiver. That had gone a lot better than he had expected. Unfortunately, he would need to find another clean phone box to call again at eight, English time.

*

Every big city, and a few smaller ones, has its share of characters like Berti. They exist, or imagine that they exist, in the grey area between respectable business people and career criminals. However, in reality, they spend more time on the wrong side of the law than the right. For this reason, they are often excellent sources of information.

Before the wall came down, Berti had been a refuse worker. He had driven a dustcart and had done so in that odd period of history when East Germany was so desperate for hard currency that it accepted the refuse of West Berlin into its own landfill sites in exchange for cash. Accordingly, Berti was one of a very small number of people who travelled daily between the two halves of the divided city.

Berti had discovered early on that a few packs of American cigarettes enabled him to find his way to the head of the queue at the tip, enabling him to be back home and off shift an hour or two earlier than the other drivers. A few more packs, or a bottle of Scotch, ensured that he wasn't selected for the random searches and inspections. When Bernard had learned of this, he employed Berti to run messages to agents in the East. And Berti had proved himself, if not exactly honest, then at least predictable. His avarice and his desires being relatively modest. And predictability was almost the same as reliability. Berti proved that he could be trusted with little tasks either side of the wall and it wasn't just Bernard who was learning to trust him. His friends in the East had little jobs for Berti to do, too.

It was a nasty shock when the wall came down, but Berti adapted – still making use of the contacts that he had made and the networks into which he was plugged, but most of all his knowledge of the black market, which had now become merely dark grey. Berti knew where to get the things that even the capitalist West couldn't provide. He knew the prices people would accept. He knew the prices that people would pay. And, most importantly of all, he knew the difference between the two. At one stage, he had seriously considered becoming completely legitimate, but when he had sketched out his business plan, he realised that that would reduce his earnings by over fifty per cent.

His one concession to the collapse of communism was to give up his job at the city council and devote himself one hundred per cent to wheeling and dealing. He sometimes mused that his address book was probably worth more than the dustcart that he had driven for years.

Although he was now a wealthy man, he did his best to give little indication of it. He dressed as he always had, drove a second-hand Opel and lived in the same apartment where he had grown up. His one outward manifestation of his new financial status came courtesy of an eye-wateringly expensive clinic in Switzerland. Berti the Limp no longer limped.

*

When Bernard got home, Emma was there. She seemed anxious to tell him something, but it was ten past four and if Bernard didn't have a cup of tea at ten past four... well, he wasn't exactly sure what would happen, but it was sure to be bad. She paced to and fro while Bernard stood in front of a cupboard, momentarily paralysed by the choice between fruit shortcakes and chocolate digestives. This had been an exhausting day in terms of dilemmas. Finally, he chose the digestives and sat at the table.

"Well?"

"I think they're smuggling drugs. Well, she is, anyway." Emma delivered these two sentences in a single rushed breath, like a small child announcing a birthday party invitation or winning a star role in the school nativity play.

"Slow down! Slow down. Do we need Frank for this?"

Emma was hopping from one foot to another like a particularly gifted tap dancer who had foolishly overlooked the 'hot coals' clause in her contract. Either this was absolutely top grade A1 intelligence or she needed to go to the lavatory.

Bernard got up to fill the kettle. It was a trick he had used before. Debriefing excited and frantic agents was a waste of time. They usually forgot some important detail or muddled the chronology. They always failed to give the right weight to various parts of their story and they never thought carefully about any questions that they were asked.

He picked up the phone and dialled Frank's number. Yes, *dialled*.

"Ah, hello, Frank, Bernard here. Would you mind popping over?"

Emma was breathing a little more slowly now and trying to order things in her head.

"Yes, yes, if you wouldn't mind. Okay, see you in five minutes."

When Frank arrived, he was carrying a spiral-bound notebook. He placed it on the kitchen table, then took out two ballpoint pens – one blue, one red – and put them neatly to the side.

Emma sat down. Frank took a pipe from his right jacket pocket and a tobacco pouch from his left. Bernard placed a cup of tea in front of him and nudged a plate of chocolate digestives in his direction. Plain chocolate, not milk. Bernard knew that Frank preferred milk chocolate and that if a plate of those were placed in front of him, the entire debriefing would take place to a background of munching.

Frank glanced at the biscuits and then at Bernard. He wasn't angry. Just disappointed. He held Bernard's gaze for a beat.

"Yes, I think this is probably worthy of a pipe."

"You don't mind, Emma?"

She didn't. She knew very well that her grandfather and now Frank had been deliberately taking the heat out of the situation, allowing her to calm down and gather her thoughts. Part of her resented it. Part of her was grateful.

Bernard nodded.

Emma began, "Mr Keller is brought a coffee each morning at about ten o'clock. In his office, on the first floor of the kitchen wing – at least that's what we call it. Sometimes Mrs Keller is with him. Her office is over the other side of the main building."

Bernard nodded. Frank nodded.

Emma took a deep breath. "Lately, I've been going in early so that I can be the one to take his coffee up. So far, his door has always been closed, so I listen for a bit. Not too long, though. Not because I can't be caught lingering outside the door – there's little chance of that – but because I don't want the coffee to get cold. That might be suspicious."

Bernard nodded once more. He was wearing a curious expression. It was one that Emma had rarely seen and Frank, never. If it had been anybody else, you might have said that it was an expression of pride. All grandparents are proud of their grandchildren. Whatever their faults and limitations, they can always find something to mark them out as special. Not top of the class? Doesn't matter; they have the biggest smile. Poor at sports? Not important; they always enjoy the game, win or lose. Of course, it makes it just a little easier if the child is a perpetually successful high achiever. By most people's measure, Emma would qualify, but what made Bernard inwardly beam with satisfaction was the point about the lukewarm coffee. Nobody had taught her that. It was instinctive tradecraft and that is what made him warm and satisfied inside.

"So, this morning, Mrs Keller was in Mr Keller's office. They were talking in German. More shouting, really. It was quite a row. I listened for a minute and then knocked. Mr Keller told me to come in."

Frank was taking notes. Without looking up, he said, "Where was each?"

"Mr Keller was perched on the edge of his desk. Mrs Keller was sitting on one of the chairs next to the coffee table."

"What did you hear before you went in."

Emma took another deep breath. "Mr Keller said something like, 'Smuggling drugs! It's stupid. It's unnecessary. Look what it's led to. I don't want you to do it again.' Then he said something like 'The chance is more than the prize' or something. My German isn't perfect."

Bernard nodded. Frank underlined the last few words of his notes. "Do you remember, before which of the two said, '*Alles paletti*'?"

"Both of them. One said it, the other repeated it as if in agreement."

Frank looked sharply at Bernard. Bernard just indicated that Emma should continue.

"Then she said, 'Do you want to be stuck here forever? We have to take risks.' And he said, 'We won't be here for ever. My merry-go-round will give us all the money we need. We just need a little time.' And that's when I knocked on the door."

"Merry-go-round?"

"Carousel – *karussell* is the German word."

"And when you went in?"

"They were glaring at each other. Neither said anything. I left pretty quickly."

"Did you hang around outside?"

"I was intending to, but I heard Mrs Keller getting up, so I hurried down the stairs."

"Hear anything else? Did she say something from the doorway?"

"If she did, I didn't hear it."

Emma looked from her grandfather to Frank and back again. Had she done well? For some reason, she craved validation in a way that she never had from her parents. Was she a good agent? Had she performed better than her elder brother? The expressions of both men gave her no clue, but Frank's pipe had gone out and her grandfather's tea was undrunk and cold. *Yes!* One point to Emma.

NINETEEN

Frank was not a regular churchgoer. In fact, if you didn't count the occasional wedding and the sadly not-so-occasional funeral, he wasn't a churchgoer at all. He was an atheist or, perhaps more accurately, a semi-lapsed atheist. If he was honest with himself, and this was one of the subjects where he had a less-than-perfect record, he was drifting towards agnosticism. Either way, here he was, picking out a tie.

Frank hadn't actually bought a tie in years. His somewhat limited collection of ties comprised mostly of ones that he had been given either by visiting officials from other countries or ones that he had been gifted on his own overseas trips. He had French Customs, Dutch Police, Guardia Civil from Spain. He never wore that one, wasn't sure why he still had it. Even the black one that he wore at the now all-too-common funerals was actually a uniform tie that he had found at the back of a cupboard in Custom House. He chose the FIOD tie, the Dutch Financial Crimes Police. It was the most muted and had only a very small logo.

Because he was an atheist, and because he was a famously appalling parent, and because he was equally famously grumpy, unapproachable and fierce, this was actually the first time in his sixty and a half years that Frank had been asked to be a godfather. And he was actually rather touched. And for that reason, he was more than willing to swallow a large dollop of hypocrisy. Not that he had any objection to rejecting Satan and all his evil works. You might even argue that he had spent his whole life doing that, albeit on a more practical and less theological basis.

The other factor – and this was truly absurd, as he himself would have acknowledged – was because the christening was to take place in a Catholic church. Frank was an atheist, but he was a *Catholic* atheist – which was to say that he was a Celtic supporter. In his younger days, he had stood on the terrace at Parkhead and sung along with the rebel songs and goaded Rangers fans with threats of the inquisition. And so, he had agreed. He would be godfather to Caroline Frances Lake. The 'Frances' bit hadn't exactly swung it, but it had helped.

He put on his best suit. It used to be his 'court' suit, but he had probably given evidence for the last time. He hadn't even been called for George Bowman's inquest. And he headed for Grantham.

Frank couldn't remember exactly how many people he had managed, dozens probably. Some for a very short time, one or two for years. He had managed Joe Lake for less than a year. The last six months of his Customs' career. Joe had stepped into his shoes when he had retired. Occasionally, he would call up for a chat or to share a little gossip. Even more occasionally, he would seek advice. There had been talk of a game of golf, but new parenthood makes such plans futile. And, anyway, Frank couldn't really play. He should have asked if any more of his old team, Nottingham A, would be at the christening, but he forgot.

Perhaps Joe would be the only person present that he actually knew. He had only met his wife once or twice and then very briefly. That was okay. He would go and say the words that he was required to say, he would probably have to pose for a few photographs and then he would slip quietly away when he thought it safe to do so – unless he got an opportunity for a little chat.

*

Catholic churches had changed a lot since Frank's youth. Of course, a lot of things had and, even if they hadn't, it was unlikely that a church in Grantham would resemble St Francis of Assisi in Glasgow's East End. That had been a dark and gloomy place, infected with the sweet fragrance of incense blended with the smell of damp woollen coats, last night's beer and the faint tang of mothballs from Sunday suits.

Frank hadn't been a diligent churchgoer even then. His faith in the almighty had been dealt a severe blow when, in 1948, despite his fervent imprecations, Scotland had lost two-nil to England at Hampden (goals by Mortensen and Finney either side of half-time, since you ask). A month later, when Rangers won the cup, it was even worse. He decided that it was more comforting to believe that there was no God than to consider the possibility that the supreme deity might be a protestant.

Now, it was all light wood and stainless steel, all bright lights and not a whiff of incense anywhere. Christening parties were the same, though. This one was in a hotel just off the A1. And the bar was doing good business. Frank wasn't exactly sure what the normal attendance was expected to be at a christening, but there were dozens present, including a couple of former work colleagues. Frank chatted to them for a little while, but they didn't want to talk about ongoing operations and he wouldn't have allowed them to anyway. He was just thinking about saying his goodbyes when he saw Lake on his own.

"Joseph!"

"Frank!"

"All seems to be going very well. I, err, I wonder if I might have a few minutes."

Lake looked around. "Listen, Frank. I am the least important and the least sought-after person here. Nobody, absolutely nobody, is interested in me. It's Bella's day and Caroline's. So, if you want a chat, I'm entirely at your disposal."

"It's actually a bit more than that. I want your advice."

If Mark Knopfler had asked him to help tune a guitar, Joe couldn't have been more shocked.

"Well, not advice exactly, more of a tutorial. What do you know about carousel fraud?"

"A fair bit. Do you want to find somewhere a bit quieter?"

The pair wandered the corridors of the hotel, trying doors until they found the snooker room.

"Ideal!" said Joe. "There's even a pad and pencil."

Frank sat down and took out his pipe.

"Is it safe to assume that you know the basics?" began Joe.

"No."

So, Joe began with the basics, input tax, output tax, VAT returns. McBride's face wasn't a complete blank, so he pressed ahead. "… And then, with the advent of the single market in 1993, everything changed."

McBride was starting to struggle, but he masked his confusion. He was sure that things would become clear in a minute and he would be able to piece it all together. But he was wrong. Joe had started tearing sheets of paper from the pad and was placing them at intervals all over the snooker table. He started quoting numbers, profit margins or, rather, loss margins. He was moving a snooker ball from one piece of paper to another. When he had finished, he looked expectantly at McBride.

"Once more, slowly, if you wouldn't mind, Joseph."

"So, this company…" Lake was pointing at a piece of paper with a large 'A' on it in one corner of the table. He placed the cue ball on the piece of paper. "This company buys goods from elsewhere in the EU, say France. And it sells those goods for a loss. Buys at one hundred, sells for ninety, say."

McBride wanted to ask why, but something told him that that would be a very naïve question.

"And this one…" Lake was pointing at the piece of paper with 'B' on it. "This one buys for ninety and sells for ninety-one." He moved the cue ball from A to B and then to C. He kept moving the ball around the table in a clockwise direction. "Each business sells for a tiny profit." The ball was now resting on the piece of paper marked 'E'. "And this company, Company E, this one exports the goods to, say, Holland. Holland sells to France and France sells back to Company A. And round it all goes again and again. And each time that it goes around, everybody makes a little profit except Company A."

McBride nodded, the question on the tip of his tongue was going to be answered in a minute, surely.

"But Company A disappears when its VAT is due, taking the VAT with it, so even though it's selling for a loss, that is more than made up for by the fact it has ripped off the VAT."

If it had been a cartoon, this is the point at which a light bulb would have appeared above McBride's head. "So, you need to control all these businesses? They are all your puppets?"

"Correct."

"And, ideally, you want the most valuable commodity that you can find and that is readily available, and you want to send it round and round the carousel as quickly and as often as you can."

"Exactly! If you've got, say, one million in capital to begin with, and if you can move the goods around the carousel once a week, you should be able to make three million in profit each quarter. If you reinvest your illicit earnings, well, it grows exponentially. If you are smart, keep creating and using new businesses, keep one step ahead of us, you can turn a million into fifty million in a year."

"Sounds easy."

"Well, not that easy. You need to be adept at creating fictitious companies, giving them convincing cover stories, probably employ a few useful idiots who will do your bidding without realising what they are involved in. You need to be skilled, manipulative and very organised, and disciplined to keep on top of everything. It's a pretty unusual person who can do all that."

But McBride thought he knew one. His pipe had gone out. He relit it, thoughtfully. "When you get to the office tomorrow morning, you might find that you have a message from an anonymous informant. He or she is promising some information about a carousel fraud on your patch. No details yet. But it would be a good idea to get it registered to you and on the system. Understand?"

Joe didn't, but he said he did.

"One last thing... the goods?"

"Doesn't matter. Ideally, you want something small, easily transported and for which there is a ready wholesale market. Mobiles phones are the most popular at the moment."

TWENTY

It was a good game. Michael was enjoying it. Yugoslavia scored early and doubled their lead early in the second half. Then, with less than twenty minutes to go, the unfortunate Siniša Mihajlović scored an own goal. A few minutes later, Oliver Bierhoff equalised, setting up a tense finish.

"I didn't know you were a football fan, Grandad."

"I was a season ticket holder at Hertha Berlin for twenty years."

"Did you actually go to any games, though? Or did you lend your ticket to shifty-looking men in raincoats who passed or received coded messages on the terraces."

Michael had said the wrong thing. *Cocky!* thought Bernard, before replying, "I'm sure that it must all seem very old-fashioned or quaint or comical to you. The world before mobile telephones and computers and databases. But there is something very important about the cold war that you should not forget."

"What's that?" Michael was suitably shamefaced.

"We won!" The old man's face broke into a sly grin. "And no. I don't think I ever attended a game."

The match finished two each and the director cut to the studio, where a handful of old pros – who were either trying to rebuild their public persona after overcoming their alcoholism or needed the cash to fund their ongoing gambling problems – began to discuss the game. It was a commentary cocktail comprising fifty per cent observations so obvious that even Bernard had made them, thirty per cent lazy national stereotypes (wouldn't it be fun if Germany entered a team that was not 'organised and efficient', you know, just for a laugh?) and twenty per cent half-baked speculation as to whether the German midfielder, Dietmar Hamann, might be on his way to Newcastle United.

Bernard turned the television off. "You are probably wondering why I asked you to come up here."

Michael confessed that he was.

"Well, I am in the process of writing my will. Please, don't. I am an old man. It's the responsible thing to do. I know that you haven't spent a great deal of time here, you or Emma, but if there are any knick-knacks, anything that might hold some sentimental value to you – well, now is the time to say so. In fact, allow me to act as a guide to the little museum of my life."

They spent the next hour walking from room to room as Bernard pointed out various artefacts and heirlooms. Michael was paying close attention. He knew for a fact that the old man had made a will less than six months previously. It was on file at MI6. So, this little charade was for a different purpose. What was the slippery old goat up to now? He was shown a few Dresden ornaments that had belonged to his grandmother and some seemingly random items of furniture with family stories attached to them – either passed down from generation to generation or made up by his grandfather on the spot, Michael couldn't tell. There were a few old photograph albums. Cricket scorebooks for Leighton Parva's 1913 and 1914 seasons, and a photograph of the team, too.

"That's my father, your great grandfather, and my uncle – he died on the Somme – and my other uncles, twins, who died at Ypres. Their names are on the war memorial outside. I don't have

160

a photograph of Edward, my other uncle. And this one, this is my grandfather, your great, great grandfather."

He indicated a photograph that had probably been taken a century before of a stern-looking man with a clerical collar.

"Was he a vicar?"

"He was vicar here. His name is in the church. If you'd ever been inside, you'd know."

Michael had been inside, for his grandmother's funeral, and he was pretty sure that that had been the last time his grandfather had visited, too. Perhaps Christmas. Perhaps Remembrance Sunday.

"All his children – my father, my uncles and my aunt – were born here. So was I. Although I left when I was about three. My father felt he had to live here with his mother. She had lost four sons in the war. But then he was posted to India and… well…"

Michael nodded. He had seen their names on the war memorial. They went from room to room, ending in the library. His grandfather always called it 'The Library', but it was more of a study really. It had a lot of books, though. Bernard indicated various volumes that were valuable or important to him or both.

"Actually, I plan to make a few small bequests to some of the people from the old days. Berlin, you know?"

He had said 'people', not 'friends', not 'colleagues', just 'people'.

"Of course, some of them may be dead themselves. I lost track of a lot of them. My last year in Berlin was mostly chaos. A lot of people disappeared, some intentionally, people scattered, literally scattered. I wouldn't know how to find most of them now."

This was it. Here it comes, thought Michael.

"Of course, they might have turned up since. Might be on file back at your office."

Michael didn't bother to tell him that the files were mostly computerised these days. And he should mention that accessing files required leaving a record these days. It always had done, technically, but in the old days a bottle of cherry brandy and a winning smile were often enough to gain five or ten minutes' uninterrupted snooping.

"I'll give you a list. Don't worry, it's a short one."

Bernard opened the top drawer of his desk, frowned as he leafed through a few papers and gave a small grunt of exasperation. Then, he noticed a hardback book on the desk itself. From between its pages, he withdrew a small piece of paper. "Here it is." He passed it over.

Name	DOB (approx.)	Last known address
Max Pfeiffer	1960	Vorburgstrasse, Schoneburg, Berlin
Gisela Sommer	1940	Walsheimer Str. Biesdorf, Berlin
Manfred Busch	1925	N/K
Jakob Schneider	1946	N/K
Renate Voigt	1945	Lutzenstrasse, Halensee, Berlin.

Michael folded the piece of paper and put it in his pocket.

"Now, let me show you the wine cellar, but I warn you I intend to drink it all. However, best intentions and all that…"

But Michael knew that the serious business was over. All that was to come and all that had occurred were just an elaborate charade. His grandfather wanted five Berliners checked out. He hated to think why.

Michael declined the invitation to remain for Argentina versus Jamaica, but he did agree to wait until Emma returned from work at about four.

*

The two siblings agreed to take a little walk. They left The Old Vicarage and turned left towards Leighton Magna. When he was sure that they were out of sight, Michael asked, "So, what has he got you doing?"

"Just a little spying up at Leighton Hall."

"You remember, I warned you."

"It's perfectly alright. He's just got a bit of a bee in his bonnet about the owners."

"Who are?"

"A Swiss couple: Joachim and Hanna Keller."

"Swiss?"

"Well, Grandad thinks they're German."

Michael fished the piece of paper out of his pocket. "The woman; could she be born in 1940 or 1945?"

"Oh no. Far younger – well, a bit younger."

"And the man?"

"He's a bit older. Fifty? Mid-fifties?"

Michael consulted the piece of paper again and put it in his pocket. "Well, be careful. He's a treacherous old sod and, what's worse, I think he may be losing his touch."

When they returned to the house, Argentina had just scored their fourth goal and it was time for Michael to return to London.

*

At seven o'clock, Bernard rose and, without a word of explanation, picked up his car keys and left the house. Emma had found a book and was sitting in the garden reading, while simultaneously considering her relationship with Ollie. He was working nights tonight. Well, not exactly working. He would probably be asleep in one of the unused guest bedrooms for most of the night, unless there was a fire alarm or some unforeseen emergency.

Bernard drove steadily, first to Oakham and then through country lanes, until he picked up the A47 into Leicester. He found a telephone kiosk outside a sub post office. He parked and studied the area. No security cameras. No traffic cameras. He entered the box and made his call.

There was a lot of background noise and Bernard almost needed to shout. He wasn't sure if he had been heard or understood. There was a long pause on the line until he heard the familiar voice.

"*Hallo, hier ist Berti.*"

Bernard gave him the number of the public telephone and waited for him to call back. It was midsummer's day, but he was starting to feel chilly. Or perhaps he was just feeling his age.

Berti called him back within five minutes. He remembered Bernard. He was surprised to hear from him after all these years, but he remembered him and he remembered that he was reliable and discreet, and that he paid promptly and in full.

"Jakob Schneider. Stasi. An accountant in the Main Second Directorate. Early fifties. I need to find him. I want to know where he is and what he's been up to. A thousand Deutschmarks. I'll call you in a few days. No, Saturday, that place in Prenzlauer Berg – is it still there? Okay, there, Saturday, seven this time. Okay."

Bernard checked his surroundings one last time and drove home.

Michael had almost reached home. He was wondering what he was going to tell his boss about his grandfather's request, because he was sure he was going to have to tell her something.

Frank was at home, sitting in his favourite chair, smoking his favourite pipe and watching the United States lose to Iran. He laughed until the tears ran down his face.

TWENTY-ONE

"We really need a snooker table," grumbled Frank, "but this will have to do."

He spent an hour explaining VAT carousel fraud to Bernard. By the end, he was quite tired.

"Well, I can't pretend that I understand every detail and nuance of this scheme, but have I, at least, got this part right? A fraudster sets up a group of companies, all of which appear to be independently owned, but which are, in effect, his creatures and he sets in chain a circular set of transactions that exploits a weakness in the VAT system and absconds with almost seventeen and a half per cent of the value of the goods each time?"

"Yes, that's just about it."

Frank felt tired, even though he had walked up Beacon Hill, past the hall and down through Leighton Magna as usual. But in a good way. He felt a sense of accomplishment, of satisfaction. He knew what he was doing. He knew what he wanted to do. It was just like the good old days.

When he was sure that Bernard had fully understood the fraud, he lit his pipe, exactly like the old days. Except that he didn't have a team of a dozen investigators, a fleet of cars, radios, cameras, access to the state's databases and physical documents or any legal powers. And that made it more challenging. But he had advantages, too. He didn't have to be so particular about following rules or procedures. He didn't require authority from above. He didn't have to worry about budgetary constraints.

"So, what's the plan, Frank? Are you just going to share your suspicions with your former colleagues and take a back seat?"

"No."

"Didn't think so. So, what is it?"

"First thing we do: we consider what we know. Then, test that against what we might expect to see if Keller is perpetrating a carousel fraud."

Bernard nodded.

Frank began counting them off on his fingers. "One: Keller is operating under a different name to the one he was born with. Might be an innocent explanation for that. Two: He's an accountant, or used to be. But there are accountants and there are *accountants*. I'm guessing that accountancy in the Stasi is not exactly like accountancy in Rutland. Would he have experience of setting up companies, registering them for VAT, VAT returns?"

"Maybe not, but it's closer to his skill set than running a wedding hotel."

"Fair point. So, what you need is some accounting know-how, some discipline and some starting capital."

"He may have that. He's been off the radar for ten years. He may have fled Berlin with a stack of cash. Or he may have earned it since. He's bought a pretty sizeable property and it must have cost a small fortune to renovate it."

"But we don't know if that's his money. He may have borrowed it. He may be fronting for someone."

"In either of those scenarios he would want to make some more money to gain his independence, whether that's financial or… whatever."

"Agreed. And if he is a frontman, then the profits from the hall aren't his and he can't use those."

"So, an accounting scheme or a VAT fraud would fit the bill nicely. But why smuggle drugs?"

"It sounds like that was Mrs Keller's scheme. Or perhaps he needed the starting capital."

"All very plausible, but, pardon me, this is more your area than mine. None of it is evidence, is it?"

"No. We would need evidence that he is behind the various companies in the carousel and that the ill-gotten booty finds its way into his sky rocket."

"His what?"

"His pocket. Or, more likely, a Swiss bank account. That's another reason why it might be handy for him to have a Swiss identity. Swiss banks are secretive enough at the best of times, but when it's one of their own citizens..."

"So, we need a filing cabinet full of VAT returns, do we?"

"VAT returns, VAT registrations, company formation documents, bank statements, transfer documents, correspondence with suppliers."

"What suppliers? I thought every link in the chain was him."

"He's got to buy the goods somewhere in the first place. And if he's reinvesting his profits, he's got to buy more. Somebody, somewhere, is supplying him with crates and crates of mobile phones, or whatever it is he's using."

"So, all we have to do is break into the hall, find this Aladdin's cave of incriminating evidence and then whistle for your former colleagues to come over the hill with search warrants and handcuffs."

"Something like that."

"Well, I don't know if you've noticed, Frank, but my cat-burgling days are behind me, and I suspect that yours are, too."

Frank was forced to concede that this was true.

"And I'm assuming that your former colleagues aren't going to be willing to break in and have a quick look round on the word of a pensioner, however well esteemed he may have been."

"That would require quite a lot of form-filling," admitted Frank.

"But it's possible that I may have a solution. You'll have to leave it with me for a day or two."

*

Oliver had proposed that they hire bicycles and planned to spend the day circumnavigating Rutland Water. Emma had been hesitant at first. Sixteen miles was a lot further than she had ever cycled before. She had buzzed round Oxford on a bicycle, but her longest journey had probably been no more than a couple of miles. She was also pretty certain that a day's cycling in June was likely to leave her hot and sweaty, and she wasn't sure she was ready for Oliver to see her red-faced and panting – at least not in those circumstances. In the end, she agreed on two conditions. The first of these being that they should stop for lunch at the Horse and Jockey at Manton. The second being that they should hire a tandem and if she grew tired, Oliver would be one hundred per cent responsible for propulsion.

Emma had known literally nothing about Rutland a few weeks ago. She didn't know it was England's smallest county, and surely everyone knew that, and she didn't know that Rutland Water was England's largest reservoir – although, to be fair, that was less well known. Emma didn't know very much about reservoirs, but somewhere in the back of her head was the idea that since they were man-made, the tracks and footpaths around them ought to be flat and easy-going for a novice cyclist. It turned out that this was wrong. It was surprisingly hard-going even with Emma providing a lot less than fifty per cent of the horsepower.

It was pretty, though. And busy, even on a weekday. There were several lithe and Lycra-clad pensioners, most of whom seemed to be carrying those ski poles – the exact purpose of which Emma couldn't determine. And then there were cyclists – proper, serious cyclists – who would arrive unannounced from behind, give one tiny ting of their bells and then race past in a cloud of dust, sweat and smugness.

The other cyclists, the smug-free ones, were all riding hired bikes – you could tell because of the alarming shade of turquoise and the way that their riders seemed to be self-conscious about the (also) hired helmets that sat on the tops of their heads like fossilised, ill-fitting berets. And then there were the dogs, dozens of them, all of them overexcited and unpredictable, many of them yapping and all of them apparently of the view that a tandem should be inspected at close quarters.

And that was just the landlubbers. Out on the water itself there were fly fishermen, standing waist-deep and wearing a sort of rubber dungaree-type garment. The type of thing that Emma imagined was only worn by sewage workers or high court judges and backbench members of parliament, who had to 'stay over in London for the night'.

Then there were canoes and sailing dinghies, dozens of them. All tacking and jibbing –or whatever it was that sailing dinghies requires – in a sort of random pattern like an aquatic demonstration of Brownian motion. And the rowers and the scullers, and the open-water swimmers and the frantic families who had just discovered that Fido had a love of water.

And all of this beneath a clear blue sky and amid green rolling hills, punctuated by chocolate-box villages. And Oliver.

It took almost an hour to reach The Horse and Jockey. Oliver had said it would be less. He had probably miscalculated how little Emma would contribute. They propped the tandem up against a fence and Oliver secured it with a bike chain that he produced from some unseen source. Emma slumped down at a table beneath an umbrella advertising a faux Danish lager. Oliver trotted inside to order drinks and to procure a menu. Only then did Emma's mind turn to the conversation that she had overheard between her grandfather and Frank.

She hadn't understood all of it. The bit about the carousel fraud made very little sense. Perhaps she would have fared better if she had seen the visual aids that Frank seemed to be using. That didn't matter, though. The key point was that the two pensioners believed that there was a wealth of, presently inaccessible, evidence somewhere inside Leighton Hall.

Emma was sure that she knew where this evidence was to be found (it never crossed her mind for an instant that it might not exist). What she was less sure of was how it might be accessed. And then the idea came to her. She was simultaneously thrilled with her genius and appalled by her immorality.

Michael had warned her. He had told her how their genial old grandfather was actually a moral vacuum with an unlimited capacity for manipulation, deceit and betrayal. He had warned her not to become an unwitting tool in whatever devious game he was playing.

But this wasn't like that. Her grandfather would not be manipulating her. He hadn't asked her to do anything. He hadn't tried to trick her or to pressurise her. He didn't even know that she had been listening behind the kitchen door. Did he?

This wasn't what Michael had been talking about at all. In a way, this was far worse. She wondered if manipulation and deceit were inheritable characteristics. And if they were, perhaps they skipped a generation. After all, Michael was a spook now. She had no idea what he did, but she was sure that it involved a lot of lying. Had he inherited a talent for that? Had she?

Oliver was back, weaving between the tables in the beer garden, a pint of lager in one hand and a half pint in the other, a pair of menus between his teeth. Emma was slightly disappointed. He hadn't asked her what she wanted to drink and he appeared to have made a rather annoying assumption. Then, he put the pint glass in front of her and the half in front of himself. He removed the menus.

"I have to drive home, you see."

Now, that was more like it. Dear, sweet Ollie. Was she ready to manipulate him? To betray him? For the sake of some wild idea that her grandfather had about a tax fraud she didn't even understand?

They both had ploughman's lunches – or ploughmen's lunches, whichever it was.

"Are we halfway round?"

"Very nearly. I thought we might take it a bit easier on the way back, perhaps stop for a coffee somewhere."

Emma approved of this idea. They had plenty of time. There was no work today. People rarely got married on Mondays and even more seldom when England was playing in a World Cup match. No wedding tomorrow, either. Oliver was making various suggestions for the day's activities from the back seat, but Emma was vetoing any that might require a lot of physical exercise. She was starting to feel the effects of two hours' cycling.

*

Phillipa Templeton learned back in her chair and steepled her fingers. "What's the old dog up to this time?"

"Skulduggery and mischief."

"I beg your pardon."

"It's what he calls it. I don't know what he's up to. He brought me up to Rutland on some ridiculous pretext in order to give me that list of five names that you have on your desk."

She drummed her fingers a couple of times, pursed her lips and gave a little 'tssk' sound. Then, she turned to her computer keyboard and started tapping. Michael couldn't see the monitor.

"And you think that his real interest is probably this Jakob Schneider?"

"I don't know, but it seems the likeliest."

She tapped some more. "Hmm. You may be right. Did you tell him that you would be telling me all this?"

"No."

"Do you suppose he guessed?"

"You know him as well as I do."

"Hmm. Well, yes. Leave it with me for now. And don't get any silly ideas about trying your boyish charm on the women in central records."

"Because you've already warned them?"

"Because you are not nearly so charming as you think you are. I'd hate to see your delicate little ego get bruised."

Suitably chastened, Michael rose, left Phillipa's office and returned to his desk.

Phillipa picked up her phone. "Yes, Phillipa Templeton. I've just ordered some files from the registry. Can you bring them up straightaway? Thank you."

She replaced the receiver and, for the second time, said, "What's the old dog up to this time?" But this time, she said it to herself. Was there just a hint of affection in the tone? Nonsense! Sentimental nonsense! This was a practical problem that required a practical solution and misplaced sentimentality would certainly not help. Still, the old goat...

TWENTY-TWO

The clock struck eight and Frank tried to compose his face, such that it no longer looked like the entry for 'schadenfreude' in an illustrated dictionary. He had been beaming and chuckling ever since Dan Petrescu's last-minute winner ten hours earlier. He laced his walking boots – a combination of practicality and proletarian shame had cast the brogues to the back of the cupboard – and took a pair of penguin biscuits from the tin beside the kettle. As he reached his door, he checked his expression in the mirror one last time. Still some work needed.

Frankie was distraught. And Maisie was failing to console him.

"But England lost! They lost to Rummy-yah."

"Simon says it doesn't matter. He says so long as England beat Colombia, it will all be alright."

Frankie was puzzled. The intricacies of the FIFA qualification system were a bit much for a five-year-old. He looked to his grandfather for reassurance.

"Never mind, Scotland are playing tonight, against Morocco."

Frankie closed his eyes and frowned intensely. "A red flag with a green star," he said, at last. "We have all the flags in our classroom at school. I like the South Africa one best. It's got all the colours."

Frank smiled benevolently and asked him what the Scotland flag looked like. Frankie closed his eyes again and his grandfather slipped the penguin into his pocket. Maisie saw it, but he gave her a conspiratorial wink and tossed hers over. She dropped it, but stooped and scooped it up before Frankie opened his eyes.

"It's blue, with a white exxy cross. England's is white with a red plussy cross."

Maisie had hopped into the car. "Can Rocky come to school with us today?"

Rocky had already cast his vote. He was standing on the driver's seat with his front paws on the steering wheel.

"Rocky wants to drive," said Frankie, excitedly.

Michelle emerged from the house at this moment. "Dad! You and I need to have a conversation." She seemed to occupy a position midway between testy and amused. "About a monochrome flightless bird from the Antarctic?"

Frank treated her to an expression that said either, 'I have no idea what you are talking about and am entirely innocent' or 'I'm a grandfather and it's my prerogative.' He gave a low whistle and Rocky reluctantly leapt from the car, taking the most indirect route via all four seats and the boot, and came to sit at Frank's side.

Frank waved until the Volvo was out of sight as he did each morning. He checked one pocket for pipe, matches and tobacco, and the other one for Rocky's lead, then headed for the gate.

Ron was waiting, as usual, at the foot of Beacon Hill, by the sign giving thanks to the historical commitment of Peter Roberts. Frank nodded and took out his pipe. The pipe was only for the downhill part of the journey, past the hall and towards Leighton Magna. The meadows had all been mown, but the wheat and barley were turning gold. Rocky scurried ahead to inspect the hedges and ditches and Ron and Frank strode along, in silence, as usual.

Frank mused upon how little he knew about his companion. He was pretty sure that Ron had lived here his whole life, although he probably had had to do some military service. Frank was sure that painters and decorators were not part of a reserved occupation. If he had been a teenager in the early part of the war, he was likely in the army or, perhaps, the Royal Air Force by the end.

RAF Cottesmore was only a mile or two away. Perhaps Ron had spent the war painting it. Or maybe he had been a dispatch rider. He certainly knew a lot about motorcycles, but that may have been due to his enthusiasm for speedway. Speedway and crown green bowls were Ron's only public passions. As far as Frank knew, nobody was aware of his secret identity as a crossword compiler.

They had reached the hall and were passing diagonally across the car park. "Ron, that old escape route, the one the Germans built and the borstal boys used to use to sneak out for a fag. Do you suppose it's still there?"

Ron considered this. "I doubt it. They did a proper job when the place was renovated a few years back. Probably tidied it up, like."

"But where was the exit?"

Ron frowned. "Easier if I show you."

But Ron didn't alter his course at all. They walked past the corner of the building as usual. Then, he stopped and turned. "It was just about here – you see those small arches. That was the windows for the cellar, like. I think it was the end one."

Frank glanced about and went to inspect.

*

Bernard's grandfather clock struck ten and his electric kettle boiled at exactly the same moment. Ten seconds later, Frank and Rocky arrived at the back door. Frank looked a little tired. As he removed his cap, a bead of sweat ran diagonally across his forehead. There was a brief battle between the force of gravity and the absorbent qualities of a shaggy grey eyebrow, but before either could triumph, Frank drew the back of his left hand across his eyes and rendered the contest null and void.

"Good morning, Francis. I am feeling especially pleased with myself this morning. I was pondering our little conundrum and I think I may have had a brainwave."

Frank slumped into a kitchen chair. He wasn't sure that he was properly ready for a brainwave.

But Bernard hadn't noticed. He reached into a low cupboard. "May I?"

Frank nodded and Bernard tossed a Bonio towards Rocky. He snatched it from the air like an expert slip fielder – no, not like that. He caught it in his mouth, obviously. He was a dog. Rocky crunched and swallowed the biscuit before trotting off to the corner, where Bernard had thoughtfully set out a bowl of water. Within seconds, there was the sound of grateful lapping and sloshing.

"I'd have liked a dog, but Karin was allergic or intolerant or something. Even considered a Mexican hairless at one stage, but there are limits."

"What's stopping you now?"

"Oh, I don't know." He cocked an ear and nodded towards the door.

"So, Francis, what are our objectives and what are our options?"

"Okay, objectives: we want to find and see as much evidence of a carousel as we can. We don't need the documents themselves – in fact, pinching them would be counterproductive. We'd have a problem with our chain of evidence and, worse still, their absence might be noticed."

"So, we just need to see them. What are we talking about? Suppose I could magic you into Keller's filing cabinet. What would you want to see?"

"Okay, first thing I'd want to know: the names of all the companies in the chain, their addresses, the names of their officers, directors and company secretary, and their addresses, too, ideally."

"And second thing?"

"The VAT registration details, the nine-digit VAT number, the certificate of registration, including the date of registration.

Finally, I'd want to see any invoices, bank transfer details and shipping documents."

"Would he need to keep those?"

"Mostly no, but he's an accountant. He might not be able to help himself."

"So, company details, VAT details, banking details, shipping details. How many companies are we talking about?"

"That's impossible to say. If he's just started, it might be three or four. If he's been at it a while, it might be thirty or forty."

"So, a quick peek probably won't do?"

"Almost certainly not. We would need to be alone and undisturbed for at least an hour."

"Which brings us to the second half of my question. How do we get in?"

"Well, there are two options and I'm not crazy about either of them. Option one: We wait for a night when the hall is unoccupied and we break in."

"You're not serious!"

"It's not quite as crazy as it sounds. There's a way in. It's a long story, but basically you can get in through an old entrance to a disused cellar. From there, you can get into the kitchen and then upstairs to the suite of rooms including Keller's office. From what Emma has told us, that is the likeliest location."

"It's all a bit 'Escape from Colditz', isn't it?"

"Worse than that. There's probably motion sensor alarms. Security cameras. All sorts of stuff."

"I am already inclining towards option two. What is it?"

"Well, it's my preferred one, too. We gatecrash a wedding. Pick a moment relatively late in the evening, after the meal, after the seating plans. Walk in dressed as guests and sneak upstairs."

"Are you sure this isn't just an excuse for you to put on your kilt?"

"I think that might make us a little too noticeable, don't you?"

"Good knees, have you?"

"They are excellent, since you ask, but the McBride tartan is especially attractive. It's a bit like the Black Watch, but with a thin yellow stripe."

"I can foresee a lot of problems."

"So can I, but it's that or crawling through cellars."

"Either way, there are going to be a lot of locks between us and what we want to see. Supposing the key documents are in a safe?"

"Locks I can probably manage, though a safe would be beyond me, I'm afraid."

"And then we'd have to find and wipe the tapes with the security footage. Do you even know where those are?"

"No, but I assume your granddaughter could find out."

"I don't want her any more involved than she is already. She's just a child, really."

On the other side of the kitchen door, Emma was affronted. Affronted and offended. And bloody angry.

"So, if we go with option two, when do you have in mind?"

"Is there a wedding on Friday?"

"Why Friday?"

"England versus Colombia – additional distraction."

"Let's think about it some more."

"Also, I don't want to miss next Thursday's pub quiz."

"Do you think they'll be one?"

"Oh, I think I can guarantee that."

Emma retreated from the door, climbed halfway up the stairs and made sure that she descended as noisily as possible.

"Oh, hello, you two!" she said as she entered the kitchen. "And hello, Rocky. Who's a good boy? Who's a gooood booooy?!"

Frank and Bernard exchanged looks. Bernard nodded. Frank nodded.

Emma began making herself a cup of coffee in the way that only students can. She used the kettle, two mugs, a cup, a milk bottle, a jug, a whisk, an egg poacher, a soufflé dish and a frying pan. Or at least that's what it seemed like to Bernard.

She took her coffee outside. She needed to think. Was her grandfather, who must be about a hundred years old, really going to gatecrash a wedding so he could sneak into Keller's office? The only thing he seemed to be concerned about was that he didn't have the gelignite required to blow a safe.

The old boy had clearly said goodbye to his last marble. This was insane. Not as insane as trying to tunnel in through the cellar obviously. Actually, she needed a whole new calibration system for measuring her grandfather's loopiness. And that crazy old Scotsman was encouraging him. The pair of them were going to wind up behind bars, either prison or, more likely, some sort of asylum.

Emma needed to think. She had an hour and a half before she needed to be at work. Unfortunately, Ollie wouldn't be there. He was doing the night shift. *Oh God.* She was going to have to do it herself, wasn't she? That crazy idea that had come to her and that she had dismissed. Either she burgled Leighton Hall or... she shook her head again. He's gone crazy. Now, the big decision. Was she going to take Oliver into her confidence? 'Oh, darling, you wouldn't mind helping me burgle the place, would you? Only, my grandfather thinks there's a carousel fraud being perpetrated from Keller's office. No, sorry, haven't a clue actually. I only heard the term for the first time a day or two ago. Something to do with VAT, I think.'

But what was the alternative? 'Oh, darling, I know that I've only known you two weeks, but what do you say to abusing our employer's trust and having a night of wild passion in one of the unused guest rooms? And, by the way, don't worry if I've got to get up in the night. I just need to go and jot down some details of company secretaries.'

*

"What do you think she'll decide?" asked Frank.

"I think she'll have a jolly good think about it and probably won't have decided by the time she comes home at around six."

"And then?"

"Then I'll ask her to do me a favour."

"And you think that will work, do you?"

Bernard was ever so slightly offended. Of course it would bloody work. He had been manipulating people since Frank was in short trousers. Would it work? The very idea!

TWENTY-THREE

In the movies, or even in episodes of *Scooby-Doo*, our intrepid heroes blunder into the offices of the sinister corporation / supervillain's secret lair / old, haunted fairground without any contingency plans or exit strategy. Amateurs! Although, to be fair, the *Scooby-Doo* gang's record speaks for itself. Frank was not an amateur. He had a back-up plan. He didn't expect to use it, but if he had, it wouldn't be a back-up plan, would it? It would be *the* plan.

They had to approach the hall from the east. That way, they could take advantage of a screen of rhododendron bushes and avoid the gravel drive that Frank knew from experience would make a noise like a brontosaurus eating cornflakes. So, from the east.

This meant driving the short distance to Leighton Magna and approaching via the Ashcombe Road. Frank parked his old Ford outside Ron's cottage. There was a light on upstairs. Frank could see the silhouette of his friend hunched forwards over a desk. Ron was probably working on a crossword; four down, sharing relatively equally (4-7).

Bernard was filling his pockets with sweets and biscuits.

"It's not a bloody picnic!"

Frank had really thought that his days of skulking in the bushes at two in the morning were behind him. But at least he knew how to do it, which was to stay bloody still. Bernard was fidgeting and shuffling like a toddler in the queue to see a department store Santa. Frank couldn't even light his pipe and he certainly wouldn't be able to do so once inside. He had tried to stock up his body's nicotine reserves by smoking three back-to-back earlier and now he felt a little light-headed. He was bad-tempered and grumpy. Scotland were out of the World Cup and he had had to endure Rocky's big brown eyes when he left him behind. And now Bernard was muttering to himself.

A downstairs light turned on and off again twice. "At last."

The two pensioners made their way to the building. They would have liked to have crept, but they were a little too stiff and cold for that. And Bernard badly needed to use the toilet. What was wrong with the man? They had spent two hours in the bushes for goodness' sake. Typical officer class.

Bernard tapped lightly on the window.

It opened slightly and a hand emerged, holding a large bunch of keys. "I've turned the alarm off, but just in case the code is 220674. You've got two hours."

Frank took the keys and, with Bernard, walked – a little closer to creeping now but still not in full stealth mode – around the corner to where there was a white door. The fourth key he tried opened it. Both men entered, paused and listened. Silence. Frank pulled out a torch, but he didn't switch it on. He waited to see if his eyes adjusted sufficiently for it to be unnecessary. After a few seconds, he decided that he didn't need it. To their left was the set of stairs that led up to the corridor at the end of which was Joachim Keller's office and the other three doors. They took the stairs, growing in confidence with every step. If something was going to go wrong, it was likely to have happened by now. Of course, they were growing further from their means of escape with every step, too.

Frank opened the door to Keller's office first. They had limited time and had agreed that it made sense to split up. Frank was by no means a VAT expert, but he was likelier to make sense of the business records they expected to be behind one of the other doors than Bernard. Bernard would search Keller's office. It would have to be done very carefully. No sign must be left that anybody had been there. It had to be assumed that Keller was organised and watchful. A Stasi accountant would be exactly the sort of person to know where he had left any paper clip. Or perhaps he wouldn't. Safest to assume so, though.

Bernard entered and closed the door behind him. Frank could hear his footsteps across the room and then the very faint rustle of a blind being drawn, followed by the tiny 'click' of a torch being switched on. Frank was relieved to see that there was no sign of light under the closed door.

Frank tried three keys in the first door before it opened. He paused and listened. Inside the room, he would be less able to hear anybody moving about in the building. All was silent. He took a deep breath and pushed open the door. Empty. The room was completely empty. Fighting a sense of anticlimax and frustration, he stepped out again and relocked the door. Time to try the second.

This time, the room was not empty. Frank closed the door and the blinds, then flashed his torch around. There were four four-drawer filing cabinets on each of the two side walls, and a small table and chair in the middle of the room. The sole window faced east across parkland and down to the road from Leighton Magna to Ashcombe. The light was still on in Ron's cottage. No, there it went, off.

Aside from passing traffic, there was nothing and nobody out there to see a light on. Frank decided to risk it. He couldn't examine thirty-two sets of files by torchlight.

The filing cabinets were all locked, but they were from the same manufacturer that supplied civil service filing cabinets. And that meant that Frank had a universal key. Any investigator who waited to be told the information contained within his manager's files wasn't worth the name, in Frank's view.

He opened the first cabinet and pulled out the bottom drawer. It was full of hanging files, each of which bore a small label indicating its contents. The second drawer up was the same and the two above that. Frank closed the top three drawers and examined the bottom one. It appeared to be full of supplier invoices from companies whose names began with the letters 'T' through to 'Z'. There were a lot of bills from Uppingham Laundry Services.

A quick look indicated that the invoices appeared to be for the financial year 1995-1996. The three drawers above were the same. The next filing cabinet was for the following financial year and the next for 1997-98.

Frank tried to remember the name on the box of cava. He couldn't. It didn't matter. It probably wasn't sold to Leighton Hall by the bodega itself. There would be a middleman. More than one, probably; a legitimate wine merchant and whoever had hidden the drugs in the corrugated sides. He didn't have the time to examine every invoice looking to identify the supplier. There was a good chance that it wouldn't even be there. He turned to the fourth filing cabinet.

This one seemed to contain invoices and other documents relating to the renovation of the hall. Not important – although, hold on. He studied the contents of the top drawer again. It included invoices from the solicitors who had performed the conveyancing. He took a file over to the table, sat down and pulled a notebook from his pocket. It took him five minutes to note the details that he thought he needed. It was now three o'clock. Time to perform a small check. He crept to the door, turned off the light, opened it an inch or two and listened. Nothing. Good.

Frank returned and made sure that the first four filing cabinets were closed and locked. He now turned his attention to the four filing cabinets against the other wall. The first gave him what he wanted. There were twelve hanging files. One for each company. Each contained the company formation documents including details of address, company officers and shareholders. In each case, the company had been created and registered by a business that existed for precisely this purpose. It was a creator and purveyor of 'off-the-shelf' companies.

The next set of documents related to the transfer of ownership to the companies' first 'proper owners'. Each had a single director and a company secretary. They were always one man and one woman, and although they had different surnames, they frequently had the same address, mostly in the East Midlands. Frank took the files to the table and started taking notes.

Next in each file was a photocopy of the form VAT 1, the application for registration for VAT including details of the company and its intended nature of business. They all seemed to be registered at different addresses in the East Midlands and all gave their business as 'General Trading'. Next were the certificates of VAT registrations, issued by Customs and Excise in response to the applications and usually dated about a month later. Frank noted these, too.

The next drawer down was full of invoices. There were too many to note all the details, but it was clear that they mostly concerned transactions between the companies from the drawer above. There were also details of companies in France, Belgium and Holland. Frank noted these and checked his watch.

The bottom two drawers contained reams and reams of headed invoice paper. One for each of the companies. Frank helped himself to one copy of each. It was five to four. Frank checked that everything was exactly as he had found it. He locked all the filing cabinets, turned off the light and opened the blinds. Doing so, he saw the first peach-pink evidence of the coming dawn.

Finally, he stood listening at the door. He could hear somebody coming up the stairs and they sounded like they were in a hurry. He opened the door an inch and saw it was Emma.

"Keller! He's coming!"

"What?"

"You must have triggered a silent alarm or something. His car's just arrived."

Frank quickly checked that he had turned off the lights and relocked every door. Bernard was coming out of Keller's office. It was too dark to see if his expression signified satisfaction or frustration.

"We've got to go, quickly!"

They hurried down the stairs. Emma leapt down three steps at a time, landing like a butterfly or a ballerina each time. Frank was walking fast. Bernard was performing a sort of high-speed shuffle. The man was seventy-seven.

A light came on in the main hall as Keller entered. The three had no time to do anything except duck in through the nearest open doorway. And they dare not catch Keller's eye by closing the door. Instead, they pushed on through a room used for storing saucepans and cleaning products. There was no other exit. If Keller had seen them or if, for any reason, he chose to enter this room or turn on the light, they would be exposed.

"This way!"

Emma opened what had appeared in the gloom to be a cupboard door. It led to a set of stairs down to a cellar. She ushered the two geriatric burglars through it and stepped through herself just as the light came on. Had she been quick enough?

There were just a few seconds to take stock of the situation. On the positive side, they hadn't been discovered yet. On the negative side, well, just about everything else, really. They were trapped in a cellar that had no other exit. Keller, it had to be assumed it was Keller, was in the room above and if, for any reason, he chose to check the cellar, there was going to be some explaining needed.

Even if he didn't, how long could they remain where they were? The staff would be starting to arrive in a few hours and even with Bernard's *sangfroid* and *savoir faire* and other qualities that really just amounted to being a former brigadier, it was expecting a lot for Emma and two pensioners to casually emerge from the cellar into a busy kitchen and just stroll off as if it were the most natural thing in the world. They were trapped.

Bernard had arrived at the same conclusion. Emma was starting to panic, while simultaneously feeling furious with herself for being in this situation. It was worth at least five points to Michael. All three stood frozen and in silence. Bernard could hear footsteps in the room above. Then, he became aware of something. At first, he couldn't quite identify what it was. Something had changed. There was a very slight movement in the air, the very faintest of faint breezes. Frank earnestly hoped that it was Plan B.

"Frank?"

Frank turned on his torch and tried to point it at the sound. In the far corner of the cellar was a smallish arch-shaped aperture that framed the face of Ron Godsmark.

"This way."

Ron led them through the hole in the wall, across what seemed to be an abandoned and forgotten wine cellar, through another entrance that was concealed, now partially concealed, behind decades' worth of cobwebs and finally up a steep slope, until they emerged through another arch-shaped hole into the fast-breaking dawn.

The quickest way off the premises with the smallest chance of being observed meant walking across the lawn until they were behind the rhododendrons that shielded the path down to Leighton Magna. It wasn't until they reached the edge of the village that anyone spoke.

"Well?" began Bernard. "That was exciting!"

Emma was furious, frightened and confused, but mostly furious. Furious because she had no idea what she was going to say to Oliver to explain her sudden absence. Furious because her grandfather had led her into some bizarre yet perilous expedition and most furious of all because she had to acknowledge that her brother, Michael, had been right. The twinkly-eyed, tweed-clad, kindly old septuagenarian was bloody dangerous company.

And who was this other old man who had arrived in the nick of time and led them through what could only be described as a secret passage? This was the sort of thing that happened in *Famous Five* books, not in 1998. Unless, perhaps, there was an exception for Rutland.

"And successful," said Frank. He fished his pipe, a Falcon, with its straight steel stem and interchangeable bowls, from his pocket and began filling it.

Emma couldn't believe it. A secret passage, a moonlit escape, inches from discovery and... and whatever that might have meant. And these three old sods were calmly walking down a country lane, smoking a pipe, discussing their deeds and generally feeling very pleased with themselves.

They reached Ron's cottage at about half past four. At no point had he explained his presence. Emma didn't know if he had been there by design, as part of some back-up plan that her grandfather had decided she didn't need to know about, or if he was just the sort of person who wandered around the hall's grounds at night on the off chance that his friends might need to make a hasty and furtive exit.

Ron gave them a sort of one-finger salute and disappeared into his cottage. Bernard turned and peered through the early dawn light in the direction of the hall. He could see the lights on in the upstairs rooms. Presumably, Ron had seen something similar. He truly was a remarkable man.

The three continued back to Leighton Parva.

"Did you get a chance to look at everything?"

"No, no, I didn't. There were three more filing cabinets in what I'm calling Room Two and I never even looked in Room Three."

"Want to go back?"

Emma couldn't believe her ears.

"No. On balance, I think it might be pushing our luck a little."

"Yes, you're probably right."

They were just impossible, both of them. She didn't know which one was worse. She decided that she needed to try to return and explain herself to Oliver. Not least to ensure his silence. She set off up the hill, rehearsing various excuses and explanations in her mind. None seemed remotely plausible. And if that were a criterion, then she certainly couldn't tell him the truth.

*

Frank would ideally have liked to go directly home and straight to bed, but Bernard had insisted that they have a debrief while the events of the night were fresh in their minds – and this debrief should be accompanied by bacon and eggs.

"I'm surer than ever that Keller is running a carousel fraud. He seems to have about a dozen off-the-shelf companies all registered for VAT as general traders."

"And he owns and controls them?"

"On paper, no. But he has all the documents and he's got blank invoice paper for them all. He produced a sheet from his pocket, by way of example."

"And bank accounts?"

"I don't know. In one of the filing cabinets I didn't get to, possibly. It doesn't really matter. What matters is that he can be linked to a company that imports the goods, sells at a loss and then disappears with the VAT. There appear to be two of those."

"So, you tell your former colleagues what you know. They turn up with handcuffs and search warrants and the Kellers spend the next ten years in the chokey?"

"Perhaps. From what I can see, Keller seems to be fairly new at this game and the numbers aren't large. There's a lot of this fraud going on at the moment and resources are limited. Even if it is taken on as an investigation, nobody will be going to prison for ten years. The maximum sentence for VAT fraud is seven, then knock off a bit for first offence, maybe a third for a guilty plea. I'd say, possibly, two years. And most of that will be spent in an open prison. Low-risk prisoners, you see?"

"That's not a lot for a pair of drug smugglers who murdered George Bowman."

"No. No, it's not. But we can't prove either of those things."

Frank was a professional, a pragmatist. His currency was what could be supported by evidence, legally admissible evidence, what could be proved. He would have approved of the decision to prosecute Al Capone for tax evasion.

But that was not Bernard's currency. Nor had it been his world. Bernard wanted justice.

*

Frank and Joe Lake were in The Wheel. It was the only pub in the Vale of Belvoir that stayed open during the afternoon. Strictly speaking, that wasn't entirely accurate. It was more the case that The Wheel would, if required, open in the afternoon.

By chance, Joe and Frank arrived at the same time. They parked in the car park at the back. Frank's old Ford beside Joe's Volkswagen. The two men shook hands and headed towards the pub. To one side was a wooden workshop that had probably been standing for fifty years and leaning slightly for forty of them.

"Hallo!"

A grimy face appeared from underneath a Renault.

"Any chance of a pint?"

The landlord of The Wheel rose and helped himself to a generous measure of Swarfega, wiping his hands as he walked towards the pub's back door. Five minutes later, Frank and Joe were sitting at a small table in an otherwise unoccupied pub, the only sounds the rhythmic ticking of the mantle clock and the arhythmic sounds of the publican addressing the Renault's transmission with what sounded like a sledgehammer.

"Have I the pleasure of meeting my anonymous informant?"

"You have. Let me show you what I've got."

It took twenty minutes for Frank to lay it all out. Joe sat there, nodding, sipping his pint and hoping that he wouldn't be conducting one-man investigations when he retired.

"Okay. It certainly looks like a carousel fraud. Maybe it's in its early phases. Maybe it's small. But if all the evidence is under one roof, it might appeal to a team who want a quick win. There is a problem, though."

"Which is?"

"If I come into the office and tell them that I've got an anonymous informant who has dropped a fully formed VAT carousel fraud literally in my lap and that fraud just happens to be taking place one mile from Frank McBride's house…"

"I take your point. But you're a bright boy. I'm sure you'll think of something."

TWENTY-FOUR

Alan Hawkins returned the handset to its cradle. Alan Hawkins, Assistant Chief Investigation Officer, Branch 11 (midlands), National Investigation Service, HM Customs and Excise. That's what it said on his business cards. But why? Somebody, for reasons that Alan did not know or understand, had ordered him 250 business cards. Alan had been in the job for almost forty years and had never handed anyone a business card. Neither did he expect to do so in the few months that stood between him and retirement.

His first instinct was to throw the whole box in the bin. But, actually, he couldn't find the bin. It was probably in his office somewhere. To be fair, there could have been a full-sized skip somewhere in his office and it wouldn't have been visible to the naked eye.

Many people had actually compared his office to a walk-in skip, but that was unfair. Alan had a system. He knew where everything was. Apart from the wastepaper basket. It was probably somewhere in that corner. He picked up the box of cards, weighed it carefully like a darts player contemplating a bullseye finish and tossed it lightly into the corner, where it may, or Alan may have imagined it, have made a faintly metallic sound, such as you would expect from 250 small pieces of card meeting a litter bin.

This important piece of filing completed, he turned his mind to the phone call that he had just finished. Some people found it hard to stay away when they retired. They would 'just pop in' to the office from time to time, to catch up on gossip, to inhale the ambiance. Over time, the visits became less frequent, less fulfilling. The sad fact was that once you were retired, people didn't really care. Alan was not going to make that mistake. He couldn't bear the thought of overhearing some young officer inquire who that old codger in the tea room was, talking about operations he had never heard of and people he had never known.

Alan was pretty confident that Frank McBride was the same. To the best of his knowledge, he had never 'just popped in' to the Nottingham office since he retired six months ago. And yet it was to Frank that he had been talking.

Frank made a persuasive case. He outlined a plausible political environment – office politics, that is. Frank rarely spoke about actual politics. He set out various operational considerations, the needs of the service, the needs of staff, both junior and senior. It was a piece of well-reasoned and virtually unanswerable piece of advocacy, but it didn't fool Alan for a minute. He had known Frank far too long.

"I wonder what the old bugger really wants? Or, more accurately, why he wants this?"

But whatever his motivations, the case that he had made was an excellent one. And Alan couldn't see any obvious downsides. He picked up the phone. Then, he put it down again. He really ought to know this number by heart, but he didn't. He had it written down somewhere around here.

"Hello, Julie." Julie was the Senior Investigation Officer who led Nottingham B, the Nottingham's office VAT fraud investigation team. "Listen, I've just been going over the quarterly figures. And obviously I've noticed that your team hasn't knocked an operation in the past three months."

Julie was recently appointed; she didn't know Alan well, having transferred from London. "That's true. As directed, the team has been one hundred per cent focused on these VAT carousel frauds. We've a number on the books at the moment and I don't need to tell you how complex and time-consuming they are."

"Oh, I quite appreciate that. And it's not intended as a criticism in any way. Your focus is absolutely where you need to be…"

There was a 'but' coming. Julie was certain.

"But…"

Julie braced herself. She was about to be asked to perform the impossible, wasn't she?

"I wanted to know if you thought it likely that you would knock a job or, better yet, two this quarter."

Julie conceded that there was very little prospect of that.

"The thing that concerns me, Julie, is that you have a bit of a mixed team. There are some very experienced and capable officers, but there are some very junior ones, too. I'm guessing that you have some who have never sworn a search warrant, never executed one, never arrested anybody and never interviewed a suspect."

Julie conceded that this was so.

"And even among the old hands, there must be some who haven't been out of the office to play for many months."

Julie admitted that this was also true.

"So, I think it would be helpful – for professional development, for morale and also to indicate to those upstairs, who don't always appreciate what it's like in an operational team – if we could knock a job, even if it's small one, in the near future."

Julie tried to suppress a sigh.

"Now, I might have something here that fits the bill. Operation Bauhaus, I think it's called. A small carousel fraud. Probably just two targets and only been running for a few months. Down in Leicestershire somewhere or Rutland, same thing really. I've been looking at the intelligence package." (This was a lie. Alan had never heard of it thirty minutes earlier and everything he knew he had been told by Frank.) "It seems to me that it might be a nice little job for the youngsters and for the others to blow away a few cobwebs – you know, get them back to match fitness. The money probably isn't that much by carousel standards, maybe a million, but it all helps the figures. What do you think?"

Julie had only the vaguest knowledge of Operation Bauhaus. One of the senior officers in the drugs team had learnt of it from an informant. Alan had made a decent case and it would certainly take the pressure from above off her. It would probably be good for her popularity with the team, too. Carousel frauds required a lot of frankly tedious desk work. Customs investigators like nothing better than kicking down a few doors and feeling a few collars. She promised that she would give it serious thought.

"Excellent. Excellent. There is just one further thing. I'm meeting the chief in two weeks. I'd love to be able to tell him that we'd just knocked a carousel fraud. It'd be quite the feather in Nottingham's cap."

And there it was! The impossible request. Knock a VAT carousel fraud investigation in less than two weeks.

Alan leant back in his chair. He felt good. He had done Frank McBride a favour – two, actually. And even if he didn't know how or why, it still placed him in a very exclusive club. Frank McBride never asked anyone for favours or understanding, or forgiveness for that matter. Frank owed him one, possibly two, and that made him feel good inside. He would have felt better if he had understood why Frank was calling in a career's worth of favours, but it was Frank McBride. Sometimes you just had to accept that you would never know.

*

Philippa Templeton really didn't have time for this. In truth, she spent hours each day doing things for which she didn't have the time. That was part of the reason why she was regarded as a rising star in MI6 and also the reason that she seldom got home before nine, had no social life, no hobbies and no partner. She sighed. As if the troubles of the world weren't enough, she had to worry about whatever Bernard Taylor was up to now.

And she resented having to write it down, in longhand, with an actual pen. Usually, she would purse her lips and pause for a few seconds, then her fingers would fly across a computer keyboard and another issue would be off her desk and down a cable to either a satisfactory conclusion or a pit of confusion, incoherence and, most of all, plausible deniability. This time, she wanted no digital trail that would lead back to her. She didn't exactly know why. She had been happy to put her initials and her fingerprints on far weightier, far more sensitive issues than this. It was just that this time, this time – well, she just didn't trust the old goat. And she trusted him even less when she couldn't determine his motives and his intentions.

She looked again at the list.

Max Pfeiffer – Politician. Never quite capitalised on his dramatic arrival on the scene in 1990 and probably losing what little influence he once had.

Gisela Sommer – Died 1990. One of Bernard's agents.

Manfred Busch – Died 1994. Former proprietor of a bar near the Brandenburg Gate.

Jakob Schneider – Former Stasi, left Berlin 1990, destination thought to be Austria or Switzerland.

Renate Voigt – West Berlin police officer, currently head of the Vice Squad.

Bernard could have traced Pfeiffer or Voigt pretty easily himself. It wouldn't have been hard to establish that Busch was dead. So, his genuine interest was Sommer or Schneider. Michael Butcher had thought it might be Schneider. Phillipa's instinct told her it was Sommer. Might be both, of course.

What harm could there be in adding an extra level of detail to what she had Michael tell Bernard? She looked again at the reports. There were rumours that Schneider had absconded with Stasi funds. But these rumours always existed when somebody disappeared, and Schneider had been an accountant. That was sure to amplify them. No harm in letting Bernard know that. The second report was the one that was giving her a headache. Gisela Sommer had been murdered. Stabbed. And the evidence suggested that it had been a professional.

But if she gave Bernard the minimal amount of information possible, what would he do and why? Phillipa was sure that she needed to know what the old goat was up to. The best way to achieve that was to give him enough information to make his next move, observe that and then react accordingly.

But how much information was the correct amount? Give him too much and his next move might be his final move. And then it would be too late to prevent him doing whatever the hell it was he was doing. If she told him Sommer was stabbed, it might be enough to trigger him. If she merely told him she was dead, he would likely seek out the death certificate. Then, Phillipa would know for sure that it was Sommer in which he was interested. And she really didn't have time for this. She reached for her phone.

"Tell Michael Butcher I'd like to see him, please."

*

Bernard put down the single sheet of paper. He was angry, hurt and upset, but most of all angry. Gisela was dead. It didn't say how. It didn't say when. As if she had never existed. Gisela had been the littlest of the little people. Born in wartime, in what history would later decide was a hundred metres the wrong side of the wall.

Orphaned by three. Raised by the benevolence of the German Democratic Republic. Never married. Never engaged. Never even loved or been loved, so far as Bernard knew. A lifetime of drudgery and want, punctuated only by risking her life, literally risking her life, to aid people that she would never meet. And all anyone had to show for her existence was: 'Died 1990, no further details'. He wondered what had become of her dog. Poor, poor Gisela.

More practically, this news meant that his most useful source of information about Schneider was gone. Perhaps that was why she was dead. Frank had scoffed at the idea that an accountant might be a ruthless killer, but Frank hadn't spent decades watching the Stasi from across a city and then across a wall. He looked at his watch. It was almost time to speak to Berti the Limp. Tonight's call would be from a payphone in Peterborough. He wondered whether he really was getting a little too old for this.

Berti was apologetic. There was little that he knew. Little he could discover. Schneider had disappeared. The consensus on the street – or wherever it was that this particular part of Berti's spiderweb extended – was that he had disappeared rather than 'been disappeared'. But Bernard knew this. Jakob Schneider was sitting in The Old Vicarage in Ashcombe.

The only thing that Berti could tell Bernard was that there were rumours that Schneider had disappeared with his girlfriend. The physical description could have matched Mrs Keller, although it could have matched a lot of people. That wasn't significant. Berti couldn't say much more about her. His sources didn't want to, at least not the reliable ones.

Bernard could imagine Berti shrugging at the other end of the line. This was not A1 intelligence. It wasn't even C3 intelligence, but one man, an old drunk who claimed to have once worked in the Stasi's Executive Group XVII, said that he had known the woman slightly. He had called her 'Die Klinge'[2] and said that she was an assassin.

Bernard didn't react – at least not at first. There was a long pause, before he finally said, "Berti, do you know how to get hold of a death certificate? I'm looking for a cause of death. Yes, I've got the name."

He thanked Berti, told him that he would express his gratitude more tangibly when he was next in Berlin and hung up. By the time he was halfway home, a plan was beginning to form in his mind.

*

Bernard was going to need accomplices. What he had in mind was not a one-man job. There are two types of accomplices: the unwitting and those that are part of the conspiracy. As a general rule, Bernard preferred the unwitting kind. This ruled out Frank. The chances of being able to dupe Frank into unconsciously assisting were zero. And Bernard was pretty sure that Frank would not approve, which made things more difficult still. It wasn't just that he could not count upon his friend's assistance, he had to make sure that Frank knew nothing about it.

It wasn't an overly elaborate plan – Bernard hated those – but it did require one very simple preliminary step. A tiny, tiny crime. Hardly a crime really, a minimal act of theft. And that task, that infinitesimal piece of larceny, fell to Emma. But Emma wasn't home. She was out at the cinema with Oliver. Bernard would ask her later. Or perhaps tomorrow. And he would ask Ron tomorrow as well. And do a little shopping.

---

2   The Blade.

TWENTY-FIVE

Frank was on babysitting duties. Simon and Michelle were going out and Michelle was nervous, even Simon was nervous. And this time, Simon was the one worrying about what to wear. They had been invited to Simon's boss's house for a barbecue and to watch the match between England and Colombia. These 'semi-social but he's still the boss and he's watching you' occasions were always difficult, but this had an extra dimension.

As far as he knew, this was not a general work colleagues' event. They were bad enough. It was Sid – Simon's boss – his friends and neighbours, and Simon and Michelle. Simon had received a promotion quite recently, but this had all the hallmarks of being sounded out for another opportunity.

Simon considered himself a football fan. He had been a season ticket holder at Nottingham Forest at one time. But meeting Michelle and becoming a de facto stepfather had changed that. Frankie wasn't old enough for football yet and Maisie wasn't really that interested. He didn't know whether Sid was a fan, much less what his friends and neighbours might be like. Did he turn up in a replica shirt with the cross of St George painted on his face? Did he ignore the football and dress as if it were just any old barbecue at the boss's house? And what was that exactly? He was also pretty sure that Sid was Hindu. Sid was short for Siddharth. Did that mean no beefburgers? Did it matter? And supposing England lost and were knocked out of the World Cup.

On a personal level, England's loss would hurt Simon, but he was sure he could keep a lid on it. Unless Sid's friends and neighbours wanted to go on a disappointment-fuelled rampage and upturn and immolate every Volkswagen on the street. How was he going to continue to make small talk with Sid's wife if that fool Tony Adams gave away a penalty? And Simon was a nervous drinker. He drank more and faster if he was anxious and this was an occasion built for anxiety, even if Alan Shearer scored a hat-trick in the first half.

Michelle was nervous, too. For all the same reasons and because she didn't want to let Simon down. Frank was reassuring her, calming her, telling her that everything would be fine. This might have been a little more effective if it hadn't come from the man who had punched the second secretary at the British Embassy in Bangkok in the mouth when he should have been making polite remarks about the Ferrero Rocher.

In the end, Simon settled for a pair of khaki shorts and a 1966 replica England shirt; Michelle for a flowery summer dress. Frank waved them off at half past six and retired to the garden with Rocky and his pipe while the children ate fish fingers and chips.

*

For somebody who had never played the role of the business person's loyal and supportive partner, Michelle was doing a good job. She and Sid's wife, Pooja, were getting on extremely well. They shared a sense of humour and had been amusing each other with observations about men and barbecues for half an hour.

"Pooja! How do I know when a beefburger is done?" Sid's voice emerged from somewhere among a cloud of black smoke.

"How would I know? Ask one of the Christians to cook it for you!"

Simon and Michelle had agreed that Simon would drive. It seemed like an extra precaution against him getting too nervous or excited and overdoing it on the beer. To make sure that his bridges were truly burned, Michelle accepted a second, quite large, glass of rosé. Simon saw. Message received.

While Sid was struggling with the barbecue, Pooja was definitely not struggling with the wine. "It'll be burnt or poisonous or both, but, honestly, I don't mind. One evening away from the stove is like a little holiday."

Michelle felt the same.

"I don't really care for barbecues. When we were in Texas, there was at least one a week."

Raj and Pooja had spent a couple of years at the company's head office in Houston. "Please don't misunderstand me. America is lovely. At least for a year or two. But I was glad to get back home to Leicester. Anyway, I shouldn't be putting you off."

That was an odd thing to say, but Michelle didn't get the chance to query it because Sid announced that cremated meat was served and everyone began to gather by the garden table. Despite Sid's claims of a lack of expertise, the food was very good. There were burgers for those who wanted them, but Michelle preferred the lamb that Pooja had prepared and Sid had cooked.

The match kicked off at eight. Michelle gave Simon's hand a little squeeze. It was all going well. Everything was going to be fine, providing that the England football team didn't put Simon's good behaviour under unbearable strain. The team started well and Simon relaxed slightly.

"Do you think he's picked the right team, Simon? I'm not sure about Anderton."

Simon was about to say that he agreed, because he did, but he didn't want to be one of those people who agree with their boss's opinion on all things, even those unrelated to work. He opened his mouth and was suddenly paralysed. What should he say? Had he left it too late to say anything? It wouldn't be a casual reply. It would look calculating. *Oh God, what was he going to say?*

At that moment, Darren Anderton smashed a right foot volley into the top corner. Sid's friends and neighbours cheered. Other cheers could be heard down the street. Sid was jumping up and down, arms in the air and roaring.

When everyone had settled down, Simon leaned over to Sid, "Yeah, you're right. He's rubbish!"

Sid roared with laughter.

Ten minutes later, England won a free kick thirty yards from the goal.

"Oh, I've seen this a thousand times," said Simon. "Everyone gets all excited, the drama builds and then it either goes directly into the wall or twenty feet over the bar."

David Beckham curled the ball into the bottom left-hand corner. Sid roared, first with joy and then with laughter.

"Simon, we are both experts!" He laughed some more.

England were still leading by two goals at half-time. Sid had invited Simon into the garden and they were pacing to and fro, their heads close together and talking earnestly. Michelle was grateful that she had insisted that Simon be the designated driver. This looked serious. The second half had begun so she couldn't remain watching them, trying to decode the body language. She had to rejoin the others in the front room. Whatever was happening, she would hear about it soon enough.

*

Michelle heard about it in the car on the way home.

"Madrid? Madrid, Spain?"

"Yep."

"For how long?"

"A minimum of two years. It might be good for the kids. Different culture, learn a bit of the language, you know?"

"But you can't speak Spanish. Neither can I."

"They'll teach us – personal tuition. And they'll find us a house, and a school for Maisie and Frankie."

"I suppose you're going to tell me it's a great opportunity."

"I'm just telling you what Sid said. We have plenty of time to think about it. We don't have to decide now. And if you don't want to go, well, I'll just tell them no."

"Do you want to go?"

"I don't know. I haven't had time to think about it."

Michelle gazed out of the window as they reached the crossroads at the centre of Uppingham. "What about Dad? Maisie will miss Rocky."

*

Rocky was bounding up Beacon Hill and Frank was following him at a slightly slower speed. Ron was not occupying his usual position, resting against the fence by the beacon. The universe was being particularly capricious these days. The England football team hadn't embarrassed itself (much to Frank's disappointment) and Ron Godsmark was not in his appointed place at the appointed time. Frank decided that this extraordinary combination of events required some contemplative thought. And contemplative thought required a pipe.

He had barely lighted it when he saw Ron marching up the hill from the direction of Ashcombe. Rocky raced down the hill towards him and the pair engaged in their usual elaborate greeting, with the question of 'Who's a good boy?' being posed and satisfactorily answered several times.

When the pair reached the beacon, Ron apologised. "Sorry I'm late. I got held up at the cottage. Bernard, you see?"

Another score for the universe's tally of unlikely events; Ron uttering three consecutive sentences without being prompted by a question. Frank remedied that now.

"Bernard?"

"Arr, come round my cottage afore seven."

Frank was surprised. He thought that Bernard and Ron's relationship extended no further than the Thursday night quiz.

"Does he often come to see you, Bernard?"

"Arr. No. Well, mebbe, sometimes."

Having caught him in a talkative mood (by Ron's standards), Frank decided to take advantage. "Have you lived in Leighton Magna all your life, Ron?"

"No, no, not at all. I was born in Leighton Parva." Only Ron could have thought this was a distinction. "Moved to Leighton Magna later, worked for my Uncle Jim, apprentice painter and decorator."

Frank remembered the man with the sergeant's stripes from the photograph. "Was your father a painter, too?"

"No, no, my father was a gentleman – at least my mother thought so. More fool her."

Frank didn't understand exactly what that meant, but he was sure it ought not to be explored further. The two continued on their usual route, with Rocky racing up and down and exploring any scent he found. The hall seemed to be especially busy – the last Saturday in June being a popular wedding date. Frank cast his eyes skywards. It looked a lot like rain.

Ron, sensing his thoughts, sniffed the air and surveyed the horizon in all four directions. "T'll be a'right," was his verdict.

And he probably knew better. Indeed, by the time they had reached Ron's cottage, it had begun to brighten noticeably. Ron led Frank inside and went straight to the kettle. Frank sat at the table.

Ron's biscuit tin, the one from which he had produced the photograph of himself as a young home guardsman was on the table. Frank couldn't help himself. You can't realistically put a tin of private treasures in front of an investigator and expect him not to take a peek. There were the photographs he had seen. And a few more. Oh, Ron had been a lance corporal. It said so on the front of his paybook. And then there were the medals – five of them. Frank's eyes widened slightly. He was not a military aficionado by any means, but he recognised that medal. Anyone would. On the reverse, it read: 'Lance Corporal RA Godsmark, 5770069, 2nd Battalion, Lincolnshire Regiment. 7th June 1944'.

"I haven't any more of those sweeteners. Do you want sugar or go without?"

Frank leaned back from the tin. He wouldn't have believed it. Ron? And yet there it was. No passport, though.

"Just one sugar, thanks, Ron."

*

Bernard had ordered a taxi to take him to Oakham. From there, he took the train to Peterborough. He spent an hour perusing the vehicles at various used car dealers. He wasn't especially fussy about what car he bought, but he did have a distinct preference for the type of dealer. Bernard was not looking for sterling customer service or a diamond after-care programme. He wanted a dealer who was used to asking very few questions and paying no attention to the answers. Kwalitee Motors seemed to fit the bill. The office was a Portakabin that had been lovingly converted into a walk-in ashtray and interactive body odour experience.

Bernard had chosen a 1994 Vauxhall Cavalier. It was a little more expensive than he had intended, but it needed to be able to travel three thousand miles in under a week, so it would have been false economy to buy an older or less comfortable car. He paid cash and gave the dealer a name and address, not his own.

Bernard then travelled to a DIY store. He spent five minutes looking at a range of hot-air strippers in a slightly puzzled fashion. After this, he was joined by a bored-looking youth in an apron who offered to assist him. The only real assistance offered, however, was that at the end of a further ten minutes, Bernard knew how little it was necessary to understand about hot-air strippers to hold down a job in a shop that sold them. Eventually, he picked the green one. It was the cheapest and it matched his car. He bought a dust mask, too. He would need one of those. And some rubber gloves.

His next purchases were made at a shop that specialised in catering for those who liked to brew their own beer and wine. Then, he visited a branch of a well-known travel agent and bought a substantial quantity of deutschmarks and smaller amounts of French francs and Dutch guilders. He stopped at a motor parts store and bought a continental travel pack, complete with stickers to shield headlights, a warning triangle and a GB sticker. He also bought a continental power adaptor. As he left the shop, a further requirement occurred to him. He needed a roll of cling film. Perhaps he had one at home.

He could put off his final purchase no longer. It was absurd that a man who had lived the life that he had, had seen what he had seen and done what he had done should be nervous. But he was. The last time Bernard had purchased condoms had been when they had been shyly offered to him at a barber's in Cambridge before the war. After that, they had been issued to him by the quartermaster.

It wasn't just embarrassment that concerned Bernard. He feared that a seventy-seven-year-old man demanding two dozen condoms, extra strong, might be a sufficiently uncommon occurrence as to stick in the memory of a shop assistant. Bernard was old. Times had changed. She didn't bat an eye.

With his shopping complete, Bernard headed back to Leighton Parva. He had already moved his Rover to leave a clear passage for his new Cavalier to go in his garage. The garage was little more than a shed really. It was built – if built wasn't too grand a verb – fifty years earlier and seemed to be held together by bent nails, poisonous glue and spit. It was for this reason that Bernard didn't use it, as a garage or anything else. There was a more than negligible chance that the mere act of opening or shutting the doors might cause the whole edifice to collapse in on itself. On this occasion, however, Bernard was prepared to risk it. The Cavalier had to be kept out of sight.

*

Michelle had decided to raise the subject of Spain with Frank at Saturday morning football practice.

"We haven't said anything to the kids yet. We'll probably say no, but, just in case, I didn't want to spring it on you."

Frank said nothing. He reached into his pocket for his pipe, but checked himself. Parents of young children could be very unreasonable where tobacco was concerned, even in the open air, even by the side of a football pitch in Rutland.

"I mean, they haven't given us any details. Haven't told us anything at all really."

Frank nodded. He was the last person on earth to criticise the choices that anybody made for their career. And the last person to give any lectures on parental responsibility. He clenched his teeth and stared straight ahead. At his feet, Rocky gave a little whine. Michelle also sensed his distress.

"And, of course, you could visit us any time – any time you wanted a little sun."

Frank stared fixedly ahead.

"And of course you can stay in the barn. I mean, we would probably rent out the house, but you could stay in the barn."

And then Frankie Junior scored. It didn't just hit him and bounce in the goal, he actually scored. The ball rolled to him. He stopped it with the sole of his foot, just as Frank had taught him. He steadied himself and, well, he didn't exactly smash it into the top corner, but he aimed at the goal, kicked it and in it went.

Simon roared. "Great goal, Frankie! Great goal, son!"

Rocky whined again.

*

Frank needed to think. This meant he needed a pipe and, on this occasion, probably a pint, too. He told himself that he had popped into The Old Volunteer in order to estimate the level of Saturday lunchtime trade, but that wasn't really true. He sat on his preferred stool at the end of the bar from where he had the optimum panoramic view. Old habit.

The amount of business being done was predictably low. There were a pair of hikers in one corner, a human collage of brightly coloured synthetic material. Frank wondered whether it was some sort of statement that no two garments should be of the same brand and that no two colours should match or even go well together. Olive green, bright orange and a shade of turquoise that should have carried some sort of health warning. There was an Ordnance Survey map spread out on the table and the couple appeared to be drinking soft drinks.

In the opposite corner was a group of three young men sitting around what appeared to be Coca-Cola. Either they had lost their nerve at the last moment or Gary had been reluctant to accept their pimply faced assurances that they were eighteen. Judging by the sullen expressions, it was the latter. Frank was instinctively sympathetic. One of them, the one with the slight fuzz on his upper lip, might have been sixteen – if you were generous. Frank would have been generous, but then it wasn't his licence. There was no way that this pub could survive. He decided to confront the issue head on with Gary.

It was as he had feared. The brewery had a formula for determining the viability of a pub. It was quite complicated and included such variables as turnover, gross profitability, net profitability and what proportion of the sales were the brewery's own products as opposed to wines, spirits and lagers manufactured by national or international businesses. All these pointed in the wrong direction, but the fatal variable was the last: the potential resale value of the pub itself.

Gary told him that a surveyor had been measuring and examining and doing whatever it is that surveyors do, and it was his considered opinion that The Old Volunteer was worth at least £400,000. And with, perhaps, £50,000 of building work, it might be worth half a million. In a week's time, Gary would provide the figures for the month's worth of trading he had done and after that he doubted that the place would remain open.

*

Emma was working the evening shift that night, starting at six and probably going on until past midnight. She had not been out of bed long when her grandfather came home. She was in the kitchen conducting a stocktake of the cupboards. Her grandfather had not been used to catering for himself and his provisions were either an eclectic mix or a ridiculous assortment, depending on your point of view. Emma was making a list, two lists actually. One was 'stock on hand'. The other was a shopping list.

"Hello, Grandad, I thought I might do some shopping tomorrow. Get a few things, you know. Is there anything special that you fancy?"

"Oh, I don't know, just the usual."

"What's that?"

Bernard actually had no idea. "I'll leave it to you. Actually, there is something that you might get for me."

"What's that?"

"A bottle of wine."

Emma was puzzled. She had been down into the cellar, where there were dozens of bottles. Good ones mostly, from what she could tell. A lot of German whites. It seemed odd that her grandfather should want her to buy something from Asda.

"I need a bottle of the house red from up at the hall."

210

Okay, the old man had clearly slipped a gear now. He had a cellar full of vintage claret and he wanted her to steal a bottle of five-pound plonk. Actually, it was probably a lot less than five pounds.

Bernard saw the expression on her face. "No. It's not what you think. I'm not desperate for bottle of *Vin tres ordinaire*. An empty one will do just as well as a full one."

Okay, he was definitely starting to lose his mind.

"There is just one thing, though. I need it to have Mrs Keller's fingerprints on it."

*

Emma was genuinely worried. She had found the proceeds of her grandfather's shopping trip and couldn't make sense of them at all. The hot-air stripper was puzzling enough, but when she found the condoms, she didn't know what to think. She found a receipt for the car, too, but it wasn't in her grandfather's name. In the end, she decided that she had to telephone her brother Michael.

Michael had been weird, even weirder than usual. He had insisted that she call him from a public telephone and at a specific time. And then he had immediately asked her for the number and called her back. She told him about the hall, what she had been asked to do, the... what was she supposed to call it? Reconnaissance mission? Burglary? And then she told him about the GB sticker, the condoms, the foreign currency. Finally, she told him about the mysterious set of Vauxhall keys she had seen on the kitchen table.

"I'm really worried that he's starting to lose his mind, Michael."

"I'm frightened that it's much, much worse than that. Look, here's what you are going to have to do."

TWENTY-SIX

Julie Sinclair put down the intelligence package on Operation Bauhaus. It was really very good. It was well written, well researched, well reasoned. It set out the important factors and identified the unknown, but avoided the twin pitfalls of speculation and wishful thinking. Opposite her was the officer who had supposedly prepared it, Chris Bolton – known to one and all as 'Monster'.

Julie had been at Nottingham B for less than six months. She didn't know her team well. She knew the officers of Nottingham A, the drugs team, even less well. And she knew Monster hardly at all. Was he the one that was supposed to be studying for a law degree in his spare time?

Julie had never worked on a drugs team herself. She liked to think that officers, such as herself, who specialised in fraud, were more cerebral, more articulate, more intelligent. After all, how much brain did it require to tear around in a fast car and then kick in a door?

But she had to admit that Monster had produced a highly professional piece of work. The case was literally ready to go. It could be knocked in a matter of days, if necessary. Her only concern was that the whole thing had been predicated by an anonymous informant. Julie hated all informants – annoying nuisances who were almost always more trouble than they were worth – and she hated anonymous informants, most of all. But the information had been independently verified. A lot of work had gone into this by somebody who knew what they were doing.

"Did anyone help you with this, Monster? I mean, Chris?"

"Joe Lake helped a bit at the beginning. It's his informant. He said he'd like to come on the knock when it happens."

Julie didn't know Joe Lake well either. She thought for a while and then leafed through her desk diary.

"Okay, start work on drafting the search warrants. Home address for the two targets and this Leighton Hall place. Check on availability, too. We'll want at least sixteen officers, so you'll need to borrow some from Nottingham A."

"Okay, what date shall I put on the warrants?"

Julie glanced down at her diary again. "Monday 6th July."

Monster's eyebrows shot up. That was a lot of work in a very short amount of time. Maybe Joe Lake would agree to help.

*

Bernard couldn't remember the last time that he had made a long road trip. He certainly wasn't looking forward to this one, but he had no choice. He had spoken to Berti and learned what he had expected, or feared. And he had made a promise, a long time ago, and broken it. Or at least he hadn't been able to fulfil it. He hadn't been able to exfiltrate Agent Gustav and now Gisela was dead. Loss of blood. A knife wound in the femoral artery.

Bernard had played the game in Berlin for forty-five years. And it had rarely been personal. There had been successes and failures. And sometimes there had been what he thought were successes and only later discovered were failures. And probably the other way round, too. That was the game. There was no keeping score; nobody knew when they had scored or how many times. And they had even less idea what their opponent had scored. There was just the game. It was a rough game. Players got hurt. People got hurt who weren't players or even spectators.

Gisela had played the game and now she was dead. And she probably wouldn't have complained. But Gisela was murdered after the final whistle. The game was over. And even though nobody really knew what the rules of the game were, that was definitely outside them.

He grunted as he applied the headlight stickers. Then, he went to the back of the car and applied the GB sticker to the rear window. He loaded his bag into the boot, checked that he had his passport, tickets, money and the address he needed to visit in France, and he was ready to go. The last thing he did was to pack the wine bottle.

It took Bernard three hours to reach Folkestone and he was already tired. He was going to have to pace himself. He had never travelled on the Channel Tunnel before and he found the whole experience very pleasant. By the time the train had arrived in Coquelles, he was feeling at least partially refreshed and estimated that he ought to be able to manage at least a couple more hours that day on his journey south.

The traffic out of Coquelles seemed to be three-quarters British vehicles. It was not yet school holidays and so he didn't see family cars filled to the brim with buckets and spades. There seemed to be an awful lot of cars pulling caravans, though, and motorhomes. Some of the motorhomes were actually towing small cars themselves. The childless and the retired heading for some summer sun.

In the opposite direction, the last of the disappointed England football fans were making their way back from Saint-Étienne. Or at least the last of those who had left at a time of their own choosing rather than following a court hearing.

Bernard didn't notice them. While on the train he had promised himself that he would try to make it as far as Reims tonight. Ideally, he would have liked to find some charming *auberge* a little off the motorway and feast on local dishes washed down by, well, not the local wine – the local wine was champagne and you can't really wash things down with champagne.

In the end, it didn't matter. It was getting late. He was getting tired. He wasn't used to driving long distances anymore, or driving abroad, or driving in the dark. He found a soulless motel on the edge of a ring road and surrounded by *hypermarchés*, *bricolages* and chain restaurants.

Bernard was somewhat bemused to discover that the motel had no staff whatsoever, no reception, no restaurant – nothing, in fact, except a machine that would dispense an electronic key card, a bit like a credit card, if a customer inserted his own card. Bernard didn't want his presence in Reims to be recorded on his credit card statement. He had gone to quite a lot of trouble to acquire a false identity and an untraceable car. He wasn't going to leave a digital fingerprint on continental Europe.

There was another motel opposite. This one had actual staff, although in terms of human interaction and personality, it didn't really exceed the vending machine. The receptionist was in training for the Olympic games – or he was if the international committee had introduced a new biathlon of chewing gum and looking bored. This kid was a serious medal hope. But he accepted two hundred francs and parted with a room key. That was all Bernard wanted from the transaction. And that was all he got.

If you were to be generous and if you didn't mind playing a bit fast and loose with the laws on misrepresentation, you might have described Bernard's room as 'clean and comfortable'. Bernard had seen more comfortable cells. There was a single plastic and steel chair, which didn't look as if it could bear the weight of a gnat who'd had a decent lunch; a dressing table that could accommodate a toothbrush or a comb, but probably not both; and a bed. The bed was thin, narrow and covered in a continental quilt that could only really justify the name if it were on a different continent. Or possibly a different planet, far nearer the sun.

Bernard was inwardly quite pleased. This was not a grand tour. It was not an epicurean odyssey. It was a mission and if it was less than enjoyable, so be it. He still had over five hundred miles to go on the first leg of his journey. The second leg was twice as long. He would stay somewhere nicer tomorrow, as a reward for completing the first phase.

*

"I'm worried about my grandfather."

Frank nodded. And then it all came flooding out: the GB sticker, the purchases made at the home brew shop, the cash, the condoms, the Cavalier, everything. Frank nodded again.

"When did he leave?"

"This morning. Very early."

"In the Cavalier?"

"I think so. It's not in the garage. I can't find the keys."

Frank nodded again. Somebody filled his pipe and lit it. It must have been him.

"Tell me everything. Every last thing."

This time, Emma set it out like a lawyer would. It was a story, but it was told logically. No details were omitted. Whenever she offered an opinion, she made it clear that that was what it was.

"I think we're going to have to search his study, library, office – whatever he calls it."

Frank thought he knew what Bernard was doing and why, but he wasn't sure how. The condoms, the bottle with the fingerprints, the home brew supplies. The challenge was going to be finding a way of either stopping him or making sure that he didn't get himself in more trouble than he could handle.

This meant that Frank was going to have to do something ever so slightly illegal himself. And involve someone else. He cursed Bernard for that. He phoned Joe Lake at home and explained the favour he was asking.

Customs and Excise had access to the computer that would match any vehicle's number plate with a description and details of the registered keeper and his or her address. But there were strict parameters about how this access was used. Doing a favour for a retired colleague definitely did not fall within those parameters. Every check was recorded. The person making the check, on whose behalf they were making it and the reason why. However, these limitations on law enforcement's ability to pry into the private data of honest, and not so honest, citizens were not foolproof.

Nick Harper was still the most junior officer in the Nottingham office of Customs and Excise's National Investigation Service. He was competent and relatively experienced, but he was still 'junior man'. It was a lottery. Some people were only junior man for a month before somebody still more junior joined the team and they were spared.

Nick was unlucky. He had been junior man for over a year. Those were the breaks. And that was why he was trudging around suburban Leicester. He started at the East end of Manitoba Road. Then, he turned left onto Edmonton Road. When he reached the bottom, he crossed the road and started back on the other side of the street. At the junction with Manitoba Road, he crossed the road and walked back up it on the opposite side.

In his pocket was a Dictaphone. A small microphone ran on a lead up to the inside collar of his jacket. As he walked, he muttered the number plates of every parked car. It was a common tactic and perfectly legitimate – well, normally.

For example, you might know that Mr Smith lived on a certain street, but not exactly where. Or you might not know which car he used. So, you recorded the number plate of every car in the street and checked them against the Police National Computer. If you were lucky, within a few hours you knew that Mr Smith lived at number fifteen and had a red Renault, and you knew its number plate. It was just a bit of a pain to have to do it this way. And that is why it was usually the junior man's job and that is why Nick was trudging up and down and muttering.

On this particular occasion, it was all a ruse. Joe Lake wasn't looking for Mr Smith and didn't care where he lived or what he drove. He wasn't looking for anyone else either. He just wanted a list of number plates of cars mostly belonging to people who lived in Leicestershire. Well, Leicestershire and Rutland actually. When he got back to the office, Nick transcribed the forty or so number plates that he had recorded and gave the list to Joe Lake. Joe added the number plate that Frank had given him about two thirds of the way down the list. In a few hours, Joe would have all the numbers checked and then he (and Frank) would know who the registered keeper of the green Cavalier that had been parked in Bernard's garage was.

When Joe told Frank, he just grunted. He was going to have to ask for another favour.

*

Michael wrestled with his various options. He considered a number of improbably innocent explanations and a variety of impractical countermeasures. In the end, he had been left with only one course of action. He had known from the start that he would, but he was dreading it.

Phillipa's Templeton's working day was busy enough without this. She scowled at the young man in front of her.

"I'm really sorry to have to come to you with this, but he's up to something. He's bought a car in a false name and a GB plate. And the last time he did something like that... well... you know."

Phillipa knew very well, but that had been different. It had been authorised, sort of. This was different. The old man had gone totally rogue. "Too late for an all ports notice?"

"Probably. He left yesterday. My sister only just told me."

Phillipa nodded. "Assuming he's up to no good, he's almost certainly headed for Berlin."

"Berlin?"

"That's where he knows people who will help him. It's too late to follow him. We'll have to get in front of him. Okay, get yourself to Berlin. What name are you currently using?"

"I'm John Harris this month."

"Okay, I'll let the local station chief know you're coming. He can put the word out. We have a few local assets who could form a surveillance team if we find him. In the meantime, we can try and track him using the motorway cameras and the toll system."

Michael nodded sadly. Bringing issues like this to Phillipa's attention, adding to her problems and workload, was not good for his career.

TWENTY-SEVEN

Bernard rose early the following day and hit the road. He had got used to the Cavalier now and was appreciating the effortless journey on French toll roads. Even the scenery improved. He left the flat plains of Picardy behind and travelled South through Burgundy, past the grand cru vineyards in their walled gardens, past Chablis, the Côte d'Or and towards Macon. Then further south along the banks of the Rhône, home to Hermitage and Condrieu. In all, he drove over four hundred miles alongside the homes of some of the world's greatest wines, before bearing west near Châteauneuf-du-Pape. And he was doing all this to buy some of the worst wine available anywhere in Europe. The irony was not lost on him.

Bernard's research had only been limited. To have made more inquiries would have been to leave a trail of evidence back to him. Nevertheless, he was confident. Chateau Bousier was not available at any retail outlet in England. Neither did it appear to be available at any retail outlet in France. The Leighton Hall house red was not sought after among oenophiles. It was cheap, it came in corked bottles and it had a nice label with a pen and ink drawing of a chateau and an address in France. For some wholesale customers, such as Leighton Hall, this was enough. It had to be. There was nothing else.

And if you wanted a glass of Chateau Bousier, you pretty much had to either get married or drive to Carcassone and buy it at the winery gate. For anyone else, this was a disadvantage. But it was precisely what made it ideal from Bernard's point of view. He arrived too late to actually make his purchase, but he was sufficiently proud of the fact that he had made it almost a thousand miles that he decided he deserved a night at a five-star hotel. But five-star hotels required a credit card at check-in. So, instead, he found an *auberge* ten miles south east of the town.

The following morning, he made his purchase. He didn't drive up a sweeping gravel lane to a chateau like the one on the label. He visited the warehouse of the local cooperative and explained in the Englishman's traditionally appalling French that he had been tasked with sourcing some inexpensive wine on behalf of the University of Sussex Students' Union. Half an hour later, he left with two cases in the boot. It was five hundred miles to the German border. He had promised himself that he would reach it by nightfall.

He stopped in Mulhouse, still inside France – just. It probably would make little difference, but it couldn't hurt to make things a little more difficult for whoever might be tapping Berti's phone. Bernard wasn't exactly sure what Berti did to earn a crust these days, but it seemed vanishingly unlikely that he was an honest and upright tax-paying citizen. Leopards might change their spots, a little, but they didn't open antelope-friendly vegan restaurants. Bernard would have been surprised, and Berti possibly a little offended, if some government agency somewhere didn't have Berti on its radar.

The railway station seemed to be the most promising site, but parking near it was far more difficult than Bernard expected. And he was tired. Really tired. It was almost seventy-two hours since he had left home and he was, at best, halfway through his mission.

He found two public telephones next to each other in the station concourse. He made a note of the number of the first and called Berti from the second. Then he asked Berti to call him back on the first number. It wasn't foolproof, but it was the best he could do in the circumstances.

He told Berti what he wanted. Berti was surprised, even a little bit horrified, but mostly surprised. He regained his composure quickly enough to start arguing about price, but Bernard wasn't in the mood to haggle. He told Berti again what he wanted and what he was prepared to pay. And he hinted, ever so gently, that he would be unwilling to accept compromises, excuses or any sharp practice whatsoever.

He knew, of course, that achieving this unholy triumvirate was impossible, but, for form's sake, he had to try. His business concluded, Bernard returned to his car and drove east. He spent the last of his francs on fuel and crossed the Rhine at *Neuenburg am Rhein* and three-quarters of an hour later, he checked into a small hotel in Freiburg im Breisgau.

*

The 4th of July was a significant date. Not because some ungrateful malcontents had put their names on a piece of paper 222 years earlier (Bernard had some fairly old-fashioned views on what he still called the 'ill-judged experiment'), but because Germany was playing Croatia in the quarter-final of the World Cup for the right to take on the hosts, France, who had beaten Italy the previous day. Bernard hadn't planned it that way, but it was very convenient. For two hours, from 9 o'clock in the evening, the attention of the whole nation would be on the match and that suited Bernard very well.

It was five hundred miles to Berlin, but Bernard preferred to linger over the first German breakfast he had enjoyed for years. It was almost nine before he set off, heading north through the

Black Forest. Bernard spoke German well, but he spoke Berlin German, and he was used to Berlin customs and traditions. He hardly knew the Germany outside of Berlin at all and the bits that he did know best were in the east, and they had probably changed beyond recognition, or at least were in the process of doing so.

He bypassed Stuttgart and had a rather unsatisfactory *autobahn* services lunch just north of Nuremburg. He considered calling Berti again, but eventually decided against it. He stopped again near Leipzig. He wanted to test his theory about how much the east had changed. A lot less than he had expected frankly.

*

Michael spent most of his flight trying to estimate exactly how much harm had come to his career, what might unfold next and how much harm that might do. On the positive side, he had identified quite early on that his grandfather was up to something and he had reported everything by the book. On the other, he feared that he would somehow be held responsible for whatever diplomatic, legal or security mess the old man created. This would hardly be fair, but Michael doubted that that would count for much.

Worse still was the fact that whatever happened, and it surely wasn't going to be anything good, it would soon be common knowledge that he was Bernard Taylor's grandson. He knew that the speculation would begin immediately that this was the reason he had been accepted as an intelligence officer (which it sort of was) and that he was neither suitable nor capable of performing the role (which he hoped was untrue).

On top of that, he had been told to liaise with Toby Drake in the Berlin office. Michael had been on the basic training course with Toby, but he had known him before that, too. They had been at university together and had disliked each other almost from the moment they met. Toby, like Michael, had been a modern languages student, but his true vocation was sarcasm and snark. All organisations have a handful of people like Toby and, sooner or later, they very often rise to the top.

*

Drake hadn't changed. The clothes were different – a conspicuously German suit, a pair of loafers. And there was just a hint of silver at the temples. Drake was twenty-three. He couldn't possibly be going grey. Perhaps he had coloured his hair in an effort to appear more distinguished. It was the sort of thing Michael could easily imagine him doing. He looked like a continental advertising executive or somebody in the accounts department at Audi. The sly smile was the same, though.

His office was just a tiny cube at the very top of the embassy, but from the way he had appointed the place, it looked like a storeroom for unwanted exhibits from the Museum of Imperial Nostalgia. There was a hookah pipe in the corner, what looked like a Zulu shield on the wall and a tiger-skin rug, which could only be genuine judging by its moth-eaten and shabby appearance. Drake himself was reclining in his chair, his feet resting on what appeared to be a pith helmet and smoking one of those ridiculous little cigars that are actually smaller than cigarettes.

"Ah! Hello, Butcher. Here to join us on the grandpa hunt?"

Michael wondered whether Drake had already learned that the object of the exercise was his grandfather. If he hadn't, he decided to give him no clue. He picked up a copy of *Stern* that had been lying on the only unoccupied chair and sat down.

"What's the latest?"

"Through the Channel Tunnel, east of Paris, down the Rhône Valley and then towards the south west. Now it looks like he's headed for Switzerland or Germany."

Michael had no idea why his grandfather might have gone to south west France. But it was at least feasible that he was now heading for Berlin. Hopefully, they could track him through the *autobahn* system.

"Latest location?"

"Heidelburg, an hour or two ago, heading for Nuremburg. Probably there by now."

Drake blew a smoke ring upwards. It met the sloping ceiling near a poster advertising the 1928 boat race. "I'm just a field guy, of course…" (there was the snark) "… and I probably don't need to know, but who exactly is this geriatric James Bond and what is he supposed to be up to?"

So, Drake didn't know. Good.

"Ex-military intelligence. Now privateering. Have you put the word out?"

"Well, naturally. I have personally spoken to our most promising sources of local intelligence."

"Who are?"

"The usual collection of spivs, spoofers, wide boys and corrupt businessmen. No response so far. But then, of course, he isn't here yet. You're certain he's heading for Berlin?"

Michael had never been more certain. He just didn't know why.

*

Bernard reached the outskirts of Berlin a little after seven. Football supporters were starting to gather in neighbourhood bars. He found a little hotel in Dahlem and checked in. Ideally, he should have liked a hotel with off-street parking, but he had neither the time nor the inclination to search the neighbourhood for one. The receptionist was concentrating on the pre-match build-up on the television and Bernard took advantage of this to enter false details on his registration form. With half an hour before kick-off, he phoned Berti again and asked him to meet at a bar in the university district.

225

The bar was ideal from Bernard's point of view. It was extremely crowded, very noisy and almost everyone in the place was less than a third of his age. This meant that they were also at least ten years younger than any surveillance officer. Bernard stuck out, but so would anybody else that he ought to be concerned about. Most of the customers were either crowding around the bar or jockeying for a position where they had a clear view of one of the establishment's three televisions. Bernard sat on a stool by the window, from where he could watch the street outside.

The match kicked off at nine. Berti arrived at a quarter past. Bernard was pretty sure that he hadn't been followed. Certainly, nobody followed him in and there were no official-looking cars slowing in the street outside, looking for parking places with a view of the exit. It wouldn't have helped them. Bernard was back on his home turf and he had chosen the bar carefully.

He led Berti through the back and down an alley into a side street. There was nobody to be seen. From there, he took an intricate route through streets, broad and narrow, for twenty minutes. The approved counter-surveillance methodology was to go somewhere busy, where a tail had to keep close for fear of losing you, and then somewhere quiet, where you had a chance to see everyone around. But there wasn't anywhere busy, except bars showing the match.

Bernard reached his hotel just before half-time. The receptionist's eyes never left the screen. Bernard and Berti walked straight past him. They were halfway up the stairs when they heard the guttural groan of distress. Croatia had scored.

*

Michael was sitting in the embassy canteen, nursing a cold cup of coffee and worrying. If his grandfather had been at Nuremburg, he must have reached Berlin by now. But there was nothing to do

226

except wait for him to surface and then either intercept him or put a surveillance team on him.

Drake entered the canteen and strolled over to Michael with a studied insouciance that could only mean he had something dramatic to impart.

"We've found him. He's at a small hotel in Dahlem – at least his car is. We think he has checked in under the name 'Ritter'."

"Can we get a team together?"

"I think you may find volunteers a little difficult to find this evening. Soccer, you see. Quarter-final, I believe."

Michael cursed. "Well, I'll head down there now. Try and get someone to help as soon as you can."

*

Michael found the hotel easily enough, but what to do next? There was nobody on the streets. It would be difficult to appear unobtrusive lurking near the entrance. There was a bar nearby from which he thought he could probably see the green Cavalier.

He reached the bar just as the second half was about to start. The mood was not good. There were at least five televisions in the bar and each was showing a panel of gloomy ex-professionals. Germany was losing. Michael ordered a Schultheiss and tried to find a spot by the window, but it was impossible. Instead, he stood on the pavement outside, watching the Cavalier and waiting.

This was unsatisfactory. The idea was to see, but not be seen. This was the opposite. There must be a better spot. He left his beer and walked up both sides of the street, looking for a spot from where he could observe both the Cavalier and the entrance to the hotel.

Finally, he found it. A launderette. It would serve for a very short time.

Bernard opened the door to his room. Berti followed him in and dropped his rucksack on the bed.

"Well?"

"I have three kilograms. Phencyclidine, usually known as Angel Dust. It's all I could get at short notice."

"Is it illegal?"

"Very; if you're caught with this in Germany, it means years in prison. In England, probably worse."

"Then it will do. How much?"

"Well, you have to understand…"

"How much, Berti?"

"Twenty thousand deutschmarks."

*

The second half was underway. The streets were deserted. Bernard went down the stairs and out of the front door past the receptionist, who was becoming very tense, but no less absorbed in the match. Bernard had bought two cases of wine, but he hoped that he would only need one. For a start, it was a bit heavy for a man of his age to carry down the street and up two flights of stairs. He almost dropped it when Goran Vlaović doubled Croatia's lead just as he was passing the hotel reception. It wasn't the goal that startled him, it was the howl.

He may have imagined it, but the wail of disappointment and frustration seemed to roll down the street like a tidal wave of horror and dismay. Ten minutes to go and Germany were on their way out of the World Cup.

In the launderette, Michael called Drake. "I need a surveillance team here, as soon as possible."

*

Bernard cleared all the unnecessary rubbish off the dressing table. The absurdly small kettle, the box of tissues and the little box containing sachets of coffee and sugar, tea bags and those little tubs of long-life milk. He took the towel from the bathroom and wiped the surface clean. He dared not use a damp cloth. Finally, he checked that his hotel door was double-locked.

He unrolled a length of cling film and laid it as a square on the dressing table. He put on the rubber gloves and the dust mask and opened the rucksack Berti had left. It contained three clear polythene bags. He took the first and, holding it gingerly by the corners, started to pour the contents, very gently, onto the middle of his cling-film square. He started about a quarter of the way in from the left edge and finished a quarter of the way from the right edge. He examined the small barrier reef of white powder that he had created, weighed the bag in his hand and decided he would repeat the process. He poured his second little mountain range almost directly on top of the first. That would do. Very gently, he put down the polythene bag. Then, he folded in the two sides of the cling film, folded the whole thing again lengthwise and, very gently, rolled it until he had what looked like a snowy white sausage about six inches long and an inch in diameter. Bernard stood back to examine his work. Just to be sure, he took another length of cling film and double-wrapped the sausage. So far, so good.

Bernard unwrapped a condom. He put it under a running tap in the bathroom until it was full and then upended it. It was now easier to insert his cling-film sausage of Angel Dust. He tied a knot at the top, briefly considered and then tied a second. And then a third. Okay, hopefully that was the tricky bit – now should come the easy part. He carefully opened the cardboard box and withdrew a bottle of Chateau Bousier. Taking a penknife, he peeled off the plastic sleeve that covered the neck of the bottle. He put that to one side. Then, he removed the cork. He examined it carefully. Bernard was used to high-quality corks that often had the vintage

229

printed on the top and '*Mis en bouteille au château*' on the side. This didn't. He hadn't expected it to, but he was relieved just the same. He wanted this to be as authentic as possible.

Bernard didn't need Archimedes to tell him that he had to pour a little wine out of the bottle to make room for the drugs, but he wasn't exactly sure how much. The obvious thing was to pour out too much into another vessel, put the narcotic sausage of doom in and then top it up. He considered the tooth mug, but it might not be big enough and it was quite wide-lipped. He could easily spill some wine trying to pour it back into the bottle. His eyes fell on the absurd little kettle. With a mental apology to any future guests who might discover that their morning coffee had a tang of Chateau Bousier, he decided it was the tool for the job. He poured a little wine into the kettle, inserted the condom full of drugs that bobbed about like a fishing float and then topped it up. Perfect. The bottle was dark green, the wine was very dark red and the drugs were mostly in the neck of the bottle.

Bernard retrieved the corking machine that he had bought in the home brew shop and the bag of corks. He selected what he thought looked like a decent cork and, with a little effort, inserted it into the neck of the bottle at only the second attempt. Then, he took the plastic sleeve – black like the Chateau Bousier original – and placed it over the bottle's neck. It sat rather loosely.

Final stage. Bernard unpacked his hot-air paint stripper, attached the continental power adaptor and plugged it in. He wished he had tested it earlier to determine how much noise it made, as it was now approaching midnight, but it didn't seem loud. For five minutes, he waved it around the bottle top like a hairdresser applying the final stages of a blow-dry. It worked. It worked perfectly. He held the finished object up to the light. From certain angles, you could just about detect the bag of Angel Dust bobbing in the neck of the bottle, but it would definitely pass casual inspection. Bernard decided that the process was a success. Only eleven to go.

For the second and third bottles, he made the drug sausage a little shorter and thicker. The plastic collar of the bottle hid it entirely. He made three more and had a little rest. He was halfway and confident that he was now a master artisan at this absurd craft. For the seventh bottle, he took the bottle that Emma had provided – the one bearing Mrs Keller's fingerprints.

It wasn't the knife that had murdered Gisela, but it would have to do. Life imprisonment. Same outcome. Bernard was being an agent of justice. He filled the bottle three-quarters of the way and inserted the condom full of drugs. He topped it up, inserted the cork and then heat sealed the sleeve. Very carefully, he put the bottle back in the cardboard case. Five to go.

It was three o'clock before Bernard was finished. He wanted to sleep, but before that he had to make sure that he had left absolutely no trace of what he had been doing. He could do it in the morning, surely? No, that was how amateurs thought. He would do it now and he would leave immediately. He left at four-thirty. Michael's ragtag surveillance team of bookies, cabbies and grifters were all dozing. Nobody saw him leave. Nobody saw which way he went.

TWENTY-EIGHT

Michael was back on duty at six. The Cavalier was gone. He cursed in English, in German and in half a dozen other languages. He considered for a moment or two, cursed a bit more and then called his sister.

Six o'clock in Germany is five o'clock in Rutland. Emma was not pleased. It took her thirty seconds to wake up. Michael insisted that she repeat back to him what he had told her. No, not told her, instructed her? Ordered her? No, not those either, although there was a hint of that. Implored her?

She dressed hurriedly and made the short journey from The Old Vicarage to Manor Farm Barn and knocked as firmly as she dared on Frank's door.

*

It was four hundred and fifty miles from Berlin to the Hook of Holland – the final, well, not quite final, leg of his journey. He ran the car almost empty of fuel until he reached the Dutch border, where he filled up using his guilders. He arrived at the ferry terminal in good time and took advantage of the spare time to book a cabin for the night crossing to Harwich. There were a few Dutch police and customs officers, one of them even had a dog, but Bernard didn't think that a dog had been born that could detect drugs whose smell was masked by the less-than-fragrant bouquet of Chateau Bousier.

And he was right – or at least no arm of the Kingdom of the Netherlands, with either two legs or four, paid him the slightest attention. He boarded the ferry without incident and made directly for his cabin. He slept soundly until the ferry's public address system notified him that they would shortly be arriving at Harwich Parkeston Quay and that all motorists were kindly requested to make their way to the car deck.

Bernard had been among the first to board and now, happily, he was among the first to disembark. It seemed to him to be a universal truth that it was impossible to exit a car ferry and travel in a straight line. It was always necessary to triple the short journey's length by snaking through an arbitrary slalom course set out in orange traffic cones. He could see the little hut with the immigration officers from the ferry itself, no more than fifty yards away, but he seemed to travel a quarter of a mile to get there.

The same was true of the Customs examination area. He could have walked there in thirty seconds, but instead he zigzagged to and fro for twice that amount of time, before he finally found the shelter of a large grey shed open to the elements at both ends.

An officer in a navy uniform stepped in front of his Cavalier and directed him into the examination area. Notwithstanding the fact that he had almost ten thousand pounds' worth of class A drugs in the boot, his first thought was that this prefaced an unwelcome fifteen or twenty minutes of tedious interaction, thus delaying his first cup of coffee of the morning.

There were three little parking spaces laid out. A second officer directed him to the furthest, the one nearest the exit. He made that little twirling motion, like the queen waving but slightly faster, which indicated he wanted Bernard to open his window.

Bernard's car was neither new nor luxurious, but it had electric windows. Lots of cars did now – soon all would. *What will become of the little twirling gesture then?* he wondered. *Perhaps people would continue to use it for generations long after the origin was lost in the mists of memory and time.*

"Good morning, sir."

"Good morning."

"May I please see your passport and ticket?"

Bernard handed the passport through the window. The officer glanced at it and nodded, presumably to a colleague, who Bernard couldn't see.

There were a few more questions: how long had he been away? Where had he visited? Bernard imagined that this was routine – certainly, the officer didn't seem to be overly excited. To someone who had passed through Checkpoint Charlie, both legitimately and covertly, as many times as Bernard, this was far from nerve-wracking.

"Would you mind opening the boot, sir, and letting us know if there's anything there that you don't recognise?"

More routine requests, he assumed. This was probably the last thing before they sent him on his way. He went to the back of the car and opened the boot.

"Your suitcase, sir?"

He nodded.

"Your wine?"

He nodded again.

"Sorry, sir."

"Yes, yes, that's my wine."

As soon as he said it, he began to feel uneasy. Had he detected a change in the officer's tone? He didn't think so. What was it? The officer hadn't accepted his nod. He had wanted him to clearly state that it was *his* wine. Should he be worried?

"Chateau Bousier. Good stuff, is it?"

"I like it."

"I'm more of a beer man myself. Did you buy it in France?"

Bernard conceded that he had. A second officer had joined them at the back of the car. Both men wore uniforms, but the one to whom he had been talking had two gold stripes. This second officer, a younger man, had only one.

"Just a quick look, sir."

The younger officer, one stripe, lifted one of the cases out of the boot. That was the one that contained nothing but nasty, nasty, cheap red wine. Then, he removed the second box. Bernard felt his pulse quickening. One stripe produced a small knife and deftly slit the Sellotape securing the lid of the box. He reached in and drew out a bottle.

This is the point, thought Bernard, *when an amateur would do something stupid like saying, 'See here, I'm actually in a bit of a hurry.'*

He said nothing and forced himself to look at two stripes. After all, it was with him that he had mostly been talking. But two stripes didn't have any more questions. He was looking over Bernard's shoulder. Bernard turned and he saw that one stripe had upended the bottle. The little white sausage was now visible, even through the dark glass, even through the inky plonk. He met Bernard's eyes and raised an eyebrow of his own.

Bernard turned back to the first officer. He said nothing to Bernard and instead addressed himself to one stripe, the younger man.

"Go on then."

Bernard turned to face the younger man.

"Ronald Albert Godsmark, I'm arresting you on suspicion of the illegal importation of controlled drugs. You do not have to say anything, but it may harm your defence if you do not mention when questioned something that you later rely on in court. Anything you do say may be used in evidence. Do you understand?"

Bernard didn't understand at all. He thought that he had been so careful.

Volunteers had not been hard to find. At six-thirty on Monday morning, there were four cars each with two officers trying to find a quiet and inconspicuous place to park in Ashcombe. This was not possible. Not even nearly possible. This was probably the greatest law enforcement presence that Ashcombe had seen since, well – did Cromwell's New Model Army count as law enforcement?

Ashcombe had an older-than-average demographic and old people often rise early. There were curtains twitching all over the village. Who were these people? They were all dressed in business attire, all sitting in late model cars of popular makes and models. All sitting doing nothing, except, possibly, waiting. But for what?

Within minutes, various theories were forming. The Jenkinsons at Elm Tree House thought that they might be Mormons or Jehovah's Witnesses. Mrs Hennessy thought they were from the TV licence people – a fear no doubt prompted by the fact that her own licence had expired four days earlier. She was actually debating whether she could sneak out of her back gate and buy a licence before they knocked on her door. Mr Wilkes-Partridge was sure that they were from Special Branch or MI5. They were here to arrest the Pembertons. Reds. She was a social worker and he had been seeing buying *The Guardian* at the village stores. About time, too. Bloody Bolsheviks!

Mr Kanwal thought that they were either well-dressed burglars or confidence tricksters. Henry Allen thought that they might be here for the half ounce of cannabis he had hidden in his old rugby socks. He wanted to flush it down the toilet, but his father was standing on the seat trying to see down the street with the aid of a pair of binoculars. Mrs Wells, who was worried about the effect that all of this might be having on house prices, decided to go and challenge them. After all, as a ratepayer, she had rights.

Monster reached for the transmit button on his Mondeo's dashboard.

"All units from Monster. We're attracting a lot of local attention. Please advise when you are in position."

"Anjali, in position."

"Ted, in position."

"Jonesy, in position."

"From Monster, knock, knock, knock."

Had this been a drugs operation, that command would have been given as if it were a war cry. Wheels would have spun, engines would have roared, officers would have raced from cars, their doors still open, like a horde of attacking Vikings. But this was a VAT job. They were wearing suits, for God's sake. Monster's Mondeo purred through the gates of The Old Vicarage and the other three cars followed at a similarly restrained pace.

Mrs Wells was left standing in the street with her mouth open, unsure as whether she should be proud of producing a reaction or affronted that these people, whoever they were, had evaded her interrogation.

*

There were four Customs cars and eight officers in Leighton Magna, too. They had all decided to wait in the bowls club car park. It wasn't overlooked. Nobody challenged them. Nobody even knew that they were there except for Ron Godsmark, who had walked past on his morning constitutional. Officers lounged against the fence, chatting, smoking, inquiring where Joe Lake had got a coffee at this time of the morning in the middle of bloody nowhere. He declined to enlighten them.

At about a quarter past seven, Monster called. Cigarettes were cast aside, ties were straightened and the four cars began a leisurely procession up the Ashcombe Road before turning off into Leighton Hall. Nobody even bothered to call 'Knock'.

TWENTY-NINE

Bernard couldn't quite believe what was happening. There were questions, but he barely heard them. He answered as if on autopilot – no, he wasn't carrying any weapons; no, he didn't have a communicable disease. He'd been arrested. He should start paying attention. Everything he said or did, everything he heard or learned might be critical now.

What was that? They were asking him if he had any medication he needed. That was just bloody insulting. He was in his prime – well, late prime. He wasn't at death's door, although he was supposed to take his statins at five each evening. Would he be here until then? Best not to ask. Anyway, who was he kidding? He could be going down for years. Pay attention.

The younger officer, the one with one stripe, was leading him away from his car now. Should he insist on being present while the search was completed? Did he have that right? What difference would it make, anyway? He tried to remember the training. Not the training he had received. The training he had given others. All those men and women he had sent across the wall. He was being led down a passage now. What was his response going to be? He could say nothing. Not a word. After all, they had just said so. 'You do not have to say anything,' they had said.

After all, they weren't going to torture him. There wouldn't be white noise in the background and an Anglepoise lamp in his face. But wouldn't that make him look guilty? Perhaps he would be better assuming the role of the confused pensioner. The victim of some terrible misunderstanding. An unwitting mule. That was better.

Or he could tell them all to go to hell and use his one phone call to call MI6. He would be out of here before you could even say, 'Sorry, Bernard, you are well off the reservation. This is nothing to do with the nation's security and you're on your own.' Okay, so not that approach.

He was being led down a second corridor now. Not frogmarched or anything like that. He wasn't even in handcuffs, at least not yet. He was being treated like a respectable senior citizen. It was vaguely patronising. Who could he use his phone call to contact? Did he even have a phone call? Nobody had said anything about a phone call. At least he didn't think they had. Perhaps that was America.

At last, he was brought before the custody officer. He knew that before anything had been said. If there was a factory somewhere turning out slightly older, slightly overweight police desk sergeants (and the evidence suggested strongly that there was), it would only take minimal retooling to convert the production line to churn out Customs and Excise custody officers. They were practically the same thing. The type of officer who had seen it all and heard it all and simply didn't care. They operated at one pace, their own, and were the type of person who licked the end of a pencil before writing. He didn't have a pencil. And he seemed to regret, if not resent, the fact. He completely ignored Bernard and began instead by interrogating the young officer. Or, at least, he raised one eyebrow in an inquiring manner, not a Roger Moore manner.

"Ronald Albert Godsmark, car passenger off the eight o'clock. Arrested on suspicion of importation controlled drugs."

The eyebrow again.

"Time of arrest: oh eight nineteen. Arresting officer: me, Jason Gates."

The custody officer seemed satisfied. He turned to Bernard, "Do you understand why you're here?"

That was a bloody sneaky question. What was he supposed to say in response to that? Literally any answer he gave would close down avenues of explanation between which he had yet to choose. He was already being led down a logical path that might lead to an evidential dead end. He nodded.

The custody officer delivered the same speech he had doubtless delivered a hundred times before in a sonorous Suffolk accent, at half the normal conversational pace and with almost no intonation whatsoever. He was asked to confirm his name. For now, he remained Ron Godsmark. To say anything else would risk things accelerating out of control before he had had time to consider his position.

There was a pause, the shortest measurable unit of time. "I have listened carefully to what Officer Gates has told me and I am satisfied that there is sufficient evidence to authorise your detention for an initial period of six hours, after which that decision will be reviewed."

When did that happen? Gates had told him almost nothing. Had there been an opportunity for Bernard to make his case? Had he missed it? The custody officer droned on like a Massey Ferguson in low gear.

"You have the right to have somebody informed of your arrest…"

This was the phone call thing, wasn't it? But it wasn't a phone call. He didn't have the right to speak to anyone, just to have them informed.

"If you choose not to exercise this right at this time, you may do so later…"

Later would be good, when he had had time to think. No point in firing his one and only shot now.

"You have the right to independent legal advice, free of charge. If you have a preferred legal advisor, you can let us know and we shall do our best to contact them. If you do not have a preferred legal advisor, you may choose from a list of local firms that we keep here. If you choose not to exercise this right at this time, you may do so later..."

Bernard shook his head. Commit to nothing at this stage. He was searched, then his belongings were listed and put in a sealed bag. His belt and shoelaces were removed. Had anyone in history ever really hanged themselves with shoelaces? Finally, he was led down yet another corridor and shown into a cell. There was no other word for it; it was a cell. And if there had been any doubt, the noise that the door made when it closed would have dispelled it.

Bernard sat on his bed and considered his position. The more he considered it, the worse it seemed to be. For a start, he was travelling as Ron Godsmark. The appearance was sufficiently similar and the age, sufficiently close. He had Ron's driving licence and passport. The car was registered in Ron's name. But this fiction could only be maintained for, at best, a couple of hours.

He didn't know exactly how Customs worked, but surely it would only be a matter of time before somebody turned up in Leighton Magna with the intention of searching Ron's cottage. And when they did, they were almost certainly going to find Rutland's king of the bowling green, in residence and very obviously not in a cell in Harwich.

Once that happened, Bernard would be forced to admit that he was not Ron. And it was going to be pretty difficult to persuade anyone that he was an innocent bystander, who had been caught up in events beyond his control, if he was travelling under an alias.

Further, they were sure to ask him about his movements for the past week. He had been careful. He had paid cash everywhere. All his receipts were in a bin in Berlin. All the evidence of his home bottling activities – the corks, the plastic sleeves, even the hot-air stripper – were in a canal near Utrecht. But had he been careful enough? There were CCTV cameras in every major city. If someone was determined enough, his Cavalier could be traced. And some cameras even had number plate recognition. He had travelled on French toll roads; there might be a record somewhere. And he had said that the wine was his. They had made him say it. They hadn't accepted a nod. He had actually said it and that was in an officer's notebook somewhere. Damn!

So, sooner or later, he was going to have to admit to travelling to France on a false passport in a car registered in a false name to buy two cases of the world's worst wine at the factory gate, having passed about a million better wines at about a thousand nearer outlets. And then he was going to have to explain why, having performed this extraordinary shopping expedition, he decided to drive a thousand miles to Berlin. And whatever he told them, he would have no witnesses to verify. He had only met Berti the Limp and the chances of him willingly submitting to be a witness in a court of law were zero.

So, what cards did he have in his hand? He could claim to be acting under duress. He could say that his loved ones were being held captive… but that was hopeless. And it would just involve more of his family. It was bad enough that he had involved Ron.

The only thing that he could think of was to send up a flare, metaphorically, and hope that the security and intelligence services rescued him. And frankly, they had absolutely no incentive to do so. In short, he was well and truly…

But perhaps someone had made a mistake. Some error of procedure or law. A technicality. People were always getting off on technicalities, weren't they? Weren't they? He needed a lawyer.

*

Gates and his more senior colleague were briefing the investigators. They needed just a few minutes to get the facts straight and then why not interview straightaway? The old man had said that he didn't want a lawyer.

"E sez e wants a lawyer now. You boys best go and get yersels a cuppa tea. Be about an hour I 'spect."

The custody officer shrugged. It made no difference to him. He returned to his crossword and gave four down some thought. A momentary glimmer of inspiration crossed his features, then he licked his pencil.

It actually took slightly less than an hour. It was just before noon when the custody officer opened the flap in Bernard's cell door. "Legal advisor," he said, in the same tone he might have used to inform someone that the postman had visited.

Bernard looked up as the door swung open. His eyes widened slightly, but he forced himself to look down again because the custody officer was still present. He waited until the door had closed and the slow, plodding footsteps had receded down the corridor. But it was the other man who spoke first.

"Now, there sits a man who very badly needs some very good advice."

*

The two interviewing officers were of approximately the same age, but the similarity ended there. Darren Greenhalgh was brash, arrogant and vain. He seemed not to realise that he was conducting an interview. Instead, he seemed to be rehearsing his Edinburgh Fringe one-man show called 'Look how clever I am'.

He fired questions at Bernard that were poorly phrased and ambiguous. It was easy to provide vague answers that left multiple escape routes open. Not that it mattered. Darren wasn't particularly interested in the answers. They were just a brief period of annoying noise in between his absolute zingers. He alternated between scorn and sarcasm, and totally failed to follow up on any loose ends, details, inconsistencies. It was like a model in how *not* to interview.

Amar Sahota, on the other hand, was listening. He sat, absorbed, quietly nodding every now and then, occasionally making a brief note. When Darren set off on a monologue dripping with condescension and spite, he leaned back and thumbed through the passport that had been on the table between them.

Eventually, Darren grew tired of his own voice or perhaps he just needed a few seconds to regroup for his next assault, because, by this stage, he was barely asking questions. He turned to Amar, "Have you any questions at this stage?"

Amar nodded. He put the passport down. "Tell me, Mr Godsmark, on what day of the week is your birthday this year?"

Bernard failed to switch gears quickly enough. He had become accustomed to Darren and being able to fend off his questions as deftly as a batsman flicking a wide delivery down to the fine leg boundary. He was almost starting to enjoy himself.

"I'm terribly sorry, young man. I honestly couldn't tell you. When you get to my age, birthdays cease to be quite so important as they used to be."

"You see…" began Amar. He picked up the passport again. "Ronald Albert Godsmark was born on the 29th February 1924. And if I had been born on the 29th February, I'm pretty sure I'd remember that I didn't have a birthday this year. So, my question is this – what is your real name?"

It was all Bernard could do to resist saying 'Bravo'. Instead, he looked at Darren with an expression that he hoped said something like: 'You see? That's how you do it, you impossibly vulgar young ass.'

Bernard looked at his legal advisor and received a small nod in response. "My name is Bernard Albert Taylor. And I was born on the 31st August 1920. That will be a Monday this year," he added, helpfully.

From then on, it was Amar who asked most of the questions. He learned that Bernard had made some very foolish investments and trusted the wrong people. As a result, he had found himself in some financial embarrassment. He had agreed, on behalf of some rather unsavoury people to whom he had found himself financially obligated, to smuggle some drugs. He didn't know what kind. He hadn't asked and he didn't expect to have been told if he had.

He had been handed two cases of wine by a gentleman of Mediterranean appearance in Arles, in the south of France. His instructions were to return home via Berlin and, if questioned, he was to say that he had spent the last week staying with friends in that city. Unfortunately, when he had been stopped by Customs, he had become flustered and forgotten his story. He had been told to travel home and leave his car parked in a position from which it could be seen from the street. He would be contacted at home shortly thereafter.

Ron Godsmark was a neighbour of his who knew nothing of what he had been doing. He had borrowed his driving licence and passport after concocting some cock-and-bull story about a television licence.

Amar questioned him properly. He probed looking for details, looking for facts that could be verified or disproved. He chased down inconsistencies. He sought to eliminate areas of ambiguity. He did a good job. And although, occasionally, his eyes seemed to shine, he maintained the same calm, matter-of-fact tone throughout.

Bernard rather enjoyed witnessing Darren's frustration turning to resentment. But he had no need, no opportunity, to butt in. Amar was proceeding calmly, smoothly, logically. Bernard thought he was wasted as a customs officer.

"Well, that is all the questions we have for the moment." Amar had completely taken control of things by this stage. Darren had been reduced to a slightly bitter spectator. "We may be back a little later. The time is now twelve fifty-nine. The time elapsed counter is reading forty-one minutes and I am suspending the interview now."

Amar removed and labelled the tapes of the interview, sealed one and gathered his papers. He picked up the passport and rose to leave. Bernard sat in silence and watched his interviewers depart. He waited until the door had shut again and the sound of footsteps had receded down the corridor. Only then did he turn to his legal advisor.

"Well, Frank, is that what you wanted?"

The Scotsman fished his pipe from his pocket and began to fill it. "Aye, that'll do. The interviewing officers will now go back and debrief their senior investigation officer on what you've said. The uniformed staff will report on the search of your car and then they'll all be told it was just a training exercise. We'll then have to provide our input to the general debriefing and then we can go home."

"I don't know whether to thank you or curse you, Frank."

"You travelled in a car that had changed ownership a few days ago. You left via Dover; you returned via Harwich – nobody does that. You had no plausible reason for your trip. Of all the cars on the ferry, yours was the only one with a single occupant. And you didn't have a single receipt. That's good in terms of not providing any evidence of where you had been, but it's suspicious as hell. Normal law-abiding people don't behave like that. Take a look at any car returning from a continental holiday and it is full of rubbish like that. You would almost certainly have been pulled."

"And…"

"Even at your age, even with your decades of public service, your knighthood, your connections, you would have gone down – not for ten years, maybe not even for two, but you would have gone down." There was a pause while Frank lit his pipe. "You really are a fool, Bernard."

"They murdered my friends, Frank. And they'll get off scot-free."

"Not quite scot-free," said Frank. "I pulled every string I had available to me. And one or two others, too. In forty years, I never fitted anybody up. I didn't let anyone else do it either. And I wasn't going to let you do it. They'll be prosecuted for VAT fraud. I know that means little to you, but they did it and it can be proved. That is what counts." He glanced at his watch. "If everything's gone to plan, they will have been arrested by now."

"Your plan, Frank?"

"And here's another plan. We're going home. That wine is going to the bottom of Rutland Water and you are never going to pull a stunt like this again."

Bernard looked a little shamefaced.

"And as for involving Ron. That was unforgiveable!"

"He was happy to help."

Frank could not disguise the scorn in his voice. He liked Bernard, but at the end of the day he was a product of the bourgeoise, the establishment. In his younger days, he would have called him 'The Class Enemy'.

"Happy to help? He was a corporal. You were a brigadier. That's why he agreed."

"You're wrong, Frank. It's not that at all. No, you are quite wrong. He helped me because... because he's my brother."

A lesser man might have choked on his pipe. Frank merely gave a slightly larger than usual puff. There was silence while Frank tried to process this information. "Ah! Yes, of course. The smoke-grey eyes, the Roman nose, the gentleman father and you left the village when you were three. Ah!"

"Ron's mother was a maid at the vicarage. We went to India. My father, our father, didn't learn about Ron's mother until we had arrived. He provided for her, a little, I think. I wasn't told. I was never told."

"So how?"

"I saw him at the war memorial. Saw the medal ribbon and looked him up. It isn't that hard if you have friends in the military records office. He was a hero, you know."

"I know he was."

THIRTY

Joachim Keller was dressed and ready for work when he answered the door. Monster identified himself and stepped inside, uninvited.

"I do not permit…"

"Is Mrs Keller here?"

"I do not permit."

"Mr Keller, my name is Bolton. I am an officer of Customs and Excise. I am arresting you on suspicion of being knowingly concerned in the fraudulent evasion of Value Added Tax. I also have a warrant to search these premises. Where is Mrs Keller?"

At that moment, Hanna Keller appeared at the top of the stairs. She was not dressed and ready for work, unless she had a second job as a model specialising in silk dressing gowns. Anjali hurried up the stairs to arrest her and supervise her dressing. Since Joachim was ready to go, it was decided that he would be taken to Leighton Hall to witness the search there. Hanna could witness the search of their home.

"But what about Erich?"

"Who is Erich, Mr Keller?"

"My dog."

Monster had a horrible feeling about this. "What type of dog?"

"He is, you call him, a German Shepherd."

Oh, bloody hell! "Is he a friendly dog?"

"Not particularly."

Oh, bloody hell! "Where is he?"

"The kitchen, I think."

Joe Lake indicated the back of the house. "This way?"

He needn't have asked; Erich was already making his presence known by throwing himself against the door and treating everybody to his *Hound of the Baskervilles* impression.

Oh bloody, bloody, bloody hell!

"I'll call the old bill dog unit," said Joe.

"Tell them to hurry."

Monster and Alan put Joachim in the back of their car. Monster made two brief phone calls and then they set off to Leighton Hall. Back in the house, Hanna Keller was dressed. Joe had expected her to be making as much noise as the dog, but instead she was exceptionally stoic. She said barely a word as she sat on the sofa in the front room while the search commenced.

On television, house searches take about ten minutes and the intrepid investigator finds the key piece of evidence among a huge pile of documents and realises its significance right away. This is not what happened at The Old Vicarage, Ashcombe. It is not what happens anywhere.

While Mrs Keller was getting dressed, the living room was searched thoroughly. That didn't take long. In houses as big as Ashcombe's Old Vicarage, where there are multiple reception rooms, the main living room is usually light on documents. And in VAT fraud investigations, evidence is mostly documents. The search was finished before Mrs Keller was dressed and so she was shown into what was now a 'clean' room, with one officer left to supervise her.

A pair of officers found and started on the study. There was only one desk, but two walls were lined with bookshelves containing lever arch and box files. In Hollywood, our hero would take one from the shelf and immediately find a list of transactions involving Swiss banks, Nazi gold, the illuminati, three cardinals and a third cousin of the queen who was also a Romanoff.

In Rutland, that is not what happened. The junior of the two officers, Paul Osborne in this case, started listing the files, labelling them and putting them in bags that he then sealed. He recorded the details of the file, the label and the seal number in his notebook. And then he did the same thing a further ninety-nine times.

The senior of the two officers, in this case Ted, and this is never explicitly expressed because it is not necessary, took the potentially more interesting area of the desk itself. In this case, the desk wasn't really a treasure trove. It mostly contained exactly the same sort of documents, just the ones that hadn't been filed yet.

There were a few diaries – those were often interesting – and some address books – likewise. Written inside the notebooks were the details of various Swiss bank accounts, passwords, access codes and others, too, for the Cayman Islands and the Virgin Islands, of both the US and British varieties.

Ted didn't know this, of course [I keep telling you, that's not how it works]. Somebody would work that out much, much later, back at the office while enjoying a cup of tea and a Jaffa Cake. Each was labelled. Each was bagged. Each was sealed. Each was noted. The officer then turned his attention to the desk itself. He prodded and poked, hoping for secret doors to spring open. None did. He removed the drawers and examined the undersides. Again, nothing. Then, cursing and grumbling, he got down on all fours and examined the underside of the desk with the aid of a torch. Nothing.

Ted stretched and then mooched about the room in what he hoped was a thoughtful manner. He lifted the corner of a couple of framed prints on the wall. Safes behind portraits were a bit *Scooby-Doo*, but you would feel pretty foolish if you didn't check. Then, he ran his hands down the edge of the curtains feeling for concealed packages. Nothing. That left floor safes. Ted tried to lift a corner of the carpet, but it was proving a bit difficult. Nobody at the briefing had said that they were confident there was a floor safe and he didn't feel like tearing up the carpet. Paul still had about twenty folders to label and bag, anyway, and it would be impossible to do so while he was still kneeling on the floor.

Ted had been an investigator many years. He was experienced. He knew the signs. He could read the situation. And right now, the situation was that he could afford to pop outside for five minutes and have a cigarette.

He passed through the dining room on his way through some French doors that led to the back garden. He mooched about the garden for a bit. He poked a pile of grass clippings with his toe. He lifted the lid on a barbecue. He even looked in the little shelter on the bird table. He saw a water butt in one corner. A water butt would be a good concealment. Many years ago, when Ted had worked at Immingham Docks, he and his colleague had often found things hidden in barrels. He lifted the lid, but the butt was almost empty. It was July, after all.

Joe Lake had awarded himself a roving brief. He wandered from room to room with his hands in his pockets, hoping that inspiration would strike. He wanted to find evidence, of course he did, but only if it was really important. He didn't want to be in the position of Paul Osborne, who would be sure to be called to give evidence in court of all the files that he had gathered and that would be 'his' exhibits. So, he wandered from room to room until he reached what appeared to be Joachim and Hanna Keller's bedroom. Alice Doctrove was searching this room.

"I've done the bedroom and the bathroom," she said. "I've just got to do the dressing room."

Joe wandered about uselessly. He pulled out a drawer of a bedside table and checked if anything was taped to the underside. Then, he did the same on the other side of the bed.

"Joe! Joe, come and look at this."

"What is it?" he walked towards the dressing room. If it had been a male officer, it would have been a fifty-fifty chance that some lingerie or sex toys had been found, but with Alice that seemed less likely.

"Looks like a safe."

Alice was kneeling in front of a wardrobe. Joe couldn't see what she had found.

"Key or combination?"

"Keypad."

"Okay, you get the camera kit. I shall ask Mrs Keller if she'd like to tell us the code."

*

Joe entered the living room. Hanna Keller was sitting on the sofa. She was upright, distant; she was haughty. Is it possible to sit in a haughty fashion? Yes, it is. She looked like Queen Victoria in one of her unamused moods. Or Women's Institute president who has been asked to share a waiting room with three slightly drunk football fans.

"Mrs Keller, there is a safe in the wardrobe in your dressing room. Would you mind telling me the combination?"

Hanna Keller's expression was a cocktail of defiance, scorn and, perhaps, just a soupçon of condescension. Who was this vulgar little tax man and why did he think that she would admit to any knowledge of any safe, or its contents? Why did he think that she would admit anything at all? And tell him the combination? It was pathetic, laughable, absurd! Actually, she was slightly affronted that he had even posed the question.

Joe shrugged and made a note in his notebook. When he returned upstairs, Alice was taking photographs. First the bedroom and the entrance to the dressing room, which was through a sort of arch, then the wardrobe with the doors closed, another with the doors open and finally the safe itself.

Joe knelt down and examined the safe. It was about the size of two shoeboxes. What he was about to do now would either make him look super, super cool or slightly foolish. Did he want more witnesses in case it was the super-cool outcome? Probably not. It was a bit unlikely.

He took a biro from his pocket and reversed it in his hand, such that the blunt end was facing forward. Using the biro, he pressed two... two... zero... six... nothing happened. Then he pressed seven... four. There was a tiny beep. A green light flashed beside the keypad and the door swung open a quarter of an inch.

"She told you the combination?" Alice was genuinely surprised.

"Nope. Just a lucky guess."

Joe got out of the way so that Alice could take another photograph. He glanced at his watch and made a note. Alice stepped back and Joe knelt again. He pulled the door fully open. He leant to one side and heard the shutter click again. He put on a pair of latex gloves and reached inside.

"Clucking Bell!" he said, or something similar. He withdrew the contents of the safe and placed them on the floor. "We need Mrs Keller up here."

Hanna Keller upright was exactly the same as seated. Haughty, aloof, a studied indifference, but with the added ingredient of being puzzled and worried as to how the safe had been opened. Had her foolish husband given them the code? Surely, he wouldn't be so stupid!

Joe began by fanning out the eight passports like a hand of cards. Two British, two Swiss, two German, two Canadian. The names were all different, but the pictures were all the same. No, not the same pictures, but pictures of the same two people, taken at different times, or at least wearing different clothes. He noted the details in his notebook. Alice put them in plastic bags.

Next came the money. Sterling, deutschmarks, Swiss francs, US dollars, Canadian dollars. It all had to be counted and noted. More photographs. Joe offered Mrs Keller the opportunity to verify the numbers and sign his notebook. She didn't say a word, but she met his eyes and wouldn't look away.

Then, there were the guns. Joe didn't know very much about guns. They were both small automatics and they were slightly different. The first looked a bit like James Bond's gun, but the end of the barrel was tapped with a screw end like a piece of plumbing. Was this what a gun adapted to take a silencer looked like? Probably.

The second was more conventional. There was a five-pointed star on the grip. He noted the serial numbers and he ejected the magazines (he had been on a course). Finally, he pulled back the slider to eject any cartridge that there might have been in the chamber, but there wasn't one.

"Gun bag!" Alice shouted down the stairs. Then, she took a few more photographs.

Paul Osborne arrived a few minutes later with two small Kevlar bags. The idea was that if you put the guns in properly, the barrel would be facing a thick wad of Kevlar and it didn't matter if the gun discharged. Joe had emptied them, but it couldn't hurt to be extra safe.

Joe had never seen a silencer before, except in films or on television, but he recognised it straightaway. More photographs.

Finally, at the very back of the safe was one last item. Joe placed it on the carpet so it, too, could be photographed.

"Is that? Is that a dagger?"

"Dagger, commando knife, something like that."

*

Joachim Keller was sitting on a chair in his office. Not his chair. He was sitting in one of the two chairs where he took his morning coffee, sometimes in the company of his wife, sometimes alone. His chair had been pushed back and an officer was searching his desk. Down the corridor, he could hear other officers searching the filing cabinets.

Joachim had only been in England for less than five years. His English wasn't perfect and he didn't know the country well. He knew, or he thought he knew, that there was no financial police such as the Italian Guardia di Finanza or the Dutch FIOD. But these people seemed very similar. They didn't carry sidearms, it was true, but English police didn't, did they? These people had search warrants. They had arrested him, handcuffed him. They were to be taken seriously. This was no routine check.

He had a vague idea that he was entitled to a lawyer, but nobody had said this to him. He had no idea what it was to be a suspect in a Western country. Back home, he would simply have waved his identification or his party card and ninety-nine per cent of all problems would disappear. Drink-driving? Please allow us to drive you home. Can't afford to wait for a traffic light to change? Perhaps you would allow us to escort you. He decided that he should say nothing, keep his options open. Hanna, he knew, would do the same.

The door to his office opened. A senior officer entered – Joachim assumed he was senior, as he was a little older than the others. He raised his eyebrows in the direction of the officer searching his desk.

"Usual sort of stuff," the searching officer said. "Next door?"

"Gold mine!" the senior officer replied, then he turned and looked directly at Joachim. He smiled at him. It was not a pleasant smile.

THIRTY-ONE

As far as the investigators were concerned, they were dealing with a greedy and dishonest businessman. They had no idea that they were dealing with somebody who ought to have been a highly trained Stasi agent proficient in the art of resisting interrogation. Keller was both, of course, but, unfortunately for him, he thought he was the latter and behaved in interview far more like the former.

It took nearly three hours to search Leighton Hall and so it was almost lunchtime before he was brought to Leicestershire police headquarters for questioning. Like all detainees, he was told that he had the right to free and independent legal advice. And like most, he elected to be represented by the duty solicitor.

The life of a duty solicitor is neither an easy nor a happy one. And an awful lot of the time, it is not a particularly rewarding one either. Their working lives are mostly concerned with representing people accused of simple and low-level crimes. Motoring offences, petty theft or receiving stolen goods. Occasionally, they might have a client accused of credit card fraud.

But VAT carousel fraud is complicated. Monster had tried to explain it three times. By the end of the final explanation, Pete Gillard still didn't fully understand, but he was too embarrassed to say so. He nodded and went to have a conference with his client.

He tried to explain to Mr Keller of what he was suspected, but he didn't seem interested. Rather he was supremely confident, indifferent almost to what was to come. What had he to fear from these little tax people with their labels and their forms? They had seemed almost apologetic when they had handcuffed him. Was this the much-feared Customs and Excise? The law enforcement of the decadent west was weak and ineffective. He tried to imagine how his former colleagues would have handled somebody accused of stealing a million pounds of the people's money. They certainly wouldn't have been offered a cup of tea. They wouldn't have had their so-called rights painstakingly explained to them.

This was a waste of his time. They were pathetic. And this lawyer! Imagine, just imagine, if this man was all that genuinely stood between him and incarceration. It was laughable. He didn't even understand carousel fraud. Keller didn't need him or his advice. He just needed the time that asking for a solicitor had bought him. Time to weave a story that would bewilder, confuse and ultimately satisfy these pathetic bean counters.

Even if he had properly understood carousel fraud and appreciated the nature of the evidence against his client, Pete Gillard's advice would have been the same. Say nothing. If Pete had ever bothered to work it out – and he hadn't; life was too short – he would have estimated that he provided the same advice to ninety per cent of his clients. Most, wisely, followed this advice.

Some were genuinely innocent and anxious to explain away a dreadful misunderstanding and a few were guilty as hell, but thought they could talk themselves out of trouble. In many cases, this was because they were encouraged by having previously persuaded themselves that they were innocent.

Then, there was the final and smallest category: those who knew they were guilty, but nevertheless believed that they were clever enough to escape justice through their razor-sharp intellect.

Pete knew almost before Keller had said anything that he was going to be in this last category. He was going to be here all night and possibly much of the next day.

Keller made just about every mistake that it was possible to make in an interview. He began by telling a provable lie. Many officers regarded a full and frank confession as the Shangri-La of investigative interviewing, but a good provable lie was almost as valuable.

Keller began by saying that he was Joachim Hans Keller and that he had never used any other name. This was a statement he would later regret, when passports in that and three other names were pushed under his nose.

Then, he conceded that a document that had been found on his desk had been written by him and was a genuine example of his handwriting. In time, the forensic scientists in the Questioned Documents section of the Laboratory of the Government Chemist would be asked to offer their professional opinion as to the author of various Companies House and VAT forms. Keller would be proved to have completed forms in at least a dozen different names.

Keller denied any knowledge of any of the people listed as the directors or company officers of the various companies used as part of the fraud. He denied knowing anything about them and claimed never to have heard of their addresses.

This was doubly foolish since all these documents had been found in his filing system and because all the names used as fictitious directors of the various companies had all been clients of Leighton Hall. Twelve different happy couples had unknowingly each become directors of businesses who conducted a huge volume of trade in mobile phones and integrated circuits, mostly between each other.

Keller was asked for the combination of the safe in his home. He initially denied knowledge of any safe, but then he changed his mind and gave a false number. He was then asked to give the code for the alarm system at Leighton Hall and claimed that he did not know it. But it was written in his address book. He claimed to know nothing of the bank accounts opened using application forms completed in his handwriting.

After forty-five minutes, the tapes had reached the end and there was a short pause. He was, again, offered a cup of tea. These people were fools. He began to hope that he would be home in time for dinner. Each question had been delivered in an unemotional tone. Each answer accepted without question or challenge. They had even thanked him for some of his denials.

*

Two doors down the corridor, in Interview Room 4, Hanna Keller was also being interviewed. She shared her husband's contempt for Customs and Excise, indeed for all western law enforcement. The only thing that created the tiniest doubt in her mind had been the fact that they had been able to open the safe. But then she reflected upon the fact that it shared a code with the alarm system at Leighton Hall. Somebody at the hall must have provided the number and they had made a lucky guess. Nothing to worry about.

Like Joachim, she had decided that it would be helpful to buy herself a little time and also to put customs under pressure. She didn't know the details, but somewhere in the back of her mind she had the idea that there were limits as to how long she could be held for questioning. The more she slowed things down, the better her chances of being released when the time ran out. She didn't want a solicitor, though. What possible use could one of them be? And she didn't need an interpreter. She had been fluent in English since university and lived in the country for five years. But an interpreter would definitely slow things down and it would give her twice as long to think about and respond to any questions. Not that she intended to answer any.

Interviews with an interpreter, even interviews with questions but no answers, take at least twice as long. The first forty-five-minute tape covered just twenty questions. Hanna Keller sat and listened carefully as each question was asked in English and then again when it was asked in German by the interpreter. Inwardly, she was correcting the translation. Externally, she didn't respond at all. It wasn't just that she said nothing, she was utterly impassive. There was no reaction of any kind, no facial expression, no body language. It was like interviewing a sphinx.

The interviewers were not the least concerned. They went through their lists of questions indifferent to the total lack of response. Hanna could explain later why she had chosen to advance no defence.

When the first tape was finished, they moved immediately to a second and kept questioning. Was Hanna Keller the only name she had used? Who was Adelade Siegenthaler? Did she agree that the photograph in Siegenthaler's Swiss passport looked a lot like her? What about Magda Kuhn? Didn't she think that that passport photograph looked a lot like her? Had she ever been to Canada? Was the Canadian passport holder, Magda Bierhof, her?

Then, question after question regarding Leighton Hall. Who owned it? When had it been bought? Where did the funds come from? What was its turnover? What was its profit? Did she or her husband have any other business interests?

The list of the 'carousel' companies was read. Did she know this one? Did she know that one? What about these people? Were they customers of Leighton Hall? Why were they also directors of these companies? It was like an irresistible force of questions against an immovable interviewee.

After two tapes, they took a break. Hanna was escorted back to a cell. The officers adjourned to the canteen to debrief the others as to what had been learned (almost nothing) and to learn what had emerged from Joachim's interview.

*

Joe Lake was in the canteen, swearing. The object of his profanity was a vending machine. It had robbed him of fifty pence and not dispensed G6, a Kit Kat. He was inwardly debating whether to give the machine a hefty kick, not because he expected that to provide him with any chocolate, but because he thought it might make him feel better. He had more or less decided to give the whole thing a good shake when he sensed a presence behind him. Glancing over his left shoulder, he saw a police sergeant. Or possibly several police sergeants, who had been merged into one large law enforcement unit to save on the cost of helmets and boots. The man was simply a giant.

"Robbed you, has it?"

Truly, the deductive reasoning of a twenty-stone police officer was quite a thing. Joe indicated that it was so. The giant grunted and pulled the machine towards him such that it was now at a roughly thirty-degree angle.

"Turn it on and off again a few times," he suggested.

Joe did as he was advised and was rewarded with not one Kit Kat, but two, and a Twix as a bonus. The giant picked up one of the Kit Kats. "Commission," he explained. And he strode off, each pace covering about a furlong and a half.

Joe thought this perfectly fair. He slipped the Twix in his pocket and started to unwrap the Kit Kat when his phone rang.

"It's me. Can you talk?"

"Yeah, give me a second." Joe left the canteen and took up a position halfway down a flight of stairs, where he could see anyone coming from above or below. "What's up, Frank?"

"You tell me."

"Knocked it this morning. Lifted both Kellers at their home address. Warrant for there, warrant for the hall. I've not seen it myself, but apparently the place was full of evidence, all neatly filed. Early estimates are between half a million and a million."

"Good, good. Anything else?"

Joe had a powerful feeling that Frank knew there was, but

he wouldn't give him the satisfaction of telling him straightaway. "She's gone no comment. He's talking himself into prison. No confession yet, but enough provable lies to sink him."

It was silent on the other end of the line.

"Oh, and you were right about the combination. Two two zero six seven four. What's that? The date Germany won the World Cup?"

"No, no, just the opposite, in fact. What was in the safe?"

"A big stack of cash, various currencies, four passports apiece, various nationalities."

"And?"

"And what?"

"Joseph!" Frank McBride had a way of making those two syllables take Joe right back to standing in front of the head teacher, having to admit or atone for some malfeasance.

"Two automatics, a silencer and a commando knife."

"Get ballistics to do whatever the hell it is they do and get whatever the hell it is they produce to Europol. Does Europol cover Switzerland?"

"No idea."

"Well, if they don't, get it to Switzerland. And make sure they don't get bail."

"It's not my case, Frank."

"And I'm retired. I have every faith in you, Joseph." There was a very long pause. "And thank you. I really mean it, thank you. I owe you one."

Frank McBride owed him one. If that wasn't worth a celebratory Kit Kat, then Joe didn't know what was.

*

There was time for one more interview of Keller before tucking him up for the night. Detained persons had rights and one of them was eight hours' uninterrupted rest. Monster thought that they might have time for one forty-five minute tape. He decided to explore the issue of the safe and its contents. Strictly speaking, it wasn't exactly germane to the issue under investigation. You don't usually need a silenced pistol or a dagger to commit a VAT fraud, but Monster thought that it might make a nice discrete topic lasting no more than forty-five minutes. Keller seized on the opportunity to make his situation immeasurably worse.

"You have a safe in your house. Can you tell us the combination?"

"No, I don't know it. It is my wife's safe. I think she keeps her jewellery in it."

"Are you sure you don't know it?"

"I'm sure."

"And do you know its contents?"

"No. I don't know. It's my wife's safe. I assume that she keeps her jewellery in it, but I don't know."

"We found a large sum in cash in that safe."

Keller was confused. Hadn't they said they didn't know the combination? No, they had asked him if he knew it. Was that a clever trick? Probably not. There was nothing about this pair that suggested they were clever – not as clever as him, anyway.

"Do you know anything about that?"

"No."

"We also found some passports?"

"I know nothing about that."

And then it began – the unbearable monotone, the indefatigable questioning, the passports pushed under his nose. Keller noticed that in one of them he was wearing the tie that he currently had on. Fortunately, these fools hadn't noticed. Yes, they had. Would he please describe the tie he was wearing? Would he please describe the tie in the photograph of the Canadian, Bierhoff?

Then, they wanted to know about the pistols. And the knife. He had told Hanna to get rid of the knife. Begged her, but she wouldn't – "But it is my signature, I am *Die Klinge*." It was sheer vanity. Why would you want to keep your signature weapon? It was foolishness!

"So, these all belong to your wife?"

Keller felt like he was at the top of a roller coaster. There was nothing he could now do to influence the journey. He just had to endure the ride. He didn't like roller coasters and he didn't like the way this interview was heading. He looked at his solicitor. He shrugged; a shrug that seemed to say 'I told you not to answer questions. I can't rescue you now.' He decided to ask for a break so that he could seek legal advice.

*

Pete Gillard now knew a great deal more about carousel fraud than he had known a few hours earlier. He had pieced a certain amount together from the officers' questions. He had also spoken to one of the senior partners at his firm. If a fellow lawyer had asked him to assess the situation, he would have said that it was clear to him that Keller had a certain level of legal exposure. If anyone else had asked him, and Keller did, he would have said that he was absolutely screwed.

"Mr Keller, the evidence is overwhelming. I consider the chances of you being charged with an offence to be one hundred per cent and your chances of conviction about the same. And having passports in four different names from four different countries means that your chances of bail are zero."

"So, I will not be released tonight?"

"No. And I anticipate further charges relating to the passports and the firearms. The cash in the safe will be seized. There will be a Criminal Compensation Order. They will want their money back. All of it. I anticipate many years in prison, followed by deportation."

Under English law, the testimony of a co-defendant cannot ordinarily be used as evidence. But Joachim Keller didn't know this. He was from an entirely different legal background. He was familiar with the prisoner's dilemma, of course: keep silent and hope your partner does the same, or confess first to earn leniency.

In East Germany, it wasn't much of a dilemma. Once you were being interviewed, there was no escape and the smart move was always to confess early and as fully as possible, while shifting as much blame as possible onto other people. This is exactly what Joachim Keller attempted to do. In the end, it took three tapes.

He listed the people Hanna Keller had killed in Berlin – there were six that he knew of and, since, the two in Switzerland, the one in France. He told them all about the cava and cocaine scheme. There had been three importations, each of a kilogramme. Surely that would get their attention. Then, he told them about George Bowman.

But no matter how much he told them, the questioning continued exactly as before. The same dispassionate requests for details, for dates, the names of other witnesses, the same polite gratitude. Why were these people so foolish? Didn't they realise that this was the case of their lives? It was like being interviewed by speak-your-weight machines. They just went on and on, making the occasional note.

"I am Captain Jakob Schneider, formerly of the State Security Service of the German Democratic Republic. I am privy to highly sensitive information. I know the whereabouts of much hidden assets."

They couldn't care less. They only wanted to know about Value Added Tax. *These people!*

*

When Hanna Keller was told that her husband had ratted on her, she refused to believe it. These people were pathetic. Did they honestly think that she would fall for as transparent a ruse as that?

Her husband? Betray her like that? A captain in the Stasi break under questioning from these people? *These* people?

And then came the details. Details that only Joachim could have known. It was true. He had betrayed her. Well, two could play at that game.

Her confession required four tapes. Although, to be fair, the confession to VAT fraud had only taken one. These tiny little people. They insisted on hearing about that first. She admitted everything – yes, yes, she had done it all. Now, let's get on to the good stuff about my husband. There were three tapes of dishing the dirt on Joachim. By the end, the investigators' heads were swimming.

And in the morning, the officers who had interviewed the Kellers had to tell the whole story again to a man from the Intelligence Service, who said that his name was Harris.

THIRTY-TWO

Frank had taken the children to see Thomas the Tank Engine. In truth, Frankie wasn't quite as obsessed with Thomas as he had been a year or two earlier and Maisie was, at best, ambivalent. That wasn't the point. Michelle and Simon needed the day to themselves. It was a big decision. And it needed to be made now.

The Great Central Railway that ran between Leicester and Loughborough was, in many respects, very like the dozens of other heritage railways that groups of hard-working and slightly obsessed enthusiasts had established across the country. Frank wasn't really an enthusiast. He hadn't been a trainspotter as a boy and he certainly hadn't been able to afford a train set. But it would be a nice day out. There would be ice creams and soot and that particular variety of nostalgia that exults in a rare Great Western locomotive and an LNER dining car and overlooks the fact that, authentically speaking, one should not be attached to the other.

Frank didn't know what Simon and Michelle would decide. They didn't know themselves. He could influence them, if he wanted to. He could probably put his thumb on the scales sufficiently hard enough to engineer his desired outcome.

He knew that he was a factor in the calculation. He could have emphasised how lonely he would be, sitting in a converted barn in the middle of nowhere. He could have hinted that his health was so poor that he couldn't visit them in Spain, that the children would forget him. There were a hundred tricks and he could have deployed whichever was best calculated to achieve the desired result, like a golfer pulling the correct club from a bag. But Simon and Michelle were an example of the sort of happy family life that was possible when Frank McBride didn't get what he wanted. So, he had almost decided that he would not interfere. Almost.

*

The dining room table was covered in estate agents' details, brochures for schools, leaflets for language schools and, in the centre, the terms of Simon's proposed contract.

When Sid had casually mentioned it at the barbecue, Simon had thought that it was a suggestion, that he would have plenty of time to decide. No. No, it had all got very detailed, very specific and very real very fast. Since then, it had become increasingly clear that he was expected to accept. He had been flattered at first. And it seemed exciting. Michelle had been very supportive. Whatever he decided was fine with her, at least that was what she had said. Since then, things had been put on a more formal footing. Sid had spoken of 'a couple of years'. Now that it was on paper, it was a minimum of three years with an expectation that he remain in Madrid for five.

Simon was reading the contract again. The numbers were large, but were they? There was a large allowance for education, but all figures in pesetas looked large and how much did these fancy international schools cost? Well, Michelle was working on that.

And the houses – large, spacious, quite a lot of them had swimming pools. But were they in a good area? How long would it take to drive to work? How much did cars cost? Would they need two? What was Madrid traffic like? It wasn't like Rutland traffic. He was sure of that. How would Michelle cope with driving on the wrong side of the road in a foreign capital? How would he?

Michelle, after a lot of swearing – including a few words that Simon didn't think she knew, much less expected her to use – had connected the computer to the internet. She had found a site relating to British ex-pats in Madrid. She now knew the going rate for maids. Yes, maids – there was an allowance. It was expected that they would employ a maid. If Frankie had been a year younger, they would have qualified for a nanny, too.

It wasn't the children that concerned Simon. He was confident that they would adapt and thrive. And he certainly wasn't concerned about Frank, except insofar as he knew that Michelle was. It was Michelle. Was she really willing to be a loyal company wife? Preparing dinner for the boss, making small talk with the other company wives at barbecues? If she said 'yes', did she really mean it? How could he tell?

Michelle was sorting through the estate agents' details. Putting them in two piles of roughly equal size. Every now and then, she would consult the computer. She moved one document from one pile to the other. Occasionally, she would make a note on a pad. Simon decided not to interfere.

Eventually, Michelle seemed to have finished her research. She rose in what Simon thought was a very 'Well, that's decided' type of manner and headed for the kitchen, calling, "Sandwich?" over her shoulder.

Simon decided to examine the notebook. It was pointless. Either Michelle's handwriting was atrocious or she had invented an entirely new alphabet. It looked like it was written in Klingon or by an eminent brain surgeon.

*

Emma didn't normally enjoy conspiracies and her experience of the previous few weeks had far from whetted her appetite. But she had to admit she was rather enjoying this one. Or rather these two, because she was a conspirator with her grandfather in a scheme targeted at Frank and she was a conspirator with Frank in a conspiracy aimed at her grandfather. Also common to both conspiracies was Ron Godsmark.

Ron was essential for the first conspiracy because Frank and Emma knew next to nothing about dogs. While it was true that Frank possessed the most faithful, obedient, friendly and loving dog in the world, the credit for this lay entirely elsewhere. Emma's home had never had a dog because her father was frightened of them, together with spiders, squirrels and, for some reason, guinea pigs.

But Ron was a genuine countryman. He had owned dogs his whole life and had supplemented his income, and his cooking pot, by beating on behalf of local shoots for years. Ron was, therefore, the chairman of the selection committee. Emma was market research and Frank was finance.

Emma had identified a litter of puppies for sale in Market Harborough and Ron had chosen a bitch that, to Emma's eyes, looked identical to its siblings. But Ron was adamant that she was the pick of the litter.

"That's the one," he had said.

*

Strictly speaking, Ron wasn't essential for the second conspiracy, but Emma insisted that he be included. Strictly speaking, Emma wasn't required either, since she had to admit she knew nothing about conveyancing (Land Law was a second-year subject). The committee for this scheme was far simpler. Selection was moot. Research was unnecessary and Bernard was providing the finance.

It had simply never occurred to Bernard that Frank might not want to go along with his scheme. That was the problem with being a brigadier, she supposed; he just assumed that people would do what he wanted.

*

Simon had given up trying to decipher Michelle's notes. He turned his attention to the two piles of house details. Perhaps there would be some clue there. He started with the shorter pile. There were seven sets of details. On some, she had marked various passages with an asterisk. He sifted quickly through them. What had they in common? They all had pools, was that it? No, this one hadn't– she had actually written 'No pool' in the margin. Wait! They all had a second bedroom with an en-suite bathroom. She couldn't be thinking... Oh yes, she was! This one had an actual granny flat. Or, in this case, a grandpa flat.

Simon wasn't sure how he felt about that. He liked Frank. And it was useful having an on-site babysitter. But there was a difference between on-site and live-in. And what about that pipe? Was this Michelle's price for agreeing to go to Spain? What about that dog?

Just then, Simon heard the sound of tyres on gravel. That would be Frank returning with the kids. He decided that he needed to be present to prevent Michelle saying anything to Frank before they had had a chance to discuss things.

But it wasn't Frank's old Ford in the farmyard. It was Ron's even older Austin Maestro. In the passenger seat was a young woman that Simon had seen once or twice in the village. She was someone's granddaughter and was working up at the hall for the summer. She hurried from the passenger seat and rushed to the rear of the car. Ron made the same journey, but at a more measured pace.

Emma – that's right, her name was Emma – opened the boot.

There was the sound of excited yapping and she removed a tiny grey bundle.

"Easy now, let her settle."

Simon looked at Michelle, who had emerged from the kitchen holding two mugs of tea. From her expression, she had no more understanding of what was going on than he did himself.

"S'a present," explained Ron. "For Bernard... from Frank," he added in what he no doubt thought was a helpful manner.

Simon looked again at Michelle. Michelle looked at Simon. She gave a tiny shrug. They both had many questions, but the only ones being posed at the moment were on the subject of who was a good girl, who was a beautiful girl and indeed who was a beautiful good girl. But the range of questions was likely to be expanded quite soon because, at that moment, Frank's Ford arrived with Maisie and Frankie Junior.

Jesse Owens was quite quick off the mark and Muhammed Ali was said to have extraordinary reactions, but neither of them could have matched Maisie in the race from Frank's car to an eight-week-old puppy. Maisie posed many of the same questions that had already been raised on the subject of the identity of the good and beautiful. But Frankie had a different question.

"What's his name?"

"She's a girl puppy," explained Frank. "She's a present for my friend, Bernard. He gets to choose the name."

"I think he should call her 'Lady', like in *Lady and the Tramp*."

"I think he should call her 'Scooby-Doo'."

"That's a boy's name."

"No, it isn't. Not necess... Not nessy, doesn't have to be. Does it, Mummy?"

Frankie turned towards Michelle and that is when she saw his face for the first time since he had arrived home.

"Francis!"

Uh oh.

"Francis Anthony Nicholson! Look at the state of your face! What have you been doing?"

"I'm going to be a steam engine driver."

"You're going for a bath. Right now. And you, Maisie."

Of course, separating small children and puppies is not something that can be achieved by verbal orders alone. There must be cajoling, promises, threats and often actual manhandling. It was full fifteen minutes before the two children, who had self-administered enough axel grease to be quoted on the international markets as standalone oil reserves, had been ushered into the house.

*

Maisie and Frankie had extracted promises that the puppy would still be on the premises when they had finished their baths, so Simon, Frank, Ron, Emma, the puppy with no name and Rocky were all drinking tea in the kitchen.

Frank saw the estate agents' details. It took him a lot less time than Simon to understand their significance. His eyes met Simon's.

"Don't worry. I'm not coming to Spain. You go. It will be good for the kids."

"But what will you do?"

"I'll manage. Something will turn up."

Emma and Ron exchanged glances.

*

Emma and Ron, together with Frank and inevitably Rocky, set off on the short journey to The Old Vicarage. Emma pushed open the back door to the kitchen and set the Weimaraner puppy on the floor. She trotted over to Bernard and sat in front of him.

"She's beautiful. What's she called?"

"Your dog," said Frank. "She's called whatever you like."

Bernard thought for a moment. "Brunhilde."

"Really?"

"I had a very good friend who had a dog called Brunhilde. Nasty spiteful little thing, it was, but still... Brunhilde."

"Well, it's your dog."

"Thank you, Frank. Actually, I have a little present for you, too."

EPILOGUE

Frank grunted. He was not, and he had never been, a handyman. He had done the bare minimum of little jobs around the house – part of the reason for his two divorces, no doubt. And now he was standing on a rather unstable stepladder, remembering why he usually preferred to employ a professional.

But he had wanted to do this himself. He didn't really understand why. Technically, it wasn't even legally required anymore, but Frank wanted it done and he wanted to do it himself. He gingerly descended and folded the stepladder, then rested it against the wall. He took two steps back to admire – well, not his work exactly. It was not perfect, but to admire what it signified.

Francis Daniel McBride
Licensed to sell beers, wines and spirits
For consumption on or off the premises

The grand reopening would be on Saturday. The pub had been closed for two weeks for refurbishment. Normally this indicated that the new landlord wanted to make his premises more upmarket, more luxurious and more fashionable. Frank had done the opposite. Most people engaged a professional interior designer to renovate their pubs. Frank had relied on Ron Godsmark's memory of what The Old Volunteer had been like fifty years ago.

Frank had stripped the carpet from the small bar, now renamed 'the public bar'. It had been a pleasant surprise to find the original stone flags underneath. He had removed the well upholstered seating, too. That was now an old church pew and a handful of hard wooden chairs. The tables had been allowed to remain, some of them, and the old sepia prints – in fact, there was an extra one of those – but the horse brasses had gone. They had been added to the lounge bar, which was mostly unaltered.

If you looked very closely, you would have noticed that one of the horse brasses was an image of a handsome young man. Only Frank knew who he was and even he had no idea where Joe Lake had found a Yuri Gagarin horse brass. There was now a dartboard and a proper blackboard to keep score. The beer was five pence a pint cheaper than in the lounge bar. Most importantly of all, in the corner was a bowl of water for thirsty four-legged customers.

Leighton Hall had ceased business. Terry and Madeline had tried to keep it going, but there was nobody to sign the cheques. Accordingly, Emma and Oliver had found themselves suddenly unemployed. But Bernard had given Emma a little bonus for services rendered and Frank had commissioned Oliver for a little portraiture work. Frank paid generously, with Bernard's money.

The Old Volunteer sign had previously borne a picture of a Napoleonic soldier on one side and a Tommy in First World War khaki on the other. Frank had commissioned Oliver to make two slight amendments. The Napoleonic soldier now bore the face of George Bowman.

There was still a Tommy on the other side of the sign, but this one was Second World War vintage, wearing a beret low over the left eye. He had smoke-grey eyes, a Roman nose and wore the single stripe of a lance corporal. On his chest, there were a set of medal ribbons. On the left, a smudge of maroon.

Oliver's fee, together with the money that he and Emma had earned that summer, meant that they were going on holiday – a touring holiday of Europe in a green Cavalier.

Brunhilde, the Weimaraner puppy, and Rocky were drinking noisily from the bowl in the public bar. Bernard was sitting on a stool at the bar. Frank was pouring a bottle of beer into a tall, thin glass.

"Berliner Kindl. And you even found the correct glass."

"That was the most difficult part."

Bernard reached for his wallet.

"No, no charge."

"Oh, come on, Frank. The place won't survive if even the owner doesn't pay his way."

"Consider it wages."

Bernard was puzzled.

"I've decided to make you the new quizmaster. Thursdays, eight o'clock."

Bernard nodded and took a sip, his eyes closed. Slowly, he returned his glass to the bar. "And you think it will work, do you? This old-fashioned bar approach?"

"I've no idea, but at least I'll have somewhere to play darts."

"And it will be the perfect base."

"For what?"

"To launch your political career."

"My what?"

"The parish council."

"Why on earth would I want to be on the parish council? And who would vote for me? A Glaswegian commie in Rutland?"

"Well, I wasn't planning on emphasising that particular element of your candidacy."

"Bernard, why? Why?"

"To unseat Peter Roberts, of course."

"And how, pray tell, are we going to do that exactly?"

"Skulduggery and mischief, Francis. We're going to cheat."

ABOUT THE AUTHOR

Michael Dane spent over ten years as an officer in the Customs and Excise National Investigation Service investigating drug trafficking, VAT fraud and smuggling of all kinds. He later retrained as a lawyer and joined the private sector where he investigated fraud and corruption all over the world. He is retired and lives in the Vale of Belvoir.